The Posthumous Adventures of
HARRY WHITTAKER

Bobbie Darbyshire

SANDSTONE PRESS

First published in Great Britain by
Sandstone Press Ltd
Dochcarty Road
Dingwall
Ross-shire
IV15 9UG
Scotland

www.sandstonepress.com

The publisher acknowledges subsidy from Creative Scotland towards
publication of this volume.

ISBN: 978-1-912240-50-0
ISBNe: 978-1-912240-51-7

Cover design by David Eldridge
Typeset by Iolaire Typography Ltd, Newtonmore
Printed and bound by CPI Group (UK) Ltd, Croydon CR04YY

For Paul Lyons, my dear friend and incisive critic

Acknowledgements

Ideas for this story came from many sources, including from *On Acting* by Laurence Olivier. For their invaluable insights and encouragement during the drafting, my thanks go to my comrades in *Writers Together*: Angela Trevithick, Bob Boyton, Chris Boyd, Colette Sensier, Eden Carter Wood, Ellen MacDonald-Kramer, Emma Bamford, Joanne Rush, Joe Watts, Julia Rampen, Magda North, Natalie Barbosa, Nick Clark, Paul Lyons, Sharon Brennan, and Toby Vaughan. Big thanks also to Ali Bacon, Debbie Collier, Elizabeth Barton, Emily Standring, Gabriel Clare Hunt, Ian Jewesbury, Janet Mitchell, Katie Wernham, Maureen Jewesbury, Pip Wheldon, and Simon O'Brien. I'm hugely grateful to dear Ros Edwards and Julia Forrest at Edwards Fuglewicz for their enthusiasm and support, and to Bob Davidson and everyone at Sandstone Press, most especially my insightful editor Moira Forsyth and Ceris Jones who hit on the title.

These our actors,
As I foretold you, were all spirits and
Are melted into air, into thin air

The Tempest, Act IV, scene I

There are no bigger questions.
Life itself is the mystery. It is all here.

CLIVE JAMES, *BBC Breakfast* interview
31 March 2015

Thursday

'... and now... yes... news just in. We're getting unconfirmed reports that actor Harry Whittaker has been rushed to hospital after collapsing on set. Stay tuned and we'll keep you updated as we hear more.'

'Sadly, we now have confirmation that Lord Harold Whittaker is critically ill after suffering what is thought to be a heart attack while filming King Lear. Well-wishers are gathering outside St Thomas' Hospital, London, anxious for news. Over now to our reporter, Gerry Matterson.'

'Thank you, Bridget. I'm at St Thomas' Hospital amidst what I expect you can hear is a large crowd, many of whom are in tears, fearing the worst. Lord Whittaker, who last year was awarded the Order of Merit, may be eighty-two, but he remains probably the most gifted actor the world has yet known...'

Harry

I snap awake into startling light. An emergency room in sharp focus. Uproar and commotion, doctors battling to save me. But thank my stars, what relief, I've survived! I am going to be fine, I just know it. The pain is gone, vanished completely, and now...

Now there's a glorious absence of feeling, almost as if I were—

'Stand back,' shouts the consultant, and I glance down and see – oh horrible – a purple face, eyes blank and empty, only inches away. A white-bearded old man in a frightening state, sprawled in the chaos, jolted by the shock to his chest.

He is me. There's no way to deny it. I struggle to yell but no sound emerges. Lips, teeth, vocal chords – save me, where are they?

The old man still has them. His mouth, sagging open, contains them. Quick, quick, I must get back inside. I will myself forward, and yes, willing it carries me nearer. Let me in, let me in... but how?... there's no way...

The crash team share my feverish need. They have magic and hope in their eyes. *Come on, you can do it,* I would roar if I could. *The great man isn't gone – this can't be the end of him.* Surely they can thump and shock him awake?

The consultant is speaking. 'No use. All agreed?' A young nurse comes running, bringing adrenalin, but he waves her aside. He's checking his watch and announcing the time, while the nurse's brown eyes fill with tears.

Not agreed, I am trying to shout. *Where's my own doctor?* Then, *Hey, be careful!* The consultant's hand zips past me – or was it through me? – reaching to give the nurse's shoulder a squeeze, and – *No, wait* – now he's closing the eyes I'm still urging to focus and blink, the mouth that should be protesting. He's drawing the tattered remnants of an Elizabethan shirt over the frail, bruised chest.

I'm dead, that's what he's saying, yet here I am, seeing and hearing like the head of a guillotined man. A few seconds is all I have left. Any moment now I'll lose consciousness forever— Or else, please, he is wrong and my heart will flicker back into life. *Wake up. Don't leave me.*

'Okay,' he says. 'I'd better speak to the press. Or is that for you, John?'

'We'll split it,' says a suit by the door.

I'm still very much here – lucid, alert – staring at the corpse with its closed eyes and mouth. Somehow it seems I've survived.

The consultant's not staring. He's sliding an arm around the brown-eyed nurse. His eyes offer her sympathy, but there's a tell-tale glint too. *You just let me die, you incompetent bastard, and you're thinking of sex?*

He lets go of the nurse. He's slipping on a jacket and tie, checking his hair in the mirror above the basin, and now off he sweeps, solemn-faced, followed by the whole faithless, frivolous lot of them, busily thumbing texts to their friends.

I want to see the press too, but I can't bear to abandon my poor body, not yet. Only the nurse stays behind – *Ellen*, I read on her name badge – shooting a secret smile at the mirror before starting to put the equipment away.

Her face becomes grave as she turns to her patient. Gently, reverentially, she begins to smooth and straighten this dead man who no longer is me. And hush now and look, just look at him. Lord Whittaker on his death bed. It's heart-breaking how ruggedly handsome he's becoming with a bit of buttoning and combing from Ellen. The purple will fade; he'll be a touch bloodless and waxen, but nothing a good makeup artist won't be able to deal with. Eighty-two years of age, yes, but strong-limbed and stern-featured, with a full head of white curls.

Sorrow engulfs me. I can't bear that he's dead.

The nurse bends nearer, caressing his cheek with the back of her hand. *Bless you, Ellen.* I approach close as close, adrift in her breath, fanned by her eyelashes. With a smile, a steady gaze, a few velvet words, I shall charm her.

The shock hits me again. I have no smile to offer. No words. There is my body, and here... here is... what *am* I? She has drawn a sheet over the face and is speaking on the phone to the mortuary, but I'm desperate with concentration, frantic again for him to wake. He must stir, must reach out for her fingers and bring them to his lips, whispering, 'Dearest Ellen, don't be alarmed. Your tenderness has saved me.'

Not a twitch, not a tremor. He is dead meat, a carcass, unable to be anyone's lover. I would kick him, but he has my feet. Damn it, there's no way to channel my frustration. For what worse fate could befall me than to be stripped of my physical self? 'The world's greatest ever actor', isn't that what *The Sunday Times* said? Only today I was the embodiment of Lear, beyond any mere 'actor', the old king himself, and now?

God, I need a drink.

The door opens, and in come two porters and, at last, a familiar face. It's my neighbour Simon Foyle of all people, red-eyed and blowing his nose. His shirt strains to contain his belly; his polished head reflects the hospital lights. Trust Simon to come haring up from Brighton – he must have heard of my collapse on the news.

One of the porters pulls down the sheet. 'Has he been identified?'

Ellen shakes her head. 'Hardly necessary.'

'I'll do it,' says Simon. 'That's Harold Whittaker.'

He speaks my name with such gentleness. *Hey, Simon*, I want to say. *Up a bit. Left a bit. Here I am. Look at me. Please.*

'Are you next of kin?'

4

'Just a friend.' He produces the business card of his failing antiques shop, but nobody bothers to take it. He has me feeling more cheerful, he is such a buffoon.

'They shouldn't have let you in, then,' says Ellen.

'There was no one to stop me. They're all out at the front with the TV cameras.' He stares miserably at the card and returns it to his pocket. 'I'm not sure who the next of kin would be. Harry had no children or other family as far as I know, and his ex-wives all hate him.'

Hey, would you care to rephrase that?

'Do you want some time alone with him?'

He hesitates.

Ah, please, let's skip it, Simon. Heaven knows how you'll embarrass yourself. Declare your long-held secret love for me in all probability. You've been on the verge of it for years. Pull yourself together, man.

He shakes his head mournfully. 'Kind of you, nurse, but no need.'

Did he hear me? Sense me? He peers into the face, takes one of the hands between his, and whispers, 'Goodnight, sweet prince.'

Could be worse, I suppose. For this cliché, much thanks.

His tears leak and run down his cheeks, and all at once I'm comprehending the enormity of what has happened. Simon is the first of thousands, maybe millions, who will gush oceans of tears. Already it's starting as the consultant delivers his news to a crowd of reporters and well-wishers. The most beloved actor in the history of stage and screen is dead. Cue blanket coverage across every television and radio channel, a tsunami of tributes engulfing the networking sites. It's Julian who should be here, managing the story, not Simon – where the deuce is my agent when I most need him?

The porters are moving in on the body, but I've no more desire to watch. The show here is over; it's time to embrace my new role. Though I scarcely know what I am, things may not be so bad. A confirmed atheist, who expected nothing but nothingness, wakes up in an afterlife bristling with possibilities. I shall head out to the crowd, find some journalists, hear their sombre reports to camera, beamed live to the nation, multiplying across the internet. Then, what is to stop me? I can go anywhere, eavesdrop on anyone, see if not touch the most beautiful women—

But help, what is happening? Try as I may – however I think it – I cannot get away from the body. I can glide along to its feet, splayed in the grey silk socks I put on this morning. I can turn, rise two feet in the air, and float back again to its head. I can insinuate myself under the sheet and slip out again, but I cannot escape it. The porters are wheeling it from the room, across to a lift, and off I go with it, like a helium balloon on a string.

Hang on. Stop. Help me please, Simon, Ellen. This cannot be right.

Richard

The pink hair drew his eye, and whenever he glanced across she was watching him too. She pretended she wasn't. Her gaze slid to the window or dropped to her magazine, whose headlines promised latest stories about celebs on *The Reality Channel*. It was the second time she'd been in today, and she'd made this banana milkshake last half an hour.

Richard scoured mugs and plates in the sink. He liked to keep busy even when there was nothing to do. As he reached for the tea-towel, he decided to tease the girl just a little.

Spinning round, he caught her eyes on him again, and his wink had her blushing almost the same shade as her hair.

Seventeen at a guess, eighteen at most, with the faces of some indie band blazoned across her top. Where were her mates? At her age, all of twelve years ago, he'd spent his time drifting about the south coast with four other lads, puffing at cigarettes and lurking in bus shelters, plotting revolution or outdoing each other with fantasies of world travel. From Alaska to Zimbabwe. Up the Amazon and down the Zambezi. He'd been doing the alphabet thing again recently, surfing the internet, telling himself it was high time he saw some of these places for real. Last night he'd googled Antigua because he'd reached 'Z' and had to start back at 'A'. He'd lost himself in images of white sand and pastel blue water. 'Luxury Caribbean getaway,' said Wikipedia. Tonight he'd take a look at some Bs. Bhutan, for example. Where was that? Who lived there? What did it look like? And Bangkok of course, firmly on his must-visit list.

He vigorously dried the last plate. Come on, Worthing! Great coffee and cake to be had here. Shake the rain from your umbrellas and take the weight off your feet. One milkshake was hardly keeping his struggling café afloat. The place would be empty right now if it weren't for the girl and Maurice, his only regular, who whiffed a bit and tied his trousers with string. Maurice was slumped in the torn leather armchair in the library corner, with an empty mug at his elbow, deep in the café copy of *War and Peace*.

Richard sighed. Something had to be done. He must stop losing money and start making some. He was nearing his overdraft limit and his credit card balance was frightening. How adventurous he'd felt at twenty-six, quitting his job as a barman, renting these tatty premises not far from the pier, starting his own café, all set to make money to finance his travel plans. That was four years ago and look where it had got him. He'd promised himself he would start travelling before he turned thirty, but the deadline had crept up and slipped past several months ago, and here he still was. He should face facts, cut his losses, sell the equipment, give notice to the landlord.

And then what? His mate Joe, who'd moved on from bus shelters in Worthing to marriage and babies in Wimbledon, had suggested a driving job – removals or minicab. Good idea. Anything would do to get himself solvent enough to go travelling.

June was a daft time of year, though, to quit making milkshakes. The sun would surely break through tomorrow. It made more sense to keep going until the dark evenings closed in, to have one final crack at turning a profit. Wi-Fi, for example. Several customers had asked about Wi-Fi. He made a note on the pad by the till.

Location was the problem he never could solve. Barely thirty paces from where the day-trippers strolled, he might as well be half a mile inland for all the passing trade he attracted. These last three mornings he'd set up a pavement board on the seafront with a big red arrow: 'This way to THE ECLECTIC CAFÉ for great coffee, friendly service and book exchange.' It had brought in several customers. None today though, except possibly the girl. Perhaps the board had blown over. 'Back in a tick,' he said, heading for the door.

He sprinted up to the promenade through the unseasonal drizzle and found the board gone, not a trace. No amount of scanning right and left persuaded it to materialise. Some bastard had stolen it. Twenty quid wasted.

He was hit by a gust of cold rain. Dismal and damp in his

happy-face T-shirt, he ran back to find the girl in a fluster, barely knowing where to look or what to do with her hands, while Maurice chewed manfully, his cheeks stuffed like a hamster's. The top chocolate brownie had gone.

'Brilliant. Help yourself, Maurice, why don't you?'

Maurice buried his face in Tolstoy, his Adam's apple working overtime.

One pound twenty. Richard bit the words back. The brownies would only go stale; the bastard might as well eat them. He retreated to his stool by the espresso machine and concentrated on elsewhere. Anywhere else.

None of his mates had got far. Joe had migrated the fifty miles up to London, not to Moscow or Singapore. Keith had fallen for a French day-tripper and was now living in Calais, big deal. And the other two had gone nowhere, one a chef, one a council clerk, sucked into being wage-slaves in Shoreham and Brighton. It was high time he set an example. If only he could pay off his debts. If only he were free of his mother.

She'd rung twice already today, guilt-tripping him that she hadn't seen him since whenever last week. 'I'll try to come over on Monday,' he'd told her, but 'try' wasn't good enough: she'd demanded a promise.

He might as well see her; there'd be nothing much else to do. Monday was a dead day for trade, Claire worked Monday evenings, and the lads rarely got together now except at weddings and christenings and on Facebook. The two in Worthing were too busy with their kids and their jobs to meet up for a pint any more. They spent their free time assembling flat-pack furniture or rooted to sofas watching widescreen TVs.

Richard rocked on his stool, flicking at the counter with

a dishcloth. He was heading the same way, spending far too much time in front of Claire's television. The three months since he'd met her already felt like forever. Okay, she was a good laugh – sexy, affectionate and cheerful. She ticked all the boxes, but, being honest, rather than have his boxes ticked on the eastern fringes of Worthing, he would so much prefer to be packing a rucksack and booking a flight.

The girl was still ogling him. For all her squirming and twitching, she hadn't taken advantage while he was out. There was only one brownie gone and Maurice wouldn't have shared it. He ought to be chatting to her, charming her, winning her repeat custom. Chin on hands, elbows on counter, he smiled. 'At a loose end, eh? No sunshine?'

She blinked and nodded, then set about twiddling her straw, lifting it to suck from the bottom, her eyes darting like fish in a rock pool. He put a second brownie on a plate, lifted the counter-flap and headed towards her. 'Have this one on me— Hey!'

Jumping up in surprise, she'd sent her glass flying, spattering the remains of the milkshake across the floor.

'For fuck's sake,' growled Maurice.

'Omigod, I'm so sorry,' she wailed.

She helped him mop up, pouring out more apologies while he told her it didn't matter at all. Then she moved herself and her magazine nearer the counter, to the table with the chipped Formica top and the wonky leg, where she sat, smiling shyly. 'I'm not clumsy, I promise.'

'You're forgiven. I startled you. Come again. Bring your friends.'

A grin lit up her face. She was easily pleased.

Climbing back on the stool, he examined the café's distorted reflection in the chrome of the espresso machine.

Maurice was yawning, turning a page, drawing the girl's attention for a moment before her gaze crept back to Richard.

Jeez, he was bored, and what was he playing at? His mother was the real problem, not the café or money. 'Man, you need to get out of there,' Joe had said last time they'd talked on the phone. 'What kind of thirty-year-old is held back by his mother?'

Richard had no answer. Joe was right, yet she made it impossible. Each time he spoke of selling up to go travelling she visibly shrank. Her eyes started hunting for comfort among her useless possessions. She would go out with her shopping bags, foraging for more things to add to the hoard, and he would worry that she was pilfering again.

She had no need to steal – his grandparents had left her well off. Emotional blackmail it was, pure and simple, with always the same choice. He could give up his life to his mother, promise never to leave, and then she'd be happy, stop stealing, eat properly, behave halfway normally. Or he could leave, and she would unravel and end up in prison or worse. She was scarcely less dependent on him now than she'd been before his one and only school trip, clinging to his hand in the bus station, shaming him in front of his friends. He'd had to lead her away, calm her down, then surprise her with, 'Got to go,' making a dash for the bus just as its doors were closing and the driver was revving the engine. 'Mummy's boy, mummy's boy,' some joker had chanted. The thump he'd dealt him cost Richard his freedom. He'd been grounded all day with the teachers while the other kids had roamed free in Boulogne and practised their French.

Maurice farted, then sighed and shambled off to the loo. He consumed more toilet paper than coffee. Richard shared an exasperated look with the girl, then put his forehead on the counter and contemplated his trainers. Get a grip. Keep things in proportion. Make a plan.

His mother was insecure – that was the problem he needed to tackle. He must swallow his impatience, stop getting into arguments with her, visit at least once a week, show her he cared. Then fly off somewhere for just a few days, bringing her back an extravagant present. Once she'd survived that, then, softly, softly, a longer trip, a week or two maybe without triggering a maternal meltdown. Building up gradually to the big one.

He looked up from his shoes. Rain nagged at the window; gusts rattled the door. Nearly four o'clock. There'd be barely anyone on the front now, just a few intrepid souls in cagoules.

For starters, he'd stop mentioning Claire to his mother – the idea of a rival unsettled her. Perhaps he should break with Claire anyway. It was getting way too domestic.

The bell tinkled, and in blew a dishevelled woman, fortyish. 'Do you have soup? I need soup.'

Wi-Fi and soup. 'Not yet. Next week,' he said brightly. 'How about a mocha with whipped cream to be going on with?'

'If that's all you've got.' She scowled, shaking out her umbrella and dumping herself on the garden chair by the barrel table. 'Oxtail I was gasping for, or tomato. Something savoury, nourishing.' She wasn't looking at him, just grumbling into thin air, pulling earbuds and wires from her bag.

Delivering the mug to her, he smiled. 'Are you local?'

'What?'

'Or just here for the day?'

She yanked out an earbud. 'I'm trying to listen.'

Richard's mobile vibrated. He glanced at the screen. Jesus, Mum, three times in one day? He would be there on Monday, he would be nice to her on Monday, what more did she want? He shoved the phone back in his pocket and drew up a chair beside the girl with pink hair. 'Come on, talk to me. What's your name?'

'Tiffany.'

'And don't worry, it's fine, but I'm curious – why keep staring at me?'

She was blushing again, mumbling something.

'What? Who?'

She showed him pictures in her magazine. Some contestant she was keen on in *Tomorrow's Tycoon*. 'You remind me of him.'

Richard pulled a face. He hated everything to do with celebrity. His personal brushes with it had put him right off.

The girl blinked at him. 'I never usually break things.'

'It's fine. I believe you.'

'I told him he shouldn't,' she whispered.

'Come again?'

'The chocolate brownie. I told him.'

'Doesn't matter. Bigger problems. Forget it.'

A teenager with a crush on him was the last thing he needed. He got up from the table.

'I could help you,' she blurted.

'Sorry?'

'Be your waitress.'

Without thinking he laughed, then saw the hurt in her eyes. 'It's not you, Tiffany. I can't afford help, is the truth. The café's bust, or nearly.'

'But that's fine.' She leaned forward. 'Just a few quid now and then. No tax nor nothing.'

He shook his head. 'It's a nice thought, but—'

'No!' said the soup woman.

He swung round. This was none of her business.

'I don't believe it.' She was looking at Tiffany, an earbud in each hand. 'Harold Whittaker's dead.'

Richard froze, shocked.

'Who?' said Tiffany.

'A heart attack,' said the woman. 'Just like that. Here one minute, gone the next. Isn't that awful?'

The air buzzed around him. He opened his mouth, but no words came out.

'Who's gone?' said Maurice, coming back from the loo.

'Harold Whittaker. It was just on the news. I can't bear it. I *really* loved him.'

Maurice looked sceptical. 'You knew Harold Whittaker?'

'Not personally, obviously, but everyone knows him.'

Maurice dismissed her with a grunt and re-opened his book. Richard made it unsteadily back to the espresso machine, where he stared at the pad that said *Bhutan, Wi-Fi, oxtail, tomato*.

'Oh, you mean that old actor bloke?' said Tiffany.

'Everyone! You see what I'm saying?' said the woman. She'd come to the counter and was appealing to Richard. 'Such a huge talent, such a beautiful man. I fell for his Mr Rochester when I was fifteen. *You* agree with me, don't you?'

'About what?' he said, dazed.

'For goodness sake.' She threw up her hands. 'Are you all stupid? I'll have one of these.' She paid for a slice of carrot cake and took it back to the barrel. 'How dreadful,' she grumbled. 'They've been dropping like flies lately.'

'Who have?' said Tiffany.

'Famous people. It jolts you. Shows it can happen to anyone.' She put her earbuds in and subsided.

Richard took a breath, fighting to steady himself. For these three the moment was passing, nearly forgotten. The woman sipped her coffee, Maurice read Tolstoy, and Tiffany stared out at the rain, tugging at a strand of pink hair.

His mobile hummed in his pocket. Mum again, and now he knew why. His father was dead.

He couldn't face her hysteria. Let the call go to voicemail. Switch the phone off. He was desperate now to be out of here, alone, to see the news pictures and think and feel for himself.

Quickly, into the back room for the spare keys and the end-of-day checklist. Could he trust her? He'd just have to chance it.

'So, Tiffany,' he said as he came out. 'Still want to be a waitress?'

Her jaw dropped.

'We'll talk details tomorrow. I trust you. Lock up for me. I have to be somewhere else now.'

She was on her feet, her eyes shining. The soup woman and Maurice were staring. He tossed her the keys and the checklist. 'Guard the brownies,' he said, and he was out of there fast.

Friday

Harry

I have to get out of here. Please, someone, let in the noise and the light. How long has it been? Will I be imprisoned for days? I can't stand it.

I thought I might self-destruct with the effort of trying to detach from my poor body as they unceremoniously stripped it, shrouded it in a green sheet and slid it, feet first, into this mortuary fridge. All struggle was useless. Whipped in along with the body as the door clanged to, here I have been ever since, unable to see a thing, feel a thing, not even the cold. All I feel is the time, only the time, passing so slowly it barely passes at all. Second, by second, by second, by second. Please, people, where are you? Come back.

Or no, rather let me wake into a new, normal day, with a full bladder and arthritic knees, the weight of the cat on my chest, his meaty purr in my face. Release me from this torture.

That absolute shit of a director! This is his doing. I was on set, clasping Cordelia's limp body to my heart and giving voice to my grief as if no one had found the words before. *Never, never, never, never, never.* I was strong, at the height of my powers. I would be alive now if that idiot hadn't kept calling for retakes and presuming to offer me notes. The jumped-up little Yank has no more notion of how to play Lear than I have of managing lighting technicians, and I was making damn sure he knew it when the vice closed on my chest. Then, too late – searing pain, pandemonium. Shouting and running, hands pulling at me, an ambulance, more shouting, noise, burning lights, and all the while the pain worsening, worsening, unable to breathe—

And now?

Silence. Impenetrable darkness. What can I do to shake off these slow seconds? I crave unconsciousness, no matter what dreams may come. The lurid colours of nightmare would be preferable to this black reality. Yet how to find sleep with no eyelids to close, no grey matter to alter its rhythms?

I've endeavoured to soothe myself by revisiting the great roles I've inhabited, the lines I've breathed life into, but such memories only serve to frustrate me. I should be out there now where I belong, soaring away, my face tilted towards the gods, each man and woman in the audience believing I'm speaking to him or her alone. I was made to perform – it was mine, it was mine.

I've recited lullabies, counted sheep, even tried plain, everyday counting: one, two, three, four... as far as six hundred, where I gave up in disgust, weary of the indifference of numbers and still wide awake. *I would not spend another such a night, though 'twere to buy a world of happy days.* I can recall an immensity of Shakespeare, yet I cannot sleep. What am I – pure mind?

In which case, meditation – perhaps that's worth a try. I learned it, way back in the sixties, from wife number two, who wore beads and kaftans, baked hash cookies and rocked, vacant-eyed, to sitar music. Tiresome woman, yet her meditation techniques had the power to calm me. Haven't had call for them in years. So... yes... empty my mind, think only of...

What? Not my breathing, for I've no breath to observe, no inhale, no exhale. A mantra then. Think only of 'om'. Take it slowly now.

Om...

Om...

Second, by second, by second, but no, damn it, the knack of the thing eludes me. My thoughts take on the tormenting rhythm of time. There's no escape from the silence, the darkness. Surely someone or something is listening? Please help me, show me how to get out of here. I concentrate my entreaties in what I hope is the general direction of 'up', but no answer comes. Truly, this is my dark night of the soul.

An eternity passes before I hear movement outside, my hearing sharp as when I was a child. Voices: good mornings and groans about needing coffee. Ah, please, soon, let me out.

'They're here,' someone says.

'That's quick. Is he ready?'

And thank God, at last comes the crank of the handle and a flood of light. A young man and a young woman in facemasks are hauling me out. Sight, sound and people. Oh thank you, thank you.

My one-time self looks quite dreadful, his mouth a grimace, his flesh whitish-blue. I'm racked with renewed pity and sorrow for him, with anguish at his being dead and lost to me. But stop this, there's no time for anguish, because now or never I must get away from him. I retreat to his toes from where I attempt to launch myself at the girl who is straightening his shroud. My mind stretches with certainty towards her sweet, pretty face. It has to be possible. She turns to walk away, and I'm with her, yes, nestling into the nape of her neck— But no, so far and no further. The girl has gone and I'm left behind, still tethered somehow, reading 'Harold Whittaker' on the label on a frozen big toe.

What in hell use is it being a ghost if I can't leave the corpse? I scan the mortuary for fellow spirits who may be able to advise me or show me the way, but if any are here, they're as mute and invisible as myself. All I see are more youngsters in white coats and a couple of black-suited fellows manoeuvring a metal trolley in through the door.

'This 'im, then?' says one of them. 'Whittaker?'

'That's right.'

'Some famous geezer, they said. Gold star treatment. We're taking 'im off to be buffed up and coiffured. Full malarkey.'

They're signing for my body, shifting it to their trolley and wheeling it away through the door they came in by, while I follow helplessly, doomed to play Siamese twin.

We're soon out in the daylight, in a yard where the insistent nag of a rapper drifts from a parked grey van. Bedraggled London pigeons huddle on a wall, above which there's a glimpse of blue sky streaked with vapour trails. Cold rain marked my death yesterday, but today sunshine pours down on the living. I make frenzied attempts to soar free. Why can't I? What's stopping me? I'm like a hawk brought up short by his jesses.

The undertakers pause to light cigarettes. One of them lifts the green sheet and peers at my face. 'Dead famous apparently.'

'Some actor,' says the other. 'Non-stop leg-overing, his ex-wife says 'ere. Probably bust a gut chugging Viagra.'

The tabloid he pulls from his pocket has the headline HARRY DIES ON THE JOB. It pictures me in a recent cast photo, fronted by my nemesis, the director. I'm looking, not at him or into the lens, but at the buxom blonde who plays Goneril. Her eyes shine at the camera, her lips are parted like Marilyn Monroe's, and I'm caught in a moment of what looks like lechery.

Nonsense, all nonsense. How the camera can lie. It's the assistant producer I've been bedding, a rather bookish brunette, not some ten-a-penny starlet. But ah God, now it hits me as if for the first time: I shall never hold a woman again.

The insolent man has lifted the shroud further and is having a good stare at my poor frozen penis. 'Makes you wonder where it's been.'

'And why the fuck they bothered,' sniggers the other.

Disgraceful. Outrageous. I make futile attempts to snatch the sheet back, but it slips to the ground as they open the van doors and shoot me onto a shelf – *Hey, be careful* – and dear me, there are other dead people in here. The hand of a young black man dangles above me. One of the men scoops it up, back to its shelf, and wedges it there. Across the aisle a grubby, grey sheet has slipped to expose an old woman whose flesh is the colour of rotting potatoes, whose head is little more than a skull. Her rictus displays gumless yellow teeth, and her shrivelled chest is exposed. Dear God, will I too come to this?

'Fuck me, what a stink,' says one of them, flapping his hands at her. It dawns on me I've no sense of smell.

The other flicks at a nipple. 'Grab an eyeful of titty, Harry-me-laddo. Let's see you get it up now, eh?'

I rage uselessly as they hoot with laughter. They're

collapsing the trolley and stowing it, screwing my shroud into a ball and tossing it at me, before banging the doors shut, cutting off the rapper's drone. The van rocks as they climb aboard, and then we're away, pulling out of the yard and driving stop-start in what sounds like heavy traffic. Where are they taking me?

The black hand comes loose again, bouncing, then swinging past me, fingers curled as if to scoop me from the air. It misses me by a whisker, sending me diving for cover. Death mocks me at every turn. In twenty-four hours I've been demoted from Shakespearean tragedy to a second-rate zombie movie.

There's a mystery here, though, because how did I see the arm fall? No connecting window looks through to the cab. The mere sliver of a gap beneath the van doors can't account for this visibility. The golden air softens the dead woman's features and lends a great thespian's nakedness some vestige of dignity. Where's the light coming from?

My attention is drawn to the upper shelf opposite. I thought it was empty, but something is stirring. A person sits upright, swings his legs to and fro and stretches his arms. A youth with blond curls, dressed incongruously in smart pinstriped trousers and an unironed T-shirt that says: *What we think, we become*. His feet, dangling above the old woman, are bare. His toes are a refreshingly healthy pink and the toenails are gilded. His smile is cherubic and aimed straight at me. I'm in no doubt he can see me. At last my beseechings are answered. Whoever or whatever is in charge has sent some angelic underling to welcome me into the hereafter. High time too, but what a scruff. Could they spare no one more senior?

What a relief!

'I can well imagine it must be,' he says.

He can hear me, or read me somehow. Wonderful! I miss the timbre and power of my matchless voice, and it requires mental effort to converse in this way. Still, needs must.

'You cannot possibly imagine the frights I've been having, young man.' I form the thoughts frantically and throw them towards him. 'Something has gone awry, you see, and I appear to be tied to my—'

'Hush,' he says. 'Compose yourself.'

What cheek. Does he know who I am? I'll give him a piece of my mind as soon as I'm set free. For the time being though, I must be diplomatic. *What we think, we become*, says his T-shirt. The actor in me is not dead; I gather myself to feel sincere warmth and gratitude. 'Yes, of course,' I agree. 'Clear the airways, eh? So you can beam me up, Scotty?'

He raises an eyebrow.

'I apologise. You must be weary of that one, dear boy. Let's introduce ourselves properly. You may not realise that I'm—'

'Hush,' he repeats.

How dare he? His face will fall when I tell him. His superiors will be furious when they hear of his cheek. But he has the upper hand here – I have to hold on to my temper. 'Harold Whittaker,' I politely persist. 'Revered actor. One of the greatest, if not *the* greatest ever. A volcano of talent erupting across stage and screen. For the past fifteen years I've been Baron Whittaker of Dorchester. That's who I am, but please, do call me Harry. And you, you are?'

Let him dare hush me now. I await his apology.

'Pickles,' he says. 'Albert Pickles. But really, don't worry. "Scotty" will do if it's easier for you – and I know who you were.' He reaches down to touch Lord Whittaker's white head.

The past tense disconcerts me, and for a moment I'm

22

dumb. Then he smiles beatifically, the very least one might expect of an angel, and I find myself experiencing a moment of almost-peace in the midst of my turmoil. For all Scotty's youth, I have to grant he has presence. I hold myself still and give him my attention. He's going to release me or explain to me what to do to release myself. I'll be out of this fix in a jiffy.

The van is bowling along. I'm hearing the roar and grind as we overtake some heavy-goods vehicle. 'There's probably no need to worry,' Scotty says quietly as the racket dies down. 'I'm told this happens in quite a few cases. You're stuck for the moment, but you should be able to detach before long. Keep an eye out for people who mean a lot to you.'

'Because?'

'Because you can go with them.'

'Just like that? No fuss or trick to it?'

'None at all.'

'Well, that's marvellous, thank you!' I've warmed to the lad. 'Such a relief, you have no idea, to know there's a way out of this.'

'I'm so glad,' he responds. 'I love to help when I can. I'm guessing you just haven't seen anyone yet that you'd like to be with. Since he died, I mean.' He nods respectfully at the departed.

I cast my mind back. Not Simon Foyle, obviously, but I soften at the memory of that brown-eyed nurse, Ellen, and the mortuary assistant just now. 'Women,' I tell Scotty. 'Pretty women, they mean a great deal to me, and I've been desperate to go with two of them so far, but it just hasn't worked. I tried, but I didn't make it across to them. Something needs fixing.'

He leans forward, flexing his toes, as the van swerves from one lane to another, sending the corpses rocking, the dead black arm swinging. Scotty is in need of a shave, I notice, or perhaps trying to grow a beard. 'These women,' he says, 'did you know them when you were alive?'

'No, but—'

'Ah, well, in that case...' He strokes the golden stubble on his dimpled chin. 'Forgive me, I have to confess I'm a little new to this job. I need to explain the situation more plainly. It's probably best if I quote you chapter and verse.'

The change in his tone fills me with unease. More guarded than at first, it's how a doctor might drop and soften his voice if the news were not good.

He recites slowly and carefully. '*After death, a spirit emerging from its body may attach itself to any qualifying host that approaches within a radius of ten metres, provided that no other spirit is presently attached to that host. If the spirit does not so attach itself it shall remain with the body, or as the body decays or is otherwise recycled, with any part or particle of the body.*'

'But—'

'Wait. There's more.' He squeezes his eyes shut in an effort to remember, before continuing, checking categories off on his fingers. '*A "qualifying host" is a person, animal, object, artefact or location in whom or in which, before death, the spirit made a significant emotional investment, or...*' He stalls. '*Or that serves...*' Stalls again. 'Bother, I always have trouble with this bit. *Or that serves, temporarily or permanently...*' He draws breath. 'Yes, I've got it, *as a medium for an idea or a message in which, before death, such investment was made.* Quite a mouthful, eh?'

'I don't understand,' I say. 'Tell me again.'

He obliges, and I listen a second time, struggling to comprehend.

24

There's a blare of horns from outside. The legalese has drowned me in bafflement, but an appalling truth stands out. Unless I come across something or someone that I cared about quite considerably, I am facing a waking eternity in an urn.

'That's the meat of it,' he says brightly, 'and that phrase – *significant emotional investment* – is the one to remember, because it's really just more of the same from then on.'

He's off again, cocky now, rattling off another verse of whatever chapter he's quoting. '*The spirit may at any time move from one available qualifying host to another. A person, animal, object, artefact or location that comes newly into existence may qualify if the spirit prior to death made a significant emotional investment in the idea of that person, animal, object, artefact or location or in the idea or message it carries.*'

He punches the air. 'Word-perfect, how about that? But you see what I mean? Grandchildren and great-grandchildren, for example. You can keep on transferring as new generations are born, provided other spirits haven't got there ahead of you.'

I stare at him, my anxiety rocketing.

'No descendants?' he says. 'Well, just guessing and by no means presuming – but in your case it sounds as if a woman you cared for will do the trick, at least to get you started. Perhaps someone like that will view the body or come to the funeral?'

When still I don't answer, he adds, a touch nervously. 'Or a man, of course, that would be perfectly fine, absolutely, please be in no doubt. Or any treasured friend of yours. Or a nephew, a niece?'

The van brakes, and the three corpses shoot forward, feet

first. Scotty waits. His smile fades. He seems sorrowful, and there's a hint of a crease on his seraphic brow. The van picks up speed again.

'Those other things you mentioned?' I manage at last. 'How about them? Objects and so on?'

'Yes, well,' he says uncertainly, 'but you need to think one move ahead. An object can be a bit of a dead end, no pun intended. A person moves around, meets other people, gives you more to see, more options down the line. Still,' he adds, 'even so, if an object comes along and that's your only choice, my advice would be to go for it.'

The bodies slip backwards again as we grind noisily uphill. This whole set-up is ludicrous; I'm scenting a hoax. 'Chapter and verse, indeed. Where from, may I ask?"

Scotty stares at me a moment, then offers his pink palms in a shrug. 'The laws of the universe?' His chuckle is musical. 'Who knows, the same may apply across every galaxy, but I'm still Earthbound myself. One level up from you, hardly any wiser, only just got my promotion.'

I'm bewildered again. 'One level up? Are you saying that you were like me?'

'A separating spirit?' He bows again to Lord Whittaker, deceased. 'Yes, that was my great pleasure and fortune. I was a railway clerk in Crewe, man and boy. My job was planning the timetables. My body survived sixty-three years until 1949. My family were around my bed when I died. I went with my dear wife at the start.'

'Sixty-three? But look at you.'

'Yes!' He flexes a bicep, grinning with evident pleasure. 'It takes some getting used to. It's a thrill being embodied and young again and knowing the difference this time.' He wriggles and stretches, making me acutely aware of how much

I'm missing my own physicality. 'Bouncy,' he says. 'That's how I've been feeling.' He demonstrates, but the van lurches and he nearly falls off his shelf. 'Whoops.'

I go through mental contortions, trying to peer down at whatever I am. 'Am I young again, too?'

'Look in a mirror,' he says, 'next time you see one. You'll find you're not anything at all.'

'Nothing?'

'Nothing.'

'But you can see me?'

'Yes.'

'What do you see?'

'I see who you are. I see into your soul.'

'But no physical me?'

'The one you imagine – yes, I see him. Very handsome, I'm sure.'

'Yes, yes, and then, if I get promoted to your level? Take me through it, dear boy. You started off by haunting your wife?'

His eyes soften. 'Not haunting exactly. She would imagine we were chatting, you know, and I would offer my thoughts, but she never knew how the thoughts came to her.' His countenance shines. 'It was a special time. The best I ever knew. I was sorry it couldn't go on forever.'

'Because she died?'

'My darling wife,' he says wistfully, 'died in 1963. I transferred to one of our sons, then to one of his children. Eventually, when that grandchild sadly died recently, everyone nearby that I cared about had a spirit already attached, so I had to let go.'

He pauses and sighs. 'Letting go is the necessary step after emotional investment. It's important to understand that.

Even after so long, it's a wrench, harder than you might think. I'm not at all sure that I've properly mastered it. Still, it's only been a few weeks and, on the bright side, now they've promoted me I've seen my wife again! She's attached to a dear little girl—'

'Listen,' I interrupt, 'how about I skip all this transferring business, let go now, be like you? I'm willing to try it.'

He rocks backward as his hand shoots to his mouth. 'Sorry, mustn't laugh, but you're a long way from that option. The first task is *caring*, only then comes letting go.'

He leans across, reaching out to me, cupping me in his hands like a bubble. 'Take heart, dear soul. Good luck to you. I hope you'll soon come across someone you cared for.'

Although he's so close, I'm having trouble seeing him. Is his radiance dimming?

'It's been a pleasure,' he says, 'but lots to do, time I was going.'

Dread of abandonment seizes me. 'Stay. Please. Don't leave me.'

The light wavers and fades.

'Come back to me soon, at least.'

'It may not be me next time.'

'But aren't you my guardian?'

His answer is barely a murmur. 'I was on call when you prayed. I'll try to look into your case. I'll come again if I'm free. Ask for Pickles 64123.'

'What's that – a phone number?'

'My name. There are rather a lot of Pickleses.'

I can scarcely see through the gloom. 'Six four...?'

'One two three. Not hard to remember.'

'So I just need to pray again?'

There's no answer. The darkness is total. 64123. We're

slowing and turning, pulling to a halt. When the men open up and start hauling the bodies out, the shelf above the old woman is empty. Pickles 64123.

They unload the young black man first and trundle him off, leaving the van doors swinging open. A fat bluebottle buzzes in and around, straight through me – ugh, disgusting – before settling on the old woman's shoulder. It runs in circles and figures of eight across her withered neck, bristled chin and gaping blue lips. Briefly it takes off, dive-bombs me again, then returns to her, disappearing up her left nostril.

Lily

The first person to realise the Caruthers' marriage was heading for the rocks had never met Martin or Lily. Mrs Jones happened to be at her daughter's bedroom window that evening, looking irritably out at the night. She'd come in, without switching the light on, to pick up dirty washing and grab five minutes' peace, for God's sake. Downstairs the dog was having a fit of barking, the kids were arguing about whose turn it was on the computer, and her husband for what felt like the ninety-ninth blessed time was shouting at the pair of them to stop shouting. Leaning her head on the glass, catching her breath, she tried not to lose her temper.

The tiny London gardens backed onto each other. With no moon to speak of, the darkness beyond the window was absolute except for a few illuminated rooms opposite, the nearest a stone's throw away and as vivid as a widescreen TV. Although the hubbub downstairs was abating and her annoyance was passing, Mrs Jones lingered to have a good look. The protective tape had finally come off her neighbour's new windows, and this was the first time she'd been able to see properly into his kitchen.

Until recently, her neighbour might as well not have existed, hidden from view, year after year, by a thicket of buddleia. But a few months ago the buddleia came down, exposing a dilapidated house, swarming with builders. The constant drilling and pounding and crashing of scaffolding at first drove Mrs Jones mad, but then curiosity took over. She'd lost count of the times she'd come in here on her afternoons off to sneak an envious look at the roofers and bricklayers and garden-designers coming and going. The house quickly sprouted a third storey, clad in synthetic slate. The yellow-brick back-addition with its rotting windows and mossy damp patches morphed into a wall of sliding glass panels that opened on a new Yorkstone patio set off by emerald turf and dwarf shrubs.

Then one day she'd seen him, chatting with an architect, pointing at plans and up at the roof. He was clean-cut, smartly dressed, his smile warm and engaging. No children or dogs were in evidence. No woman either. He was young enough to be single, and she'd allowed herself to imagine knocking ten years off her age and climbing over the fence into his arms. It hurt no one to fantasise.

A loud crash below made her jump. It was followed by silence. Dear heaven, what now? She imagined her family motionless, holding their collective breath, suppressing their giggles, her husband included, one of them hugging the dog to keep him quiet, expecting her to thunder down and say, 'Who the bloody hell did this?' whereupon they would all blame each other and tell her not to fuss. Soon she heard muted voices and the sound of the back door opening as they snuck whatever it was they had broken into the rubbish bin. She sighed and turned again to the window, her eyes drawn once more towards her attractive neighbour, lounging tonight against his new granite worktop.

It was bad manners to spy on him, a step further than watching his builders. Briefly she acknowledged this, but her conscience didn't leap into action. She would have stepped hurriedly away from the window had she chanced to witness old Mrs Briggs next door talking to thin air, or Mr Sanders two gardens along picking his nose. At least she believed that she would. But this man was just smoking a cigarette. He was unlikely ever to be more than a stranger. She rarely walked on his street; it would be hard to guess at his house number. He was like someone she might eye up on the train, she decided, or might mildly lust after from the window of a bus. He wasn't naked or talking to himself, and he could close his blinds, couldn't he? She was out of order, of course, but her daydreaming was harmless.

Not least as it seemed he was, after all, spoken for. A young woman was there, her back to the window, her hand on an iron she'd just returned to its rest. The two of them were captured in freeze-frame: he in his business suit, she in a white top and faded blue jeans; he propped against the worktop, contemplating the floor, she occupied with a pink dress on the ironing board. Apples, or maybe pears, were piled in a yellow fruit bowl on the table. Arum lilies drooped in a vase. Maybe music was playing, or the radio was on, because the two weren't speaking or laughing or looking at each other. Definitely married.

The wife wasn't moving, that was the strange thing. It must be a minute now, and still her hand clutched the iron without lifting it, and the dress lay on the board. Her head was bent, maybe in thought. Her brown hair hung in a thick

31

braid to her waist. When at last she flung back her head and said something, Mrs Jones pressed her face to the glass, but all she could hear was the renewed rumpus in the sitting room below: a row breaking out over which channel to watch.

Impassive, leaning against the work surface, examining the tip of his cigarette, the man offered no reply to his wife. Mrs Jones did her best to excuse him. Perhaps he hadn't heard her speak, or he'd responded with a grunt or a chuckle.

The wife became angry, though. She let go of the iron, turned to yell something at him, and Mrs Jones ducked away in confusion. What had she seen? She crept back to the window. It was awful – the young woman's left cheek was purple, eye to chin, nose to ear. Had he been hitting her? She narrowed her eyes, trying to see better. The colour wasn't right for a bruise. A burn would be painful, needing a dressing. It must be a birthmark.

The husband looked up, but still he said nothing, just tapped ash off his cigarette into something obscured by the window frame, an ashtray or the sink. And, oh heavens, the wife was in sudden motion, crossing the room fast towards him. For a moment it seemed she would strike him or shout in his face. But then, no, she was putting her arms round him, her head on his shoulder.

Sympathy demolished Mrs Jones's envy. She wanted all to be well for this woman. It made her smile that she was consoling her man, or apologising to him, or forgiving him, or whatever other generous thing a spontaneous hug might signify. But now, what was this? He didn't respond. He stayed as he was, propped against the work surface, arms at his sides, allowing himself to be hugged, but giving nothing back, the cold bastard. When his wife gave up on the hug and stood away, he took a last, deep inhale of his cigarette before twisting to stub it out.

She was speaking again, and he was nodding and saying something at last, smiling his engaging smile and squeezing her arm, so that she grinned and did a little mock curtsey. As she re-crossed the room to the ironing board, he straightened up and went out of the room.

In her beautiful new kitchen, across the moonless back gardens, Lily Caruthers ironed her pink sundress. Martin's words and his squeeze of her arm had reassured her. All might yet be well. There was maybe no reason to worry.

But Mrs Jones felt differently. For a minute or so longer she watched. Then she turned from the window, unhooked her daughter's laundry bag from the door and descended into the dog-smelling chaos. When she put her arms around her own husband, the hug he returned her brought tears to her eyes.

Richard

Fifty miles south in the same moonless night, Richard stared down at the glimmer of a grey cat sniffing around the dust-bins below. Harry was dead. Good riddance. He ought to be happy, but still his thoughts were in turmoil. It was going to take more than a day to steady himself. Behind him, images of Cambodian jungle temples floated steamily across the screen of his laptop, but even they couldn't calm him.

His gaze travelled along the alley of downpipes and rubbish bags towards the tranquil June sea. It was too dark to make out its colour or the line where it met the sky, but he tried to hold on to the idea of it, to put the father who'd never given him a thought out of his mind.

Thank goodness for Tiffany. In a neon-green microskirt

and with her pink hair embellished with clip-on butterflies, she'd served Maurice and the small flurry of Friday customers with efficient friendliness, shooting Richard shy smiles while he skulked by the espresso machine pretending to do the books. He'd been in no state to charm customers.

He'd found any excuse to go out. To the cash-and-carry. To the hardware store for a new pavement board, chain and padlock. To the seafront to secure the board to a lamppost and guard it. At lunchtime Tiffany had dashed up to the front with a sandwich for him. 'Don't worry,' she'd gabbled. 'A really nice woman is keeping an eye, and I've counted the cakes.'

She seemed more infatuated even than yesterday. He felt bad taking advantage. When they closed up for the evening, he'd tried to give her a fiver, but she'd backed away – 'Tips'll do fine, honest. See you tomorrow' – and run off before he could argue. He'd been so aloof and unfriendly all day, she probably thought he was trying to pay her off.

'It's not you, Tiffany,' he told the cat in the alley. It was thoughts of Harry he needed to send packing. Instead he felt... what? Rage? It made no sense. There was nothing new to be angry about, and his rage never solved anything. He'd learned as a child to stop furiously insisting that this man was his father. It had earned him only a succession of black eyes from bullies and black marks from teachers for the rumpuses he provoked. One boy had told him his mother was a 'deluded whore', repeating the phrase over and over, clearly pleased with the sound of it. Perhaps she had heard the taunt, or perhaps he had asked her what the words meant. It was sometime around then that she'd withdrawn behind her theatrical poses and begun her bizarre hoarding.

There were seventeen missed calls on his phone: fourteen

from her, three from Claire. Claire could wait, but his mother would get worse the longer he blanked her. He brought her face up on screen, swore under his breath, rang her back.

'Richard—'

'I'm coming. On my way now. Are you in bed yet?'

'How long?'

'As long as it takes me to get there.'

'You've been with that *woman.*'

'No, I haven't,' he snapped.

He cut off the call and stood a few moments glaring out at the alley, refusing to leave. Or yes, he would leave, but instead of turning his bike east towards Brighton and Hove and his mother, he would turn west and start pedalling, fast at first and then steadily, heading for Dorset or Devon or Cornwall. Penzance, the Scilly Isles, the Azores. He would chuck his phone in the sea as he went. He would change his name, never come back.

He stuffed underwear, a shirt and some bed linen into a bicycle pannier, then crammed in an assortment of groceries, half-pretending they were for his escape: a packet of chocolate digestives, a Mars bar, a roll of bin bags, some bananas and a tin of baked beans.

The laptop had gone to screensaver. He stole a last look at Cambodia, trying to imagine the heat-sweat breaking all over him, the hum of insects, but it was no use, unreachable. He logged off, bolted the front door and went out the back.

The night air was warm and a smell of vinegared chips rose from the alley. He carried the bike down the fire escape into the darkness and turned on its lights before wheeling it out through the puddles from yesterday's rain. The eyes of the grey cat glowed briefly from where it hunkered on a bin, its fur ruffled by the wind. For a short while he paused on the seafront, hearing the Channel chew at the pebbles, watching the swell break, ghostly-white, around the struts of the pier and along the ragged, receding lines of the breakwaters. Then he set foot to pedal, threw his leg over the bike, and turned the handlebar east towards Brighton.

Weights seemed to drag at his limbs, it was an effort to reach cruising speed, but when he did he felt better. With the breeze in his hair, he could imagine he was free. There were ten miles to go, the road was clear and the wind was behind him. He told himself again he mustn't rage at his mother. He shouldn't have snapped at her on the phone.

It was late by the time he turned off Hove seafront and zigzagged his way to her street. Along the dilapidated terrace all the windows were unlit, hers included, and as he chained his bike to the railings he played with the notion that she would prefer not to be woken, that he should pedal home again and come back tomorrow. But she wasn't in bed, he knew. She would be wedged in her place by the window, all set to cross-question him and wheedle him and fill him with guilt. He could feel himself becoming a child again, unmanned each time he made his feet climb these steps.

He let himself in, pushing the door against the stacks of junk mail and carrier bags that bulged with who knew what, squeezing his way past them. He pulled a face, never fully prepared for the fusty odour of rotting fabric, yellowing paper, stale dust and cobwebs. In the dark front room the TV screen flickered, a chamber orchestra played and his father's young voice – resonant, but not yet matured to its recent more sensual gravel – asserted, 'My good opinion, once lost, is lost forever.'

Edging between stacks of boxes and magazines to the foot

of the stairs, he switched on the landing light to illuminate the hall. 'Hello. I'm here.'

'Yes, I know. About time,' came her voice from the front room. 'Where on *earth* have you been? I've been ringing and ringing. Will you make me a cup of tea? Did you bring biscuits?'

'Yes.' He held on to his temper. 'Be with you in a minute.'

He wedged the pannier amongst the junk on the stairs, loaded his arms with the things he had brought for her, and pressed on through to the kitchen. While the water came to the boil, he acted fast, shaking out a bin bag and chucking into it whatever useless objects came to hand, leaving gaps that with luck she wouldn't notice. A bouquet of paper roses, a bag full of corkscrews, another of tape-cassettes, two Venetian masks, a bunch of plastic grapes, a small bust of Beethoven, a tin whistle and a set of Shakespearean fridge-magnets. Theatre props, his arse: these days she was bringing home any old junk. He topped up with newspapers and books, barely glancing at the titles, sending the spiders scurrying for cover. Futile but satisfying, a few temporary points scored. Holding the bag aloft, he eased between the teetering mountains of stuff towards the street door.

A light came on in the front room. 'Richard, what *are* you doing?'

'Nothing. Putting my bag on the stairs to go up.'

'You're not *moving* things, are you?'

He didn't answer.

'I can never find *anything* after you've been. Why didn't you answer my calls?'

'I did. I'm here, aren't I?'

He left the swag by the door, hidden beneath a moth-eaten rabbit-fur jacket, a barrister's wig, a box of Christmas tree baubles and a brass candelabra. He would smuggle it out later and dump it among the bins a few houses along. Back in the kitchen he made the tea, then set off for the front room, telling himself to stay calm, not to flinch at whatever ludicrous costume she was wearing to mark Harry's passing. Judging by the old movie she was watching, he put his money on a Regency ball-gown.

To his surprise she looked almost normal. The black dress, though a bit big for her, was stylish. Her face was brightened with blusher and with blue round her eyes. Her hair was fluffed from its usual lank skull-covering into a cloud of brown waves. Had she been to a hairdresser, a beautician even? She looked barely older than her fifty-one years, sitting straight and with life in her eyes. She smiled as he manoeuvred towards her with a mug in each hand. 'Don't spill them,' she said. 'I can't always be mopping up after you.'

He stooped for a kiss, a mug held either side of her. Her lacquered hair brushed his cheek. He smelled scent. 'You look wonderful,' he told her.

'So do you, my darling.' There was almost a laugh in her voice.

He'd expected her to be in a state of hysteria. Her voice-mails had been melodramatic variations on 'Richard, where are you?' Was she glad Harry was dead? Or could it be that the news hadn't reached her and her summons was about something else?

'What's new?' he said cautiously. 'Did the social worker come by?'

'Who?' she said. Her attention was back on the movie still playing, on young Harry Whittaker galloping on horseback through Jane Austen's green countryside.

'She said she would come.'

'Who did?'

'The social worker.'

'Nosy madam. I didn't open the door.'

He parked the two mugs amidst the clutter on top of the stone-age TV while he cleared space beside her. Her table was loaded as ever with back copies of *The Stage*.

'Be careful. Where are you putting those?'

'They'll be safe over here.'

'But I *need* them.'

'You can have them back later.'

He straightened up, looking around him. The corner by her chair where he usually sat on a big, tasselled cushion had disappeared beneath two cardboard boxes and several volumes, black with dust, of the *Encyclopaedia Britannica*. At least she couldn't have nicked those – some car-boot-sale bastard must have ferried them here. He swallowed his frustration. 'I'll be back with the biscuits and some bananas I've brought you. Have a think where I'm going to sit, Mum. Will Sid mind if we move him for once?'

'What?' She was mesmerised by Mr Darcy.

'Sid. May I shift him?'

He laid a hand on the head of the giant wooden Buddha that beamed from the disintegrating armchair beside the TV. For a moment his mother bristled, working herself up to find reasons against. Then she nodded and winked. 'I'll ask him nicely,' she said.

'What kind of biscuits?' she called after him.

'Chocolate digestives. And a Mars bar.'

He fetched them and put them beside her mug. 'Have a banana first,' he suggested, but she unwrapped the Mars bar. She would rather buy a feather boa than eat a square meal.

He hefted the Buddha over to the stack of encyclopaedias,

where it listed like the figurehead on a sinking ship. 'Thanks, Sid,' he murmured.

The television screen filled with a soft-focus, close-up image of the young Harold Whittaker. 'I wish I'd known him then,' said his mother. 'Wasn't he just *gorgeous?*'

'Yes, but can we pause him?'

She pointed the remote and the movie stopped. Richard closed his eyes for a moment, savouring the respite from Harry. Then he lowered himself gingerly into the sagging seat of the armchair, shunted close to his mother and took her hand. 'Tell me this,' he said, as gently as he was able. 'Have you heard that he's died?'

Her big blue eyes widened and Richard steeled himself for the onslaught of emotion. Then, 'Of *course* I have, darling. It's been on the news all day.'

Too right. He wasn't able to turn on the radio without hearing another hyperbolic tribute or clip of Harry's voice, and the whole world was posting about him online.

'But that's great.' He gripped her fingers. 'Great that you're okay, I mean. I thought you'd be sad.'

Her expression changed on cue, the mouth quivering, the eyes pained. 'I *am* sad,' she said. 'And so should you be.'

'I thought you'd be in shreds, but you're not.' He did his best to look solemn. 'Look at you, you're not.'

'I'm *devastated*,' she insisted. Her eyes glistened with tears. She could shed them at will. Instead of living on the money her parents left her and obsessing about Harry, she really ought to have gone on the stage. 'I couldn't stop crying last night. I was crying this morning, but then I had to go out. You wouldn't answer the phone to me.'

'I'm sorry. I should have done.'

'Pretending not to care. Pretending he doesn't matter to you.'

She was a fine one to talk about pretending. 'I needed time. I was shocked,' he said.

The tears spilled down her cheeks. 'I can't believe it. How *can* Harry be dead?'

'He was bound to go one day.'

'But your *father*, Richard, your *father*.' She accused him with those streaming blue eyes.

He looked away, at the darkness beyond the window. 'Which is why I've been shocked, okay?'

She gave a disbelieving sigh. 'Anyway, I've been out and bought this mourning dress. Do you like it?'

He refocused. 'Very much.' What a neat swerve from lamentation to vanity.

'*And* had my hair done. *And* washed and ironed my best hanky in case I cry in public.'

She produced a white, lace-edged square from the sleeve of the dress.

'Beautiful. Don't use it. You'll spoil it.'

She located a box of tissues amongst the flotsam and jetsam around her, pulled one out and dabbed at her tears. 'I can't *bear* it. I *really* loved him.'

As sincere as the soup woman. 'Yes, Mum,' he said, smiling.

'You're talking down to me, Richard.'

'I'm sure you loved him very much,' he made himself say.

In the past perhaps, but not now. Her love had as much meaning and use now as a box of Christmas tree baubles and a bag full of corkscrews.

'*Nobody* understood him.' She gazed past Richard at the paused TV screen.

Oh no, here we go. 'Except you,' he quipped cynically and saw her shrink a little, wounded, or acting wounded, same difference. He reached for her hand again. 'I'm sorry – that was unkind of me.' His job was to play along, to feed her the cues, to listen and smile and agree.

'I've seen beneath the surface,' she said.

'Yes, Mum.'

'Everyone *thinks* that they know him, but they've only seen the masks he puts on.'

'Exactly. What he wanted them to see.'

'But Richard, there's a good man inside.'

He couldn't bring himself to agree. He sat back, took a gulp of tea and examined the mug he was holding. *Save our theatres!* it demanded.

'You've never believed me, but everyday happiness frightens Harry. He doesn't know how to do it. It feels like forgetting his lines.'

As a child Richard had soaked up her apologies for his father, wanting to believe in the romance, but he'd seen through him long ago. He was just a lying Casanova who'd seduced his mother, then dumped her and never given her a second thought beyond coughing up child support and instructing his lawyers and minders to keep her off his back. Richard stared dejectedly at the bananas he'd put in her lap, then lifted his eyes to her thin face.

'I *have* to go,' she was saying. 'They'll be trying to prevent me, I know, the ex-wives and the minders, but you'll be with me, making *sure* we get through.'

'Get through what? Go where?'

'To the *funeral*,' she repeated. 'You're not paying attention, Richard. That's why I've bought this dress, and—'

'No!' He sat straight in the chair. 'It's a terrible idea.'

Images flooded in of the day she'd gone crazy when he was eleven. She'd heard or read somewhere that his father

42

was married again, and begun yelling and weeping, finally marching him out along the front and past Brighton Pier to camp on Harry's doorstep on Marine Parade. A bad-tempered housekeeper with cigarette breath had told them to push off. The happy couple weren't here, she'd said, nor likely to be any time soon. Sir Harry was filming in Spain and his new wife was away in Los Angeles.

His hysterical mother had refused to accept it. She'd insisted on waiting, unrolling their sleeping bags beneath the white-pillared Regency porch and screeching at passersby that this was Sir Harry's child, that she should be living in this grand house, not in a hovel in Hove.

People began to linger and stare. When Richard, pink with shame, had whispered that he was hungry, she'd sent him to the beach vendors for hotdogs and chips. He'd got back to find a small crowd had gathered. She was laying strident claim to VIP connections and an important job in the theatre. As if.

Eventually the law had arrived, to the cheers and hoots of the onlookers: a policeman who spoke sternly, and a police-woman who had put her arm around Richard as though he were a little kid. The policeman had told his mother she would lose her son into foster care if she didn't shape up. He'd told her to consult a solicitor if she had grievances. He'd driven them home in a squad car, his mother silent at last in the passenger seat and Richard in the back with the policewoman, who'd kept asking him if he was all right.

The black dress, the makeup, the handkerchief. Of course. He knew now why she was happy. She was planning to stage some kind of scene at the funeral. He had to dissuade her. 'They'll be expecting you to come, ready to laugh at you. Don't give them the satisfaction. Tell you what, we'll have a day of remembering him here, just you and me. You can tell me the whole story again, and we'll watch his best bits, make an occasion of it. Remind me, you first met him at...?'

'The Barbican,' she said dreamily. 'He was playing Oberon, and his crown got trampled onstage, so they sent me running to his dressing room with a new one. He held my hands to his heart, and he drank me in, Richard, you wouldn't believe it. His eyes were *so* big, painted in turquoise and blue, and his chest was bare and so *warm*.'

Memory made her radiant: it wasn't a leap to imagine her as a gullible twenty-year-old.

'He smelled *wonderful*, of greasepaint and of the sweat from being out there under the lights, spellbinding more than a thousand people. So earthy, so *sexy*—'

'Mum, okay.' Always her account of this scene had him squirming. A lecherous fifty-one-year-old togged up as the king of the fairies.

His mother persisted. 'He turned me to the mirror with the light bulbs all round it, and he put his face next to mine, cheek to cheek, and he asked me, 'What is your name?' And then he said, "Deborah Lawton, just *look* at you. You're more beautiful by far than Titania, inside and out. Your soul sings in your eyes." He poured me champagne and begged me to wait there in his dressing room. And when he came back—'

'Enough for now,' Richard said, 'but we'll make a day of it together, I promise, with non-stop Harry-movies, and I'll bring champagne, the very best champagne.'

'No,' she said. 'We have to go to the funeral.'

He leapt to his feet. 'Oh, come on. Don't do this.' There must be a way to dissuade her. 'You won't get anywhere near him. You'll only upset yourself. It'll be massive. A memorial service in Westminster Abbey, they were saying on the radio this morning. Invitation only. Crowds in the streets—'

She interrupted sharply. 'You're being stupid on purpose. I'm not talking about *that* razzle-dazzle. That's just for show. There'll be a *private* funeral earlier. Soon. There's no time to waste, Richard. We're going to find out where it is, when it is, and then we're going to be at it, both of us, and that's *final*. Harry wants us to be there.'

No argument would shift her. 'He wants us there,' was her answer to everything, as if the rancid old bugger not only gave a damn but was still alive to give it. She insisted that Richard must ring his father's agent the next day, because if he wouldn't, she would, and if he wouldn't go with her, she would go without him. She wore him down until he exploded, 'Okay. You win. I'll do it,' and slammed out of the room, throwing himself into action in the kitchen, not caring if she heard him fill bin bags and scrub surfaces.

Eventually she came and watched, pale and silent, not commenting or protesting or snatching things from his hands. Maybe this was his opportunity: he would get some house-clearance firm out of bed and summon them round to start ferrying the whole contents of the place to the dump before she remembered how she needed every last worthless item. He strode back and forth to the street with the bags.

Then she started to wail, 'Stop it. Please stop it, Richard. You're frightening me.'

Her fear wasn't fake. He dropped the bag he was carrying and let himself hug her, really hug her for the first time in years, shocked at how fragile she was beneath the black dress, feeling the pressure of her thin arms round his ribs, inhaling her perfume, burying his nose in her lacquered hair, almost crying himself.

Later, as he negotiated his way up past the heaps of theatre programmes and scripts on the stairs to snatch a couple of hours' kip, he gathered resolve. He had to think this through as a grown-up, not as an eleven-year-old kid. Harry was dead at last, that was something, and if she made a public spectacle of herself, he would just have to weather it. But maybe she wouldn't and the funeral would release him somehow. He would reach some resolution, be able to sign off on his anger. It was the nearest he would ever come to the callous father who'd never bothered to come to him.

On the landing he eased past the bundles of charity-shop glad rags, the tower of hat boxes and the rocking kangaroo, and found the key to his room on his key ring. Inside, he exhaled a sigh of release, stretching his arms in the space he kept empty of all but a bed, a lamp, a rug, a toothbrush on the washbasin, and *The Times Atlas of the World*.

He tipped sheet and pillowcase out from the pannier and gave the duvet a shake. With Harry gone, his mother might begin to turn herself round. Might accept the space he'd made in the kitchen and not fill it with jumble again. Might concede that she didn't miss anything, allow him to throw out more stuff next time. He would come for a whole day, talk to her seriously, get her to acknowledge her hoarding and stealing and smothering and clinging, to accept counselling even. He'd persuade her to sit tight in the front room while he cleared another area. Bit by bit, visit by visit, he would liberate the kitchen before making a start on the hall.

Or he would brave her hysterics and get it done anyway, calmly, hugging her tears away afterwards. With Harry gradually forgotten, her house would become normal, his *mother* would become normal. She would make friends, develop less morbid interests, and at last he could leave her.

He sat on the bed and sent two quick texts: one to Claire, saying he was tied up looking after his mother, and the other to Tiffany, praising her brilliance, telling her she was a godsend, and asking her to open up because he wouldn't arrive until mid-morning. Then he stripped and slid into bed, reaching for the atlas to lull him to sleep. Harry's death was a milestone. It might or might not mark a new start for his mother, but either way he was determined to claim his own freedom. Where should he google tomorrow? He consulted the index. Dalgety, Dalhousie, Dalmatia, Dalwhinnie...

Someone was moving below. He got out of bed and moved silently to the door, easing it open a crack. A draft of night air came up the stairs, and the noises were unmistakable now. A rustle, a clink, a soft thud. The sounds of his mother carrying the bin bags back in.

Two Wednesdays later

Harry

Dear God, how much longer? I've lost track of the days. Skewered by fear until I'm weary of fear, abandoned in this refrigerated warehouse, stacked floor to ceiling with bodies festering like bad wine in a cellar. The only sound is a tap dripping somewhere, counting the interminable seconds.

The corpse mocks me with a semblance of life where there is none. I've examined it so minutely it has become unfamiliar, as though I never spent all those years rehearsing its moves, fretting its aging, watching its weight, shaving its chin, picking fluff from its navel. Drained of the life that was me, no longer my professional tool, my means of sensual enjoyment, it has become my millstone. Desperate to be away from it, instead I can only flitter around it, enduring the impotent hours. Who knew that time could extend so as I wait for the door to burst open and the daylight to flood in, craving the raucous jests of the undertakers. I know their names now: Bill and Frank.

Sometimes they arrive empty-handed and whistling to fetch one of us out. The disintegrating hag who accompanied me here went off yesterday. The young black man, two down and one along from me, looks philosophical waiting his turn, his handsome face so serene he might be an actor taking his curtain call.

Sometimes they manhandle a new corpse from trolley to hoisting machine and slot it in among us. *What sights of ugly death!* Many are barely recognisable as human: mangled by post-mortems, smashed in accidents, crisped and blackened by fire. This is it. This is what we all come to. Meaningless husks. Refuse disposal.

Except no, here I am, still myself, as some of these ruined creatures surely are too. I beam the message yet again – *Is anyone there?* – but no answer comes, only the drip of the tap. It's hopeless: my fellow shades are as unheard and unseen as I am. Scotty smiled at me, heard me, held me in his hands, but he's 'one level up'. 'Look in a mirror,' he said. 'You'll see you're not anything at all.' We lost souls are lost to each other. The laws of the universe are cruel indeed.

I refuse to despair. *Significant emotional investment*: Scotty's phrase nags at me. He started this way himself, he said, perched on the nose of a sixty-three-year-old railway clerk, and then he jumped, or transferred or whatever the term is, to someone he cared for, and he never looked back.

Fear closes in like a smothering pillow because, although I adored my work and my home and the power that so much money gave me, and the wide, beautiful world, and life itself, God help me, all that is far, far away, out of reach, which leaves only the possibility of some person I cared about who may come to the funeral. But each person I think of is tiresome or tedious or trivial. Try as I may, I can call to mind no one, not even a woman, least of all an ex-wife, who held my attention for long, let alone earned my deep affection. Taken individually, human beings are so paltry. I've rubbed shoulders, raised glasses, been intimate in one way or another with the good and the great and the bad and the humble and found them all disappointing, no match for the marvel of humankind gathered together as a spellbound audience. Even if I have overlooked someone and whoever it is comes to see me off, how in heaven's name will I know they are there? I'll be shut away in the coffin as I was in the mortuary fridge, one second outside it, frantic to escape, and then, as the lid closes, dragged in along with the body.

I have to hope that won't matter. Within ten metres, did Scotty say? Maybe I'll sense my rescuer somehow and the coffin won't hinder me. I'll pass through the velvet and the silk wadding and the solid oak and fly to whoever it is. It had better be so because, if not, what then? I'll remain with any particle of the body, he said. I imagine riding a speck of my own dust to a crematorium worker's sleeve, later to be disgorged from a washing machine into a sewer. Or will I swirl with the smoke up the chimney and be carried off who knows where by the wind? Awful to contemplate, but the alternative is even more awful: sealed in the urn, never to see light again. I should have asked for my ashes to be scattered. Instead I specified 'interment in a modest memorial', confidently imagining myself in Poets' Corner in the Abbey, alongside Larry and Irving. Ah, take care what you wish for. I shall be alone in a stone vault in darkness and silence, perpetually wakeful, time without end. No, no, have pity.

I need to share this with someone, to beg for reprieve. 'I'll try to look into your case,' Scotty said. 'I'll come again if I'm free.' I've called on him endlessly, using the name and number he gave me, Pickles 64123, but he hasn't appeared, not a gleam, not a glimmer.

At last, some relief. The throb of an engine, slammed doors and footsteps. Sunlight streams through the doorway, and in come Bill and Frank. Thank heaven for the sheer, loutish animation of them, blowing their cigarette smoke, sniggering at some banal profanity.

The trolley they're pushing is empty. They trundle the rickety hoist into place at the far end and move it towards me.

Joy and horror, I'm the one they have come for!

They are sliding Lord Whittaker out and away, and me along with him.

I was alone in the unmarked grey van, with no new visitation from Scotty. They've brought me to the back room of a funeral parlour, where my body lies naked, face up on a table. Nearby waits the sumptuous coffin I chose for myself, not trusting to leave the choice to incompetents. I shrink from it, tugging in the other direction, straining uselessly to break free, while Bill and Frank pull on coveralls and surgical gloves and squirt disinfectant into hot water in preparation for administering the 'gold star, full malarkey' treatment they mentioned in the hospital mortuary.

'Has anyone asked to view 'im?' says Frank.

'I'll check,' says Bill and ducks into the next room. 'Nah,' he says, coming back. 'He ordered embalming, make-up, the 'ole lot, but let's skip it. What the eye doesn't see we can put in the till. It's a straight coffin job.'

The swindling bastards – but I've no time to be angry. This is it. Here I go, any minute, into the dark, abandoned by everyone.

Rigor mortis wore off days ago. These animals are running flannels across my limp corpse, flipping it on its side and making unrepeatable jokes. I thrash about uselessly. This is happening in slow motion, with ghastly inevitability.

They have my best dress suit on a hanger – Simon must have brought it to them – and Frank holds up a pair of my shoes.

'What size?' says Bill.

'Ten.'

'They'd do for my dad. D'you think?'

'Go for it. If someone wants a look, we can sort him out sharpish.'

Bill examines the suit. 'Tailor-made. Should fetch a bob or two.' He rezips the cover and goes off with it.

Then he's back, and – no – no – they're moving tables together, the high one the body is on, the low one the coffin is on. They're getting ready to tip the one into the other and me along with it. Oh Scotty – I mean Pickles – Albert Pickles 64123 – *anyone*, please help me, please, please. I lived such a bad life. I'm sorry, I'm sorry, I couldn't be more sorry. Set me free, and I swear I'll spend the whole of eternity bringing comfort to the afflicted, the lonely. Anything, anything, but let them not do this.

The body is in, slumped on its side against the cherry velvet padding, and I'm fighting wildly to get out from under it as they heft the lid from where it leans against the wall and raise it up and lower it onto me. No, no, no—

The lid is on the coffin, they're screwing it down, but glory be – I am outside it! In a euphoric moment I find myself pardoned and free.

Bill and Frank are stripping off their coveralls, heading for the front office. I'll go with them, back to the land of the living, what blissful release! But no – try as I may, I still cannot follow. I have to stay behind.

This is nonsensical. I hover above the coffin, reading my name engraved in brass. I'm still tethered, I don't understand. Then I do. Comprehension sweeps through me in a surge of new horror and helplessness. That maudlin Sunday I spent, mourning my mortality, selecting this casket, imagining myself lifeless within it – did that count as significant emotional investment?

I want to scream, but lack voice. Lack everything but an insane predicament. I batter the coffin with my silent howls.

Richard

'Gosh, I'm excited. Aren't you excited?' said Claire. She flopped down on the sofa and put her damp bare feet in his lap. Her blonde hair dripped on her shoulders. Steamy from the shower, she had a flirtatious look in her eye.

'Not half,' Richard said. Her towel was slipping, and he gave it a tug. There was a condom in his back pocket.

'Hey, stop that,' she tugged back, 'I want to watch telly. About tomorrow, I mean. I wonder who'll be there. Wall-to-wall famous faces. Will they all be old actors, do you think? He must have known dozens of young ones as well.'

Richard hunted around for the remote. 'I'm trying not to think much about it. I'm worried what Mum will get up to.'

He'd started this evening at home in his flat, but the laptop images of elsewhere had lost their power to distract him. Today's letter was O, always tricky. Oban wasn't foreign enough and Oman looked far too expensive. He'd stopped googling, logged off and come round to Claire's, to escape into sex and TV-land instead.

His mother was hard to read. Last night when he'd cycled over there she'd reminded him of Vivien Leigh in *A Streetcar*

Named Desire. In a flimsy white frock, fluttering her lace handkerchief, she'd run from room to room, pulling one thing after another from the stacks and the heaps, reminiscing, rearranging, making impromptu speeches, and all the while quivering with nerves.

'You don't need to do this,' he'd told her. 'You don't need to put yourself through it. Harry wouldn't have expected it. He'd be amazed you even care.'

She had sagged momentarily, which had him hoping she might relent, but with a grand flourish of the handkerchief, she had straightened her back and announced to the dress circle, 'Pride of place at his funeral is the very least Harry owes *us*.'

Fuelling her excitement was the fact that, wonder of wonders, they were indeed welcome, and not to the service alone, also to the reception in Marine Parade. At last she would gaze in triumph from those fine Regency windows instead of up at them from the pavement below. She could scarcely contain herself.

The service was tomorrow afternoon, four o'clock at Woodvale Crematorium, just north of Brighton. His father's theatrical agency had given Richard the number of a neighbour who was organising it, and once he was sure Richard wasn't a reporter, Mr Foyle had effusively welcomed him onto the guest list.

'His son! Well, I never – that's extraordinary. He didn't breathe a word to me about having a son. No, really, I don't doubt you for a moment – Harry was quite a rogue by all accounts. It's truly wonderful news – I'll be delighted to see you, and yes, of course bring your mother – it goes without saying – and anyone else as your guest. Please keep it to yourselves, though, as I don't want the media turning up and spoiling the day. You simply must come back afterwards. There'll be smoked salmon and champagne at Harry's. I can't wait to meet you and your mother. No, no, please don't thank me, and you must call me Simon.'

Claire was on her knees on the yellow rug, fishing the remote from under the sofa. She clicked it at the widescreen. Up popped a high-definition picture of nothing worth seeing: an old boy in country tweeds pretending to be happy that his great aunt's wooden chest might fetch three hundred at auction. The expert fingered a brass handle. 'It's a pity these aren't the originals.'

'Your mum will be good as gold,' Claire said.

'You haven't met her. You don't know her. Claire, you've got to believe me, she's going to be horrible to you. She declares war on every woman I ever introduce her to.'

He'd only ever introduced her to one, his first girlfriend from school. His mother had bombarded her with hostile questions and made scathing remarks about her looks and her accent.

'Nonsense. I'm sure she'll be fine.' All his efforts to put Claire off were useless. No one was going to come between her and this star-studded event.

He wished he'd never told her who his father was. It shamed him that he sometimes used the connection to chat up women. Even when they didn't believe him, the idea intrigued them, made up a little for his lack of money and prospects. In the singles bar where he'd met Claire three months ago, more than believing it, she'd been in awe, weaving romance around him as though he were a pauper prince in a fairytale.

Did she see him at all, he wondered, or just the young Harry playing him? She was bursting with thwarted fame-by-association, itching to tell everyone she knew. 'No,' he'd said. 'This is *my* secret. Mine, not yours, Claire. I don't want people knowing.' He would hate strangers to be staring and whispering, talking about him.

'A bit of fame would be fun,' was her take on it. 'Just think – it would put your café on the map and cheer up my clients no end.' She earned her money as a peripatetic care-worker for Brighton and Hove council, helping frail and confused people out of their beds, seeing to them in their bathrooms, feeding them and their pets, and putting them into their beds again.

She wriggled her bare toes against him. 'Do you want me to ring your mum for you? Tell her I'm coming? I won't upset her – I have a way with old people.'

'She's not old.'

'With mad people then.'

'She's not mad.'

'If you say so. Look, I'll ring her now.'

He snatched his phone from the coffee table and put it out of reach.

'She'll chat to me nicely. She'll invite me to drop in the next time I'm passing. She'll say, "I'm so glad to be getting to know you, my dear," and then,' Claire squealed and shrank in mock terror to the end of the sofa, 'she'll come after me in the shower, like that mother in *Psycho*.'

'That wasn't the mother, Claire – it was the son.' Richard leapt at her, grabbing the remote from her hand and slashing down with it – 'Eeek, eeek, eeek, eeek!' – making her scream and hit him with cushions.

He dropped the remote and kissed her, and she kissed him back, and one thing led to another. Maybe she was right, he found himself thinking in the thick of things. She might charm his mother with her warmth and her jolliness.

Afterwards, he cracked open a beer and began channel surfing. 'Bloody hell, not *Tomorrow's Tycoon* again.'

'Hey babes, I wanted to watch that,' she said, but he ignored her, pausing on the news, then flicking to some soap where three people were shouting at once, then to a woman with big breasts frying onions, then to his father in an archive chat-show clip, back through *Tomorrow's Tycoon* where a contestant was pitching to the panel of fat cats, landing finally on a weather forecast. It was going to be warm and sunny for the funeral tomorrow.

'Mean bastard,' said Claire, rearranging her towel and peeling a damp strand of blonde hair from her cheek. '*TT* is good. You should give it a go. You might get some killer ideas for turning the café around.'

He grinned. 'I've already had the killer idea. Tiffany. She's amazing. She's got a children's story hour and elevenses going. The mums have been turning up, droves of pushchairs, drinking coffee by the gallon.'

With Tiffany to help him, he'd begun to enjoy the café again, looking forward to opening up every morning, seeing its possibilities as he had at the start.

'That's clever of her.' Claire sounded dubious. 'Take care, though. My guess is she fancies you.'

'For heaven's sake – she's a teenager.'

'No need to snap.'

'Sorry, but I get enough earache from Mum about women with designs on me.'

Claire giggled. 'Me, you mean? A gold-digging harlot, is that what I am?'

'Exactly. No gold to be dug, though.'

'Which reminds me,' she said, snuggling up, 'I've been thinking. The press would give a lot for your story. It would solve all your problems. You could pay off the bank, and—'

'Good try,' he interrupted, 'but Mum had the same thought when I was a kid. I think she hoped the publicity would bring Harry back to her somehow. She got nowhere. The journalists laughed in her face, told her she was a fantasist, wouldn't touch it.'

'Of course not,' Claire said. 'They'd have been afraid of his lawyers, but it's different now – dead men can't sue, and you can back her up. You look so much like him, and they can do DNA.'

He pulled away from her. The idea made him uncomfortable. 'I don't see that it's much of a story,' he said. 'Harold Whittaker fathered a baby. So what? Who hasn't these days?'

'Yes, but your mother's the angle.'

He shook his head. He wished she would drop it.

'The press need a hook and an angle. The hook is he's just died and—'

'Have you been to journalism school?'

'Don't be silly. It's commonsense. The angle is your mum's like that batty woman in *Great Expectations*. She sits in her wedding dress and won't wind the clocks, and her cake goes all mouldy, and—'

'Stop it, Claire, please. This is my life we're talking about. I couldn't bear to be famous – can't think of anything worse. And Mum's vulnerable. Publicity could tip her over the edge. The last thing she needs is the press telling her she's Miss Havisham.'

'Go on. She'd enjoy it and you need the money.'

'I get it.' He faked a grin. 'You *are* a gold-digging harlot.'

'Yeah, right,' she said, sounding huffy, 'and that's why I've sunk my claws into such a whizz entrepreneur.' She snatched the remote from him and switched back to *Tomorrow's Tycoon*. 'It's the only decent thing on.'

He groaned, but he didn't mind really. Anything would do to shut her up and fill the time between now and tomorrow. He tried to focus on the programme. Tiffany reckoned he resembled this curly-headed ego-trip called Quentin who was out on a task now, haggling prices for bolts of cloth. He was using his charm, making the Indian stallholder giggle, her double chin wobble. She was meeting him more than halfway. Then cut to the aftermath: Quentin's arms full of patterned silk and the Barbie-doll presenter of the programme high-fiving him, trilling, 'That was so, so cool.'

'Seriously,' Claire said. 'You're more photogenic than any of this lot. You'd look smashing in the papers. Which reminds me – have you noticed my teeth?' She drew her lips back to display them. 'I've been whitening them in case anyone takes pictures tomorrow.'

'I'm dazzled.'

She laughed, and for a while she was quiet, watching the programme. Then, 'By the way,' she said lightly, 'there's something else I've been meaning to ask you.'

Her eyes were on the screen, but she had his attention.

'Thing is, it's July already, and my lease runs out first of August. Any chance I could move in with you?'

He said nothing, gathering his thoughts.

'Share the rent? Save us both a bit of money?'

'Can't you renew?'

'Nope. Landlady's due back from Seattle and needs it herself. You'd hardly notice me, honest. None of this furniture's mine. It would be just the telly and a few bits and pieces.' She looked up at him. 'Nice telly.'

'I'm sorry,' he said, 'but can I be straight too? I'm not

serious enough about us, that's the truth of it, Claire. I don't think you are either, not really.'

For a moment the silence was awkward. Then, 'Okay,' she said. 'Just thought I'd ask. See what it sounded like, eh?'

'I'll be happy to help with the flat hunting.'

'Great. Thanks.' She stared at her nice telly. 'I'll probably look in Brighton. More expensive, but I won't have to commute every day.'

Lily

A young man who worked for her husband was the next person to realise that Lily's marriage was broken.

The office party was spiralling fast out of control, the air becoming humid with sweat and free booze. The speeches had been made, most of the bigwigs had gone, and the whole of the tenth floor was now heaving with drunken dancing.

Half a year of unplanned celibacy had sapped the young man's confidence. All he had to do was find an unattached woman, he kept telling himself, and the rest should be easy: your place or mine? But the admin girl he'd just shouted his best chat-up line at had given him two fingers and, if his lip-reading was right, underlined this with, 'Get lost, loser.'

Shielding his plastic cup of red wine, he retreated to the fringe of the battle to regroup. Lower your standards, he told himself. It didn't much matter who the next woman was. Not busybody Karen, who was roaming the place spying and stirring – he would never live that down – but where was Tamara, his new boss's PA? A bit ropey to look at, but a good laugh, a good sport, and right now she'd do nicely.

He stood on a chair and peered across the crowd. Holy shit! Pussycat Christine from marketing was snogging that berk from accounting. If berks from accounting could pull pretty women, then so could he. He stood taller on the chair and stared around angrily. That bird in the red dress by the buffet, for example.

He watched her for a minute. She looked a bit lost, a bit down, no one talking to her. Age hard to tell at this distance – mid-twenties perhaps – but super-elegant with all that brown hair piled up on her head. Way out of his league, not least because something about her shouted intelligence, which he felt a bit short of right now. Hang on though, didn't they say the beautiful, intelligent ones were short of offers because nobody dared ask? And if she said no, she would say it politely; she didn't look like the 'get lost, loser' type. He drained his plastic cup and tossed it aside before climbing unsteadily down from the chair. Expanding his chest and jutting his chin, he began shouldering his way through the crush.

Before he reached her, she turned, looking for someone, and he stalled, shocked first by the shiny red-onion-skin of her cheek and then by the realisation that he'd been about to proposition his new boss's wife. He'd only seen her right profile when they came in together. Jesus. Bad move. Think again.

He wasn't altogether repelled by the birthmark. Jostled by the crowd, he wondered tipsily how it must feel to be beauty and beast in one skin. Others, he noticed, were darting glances, as if she were a puzzle they needed to solve. Curiosity held him. More than curiosity, the lure of the exotic. He very much wouldn't mind giving her one, he decided magnanimously.

He grazed the buffet, brushing her arm as he reached for a handful of peanuts, and seeing close up the ragged spatter

61

of bluish-red mottling that spread down from her cheek to her jaw.

'Are you all right, Mrs C?' Busybody Karen arrived, beaming fake warmth, standing too close and touching the woman's shoulder as she bellowed in her ear, 'Come and join in. No need to be on your own. I'll introduce you around.'

Mrs C shook her head, smiling, insisting she was fine.

'Well, if you're sure, love, but come and find me if you need someone to talk to.'

Alone again, the woman showed the whole of her disturbing face to the crowd, scanning it for her husband. She looked a bit lost, younger than she'd seemed from across the room. It was clear she'd had enough of this party: she wanted to go home.

The young man munched peanuts, looking for Martin too, wanting to see how he behaved with his unusual wife. There was no sign of him, which was odd, come to think of it. He'd had his new boss down as the life-and-soul type.

He lurched off round the edge of the party in search of him. How naff would it be to tell him his missus was after him? Might be worth it though, just to see his reaction. He wasn't among the dancers. Or in the gents. Someone was throwing up in a cubicle, but the feet in scuffed trainers weren't his. The young man pushed on to the far end of the building, where the meeting rooms and senior staff offices were shuttered and dark behind venetian blinds. Still no sign of Martin. He stood swaying a moment, trying to remember why he was looking for his boss, starting to size up the women in the group coming in off the stairwell.

Just then the door of meeting room 3 opened and Martin Caruthers emerged from the darkness. The young man stepped forward, then paused, disconcerted, because the door behind Martin was closing as though someone was pulling it from inside. Checking his flies and smoothing his hair, his boss headed off briskly.

The handle to meeting room 3 was quivering and turning. Who would the woman be? Blimey, it was Tamara, the PA. She slipped out and stood for a moment with her back to the door, glancing nervously about. The young man shrank into the stairwell as she passed. She stumbled, then stopped, leaning a hand on the wall while she raised a foot to adjust her shoe.

Here came busybody Karen. 'Ooh, Tamara, you're awfully pink. You need to go carefully. How much have you had? And hang on – no – I don't believe it!'

Karen erupted in a great screech of laughter that had everyone looking. Tamara, grinning, tried to slide past, but Karen caught her by the wrist, spluttering and gathering herself for the kill. 'You mad hussy,' she managed at last. 'Un-freaking-believable. What have you been up to? You've got your dress on inside out.'

Thursday

Harry

'But what happens with babies?' I'm yelling. 'How does this nonsensical rule work for them?'

'Babies?'

'Or people whose family and friends all die before they do.' I'm becoming hysterical. 'There must be millions of those.'

Scotty smiles. His eyes twinkle merrily. Has elevation from spirit to lesser angel released his inner imp? I could happily wring his neck for that smirk, if I only had hands.

His T-shirt today advises: *Peace comes from within.* He showed up just as the cortège was setting off from the funeral parlour, where two undertakers became four, Bill and Frank in the hearse, the other two in the limousine that now follows us, carrying Simon Foyle and Mrs Butley, my cleaner. All my furious attempts to transfer, first to Simon, then to Mrs Butley, as the coffin was carried to the hearse were in vain. I was brought up short like a stringed cork from a popgun.

Encased within polished glass, a great mass of white and gold roses and lilies dazzles in the afternoon sun as we process up Lewes Road out of Brighton towards Woodvale

Crematorium. Scotty sits cross-legged amidst the flowers at the shoulder of the coffin, the pink soles of his bare feet neatly upturned, while I spin and jump at the narrow end, demanding fairness from the implacable laws of the universe.

'People who are murdered,' I try, 'and dumped, never found, no fault of their own – are you telling me *they* get stuck with their bodies?'

Scotty's eyes follow an overtaking hatchback laden with children and small, panting dogs. 'See that window sticker?' he giggles. '*Menagerie on board.*'

'What about it?'

'Nothing. It's funny, that's all. I love families, don't you?'

'How dare you!' I fly at him furiously, only to find myself at the head end of the coffin with a close-up view of his self-satisfied back. A small, tasteless wreath of red carnations sits in pride of place here. The card, from Mrs Butley, says *Will be sadly missed*, in reference to her wages most likely.

Scotty raises himself, upturned soles and all, on his hands, rotates to face me, and backs off a little before lowering his angelic backside into the petals and foliage. 'Try to be calm,' he says.

'Calm? Are you crazy? Are you even listening to me?'

'Yes, but you're not thinking helpfully.'

'I'm pointing out the flaws in the logic. People die away from their loved ones. Happens all the time. At war, or at work, or travelling. Climbing Everest, for example. Crashed in the Amazon jungle or the Pacific Ocean. What about them? The rules are ridiculous.'

He leans towards me, his eyes at last serious. 'You care about these people?'

'The whole thing's a farce, is what I care about. The system's unfair.'

'Unfair to the people you mention?'

'Unfair in principle! Someone needs to review it, the total absurdity of it, and put my case on hold, quickly, please.'

The hearse is turning right. I glance out through the glass, and my panic enters the red zone. We're at the cemetery already, gliding through the gates and now, smoothly, inexorably, up the long, sloping valley lined with ancient trees and old tombstones. A blackbird glides over the hearse to the ground before bouncing away across the grass with its head cocked for worms. I throw myself towards it. 'For pity's sake, let me out!'

Scotty unfolds his lotus-legs, leans back on his hands and regards me as if we have all the time in the world.

'Answer me,' I beseech him. 'This makes no sense at all.'

He shakes his blond head. 'Okay,' he says carefully. 'Since you insist. Would it help you to know that the babies, those who've lost all their loved ones, the unfortunates who die far from people they've cared for, that they're happy and safe, that what you call "the system" looks after them. Would that make you feel better?'

'It takes care of them how, though?'

'I'm not up on the details. My section doesn't deal with those cases.'

I stare frantically about me. We're passing landscaped shrubbery and herbaceous beds. 'This is outrageous. I need someone competent.'

'You know all that you need to know. Try to concentrate on resolving your own situation.'

All at once, up ahead, our terrifying destination swings into view. A stone tracery of wide lancet windows, a carriage-arch between twin steep-pitched roofs, an ornate tower looming above. From one or other of these two mock-Gothic chapels

I've watched several of my fellow thespians' coffins disappear behind curtains on their way to the fire and the chimney. Did their ghosts roll through too, shrieking for mercy?

'Duty calls. Got to go now.' Scotty begins to shimmer and fade. 'Good luck.'

'Stop. Hang on. You said you'd look into my case.'

'And I did,' he says sorrowfully.

'There must be discretion,' I beg him, 'a way round this, some grounds for appeal. My genius must count for something. It has to be possible.'

His inscrutability lingers in the air for a moment, then he's gone.

The hearse and the limo are slowing and stopping by a mass of parked cars – oh please, let there be someone inside that I cared about, just one. Here's my agent's Mercedes – not him, I don't give a stuff about Julian, but there has to be *someone*.

Simon Foyle stares in at my coffin with bloodshot, lugubrious eyes. Mrs Butley stands apart, puffing on a cigarette and chortling about something with one of the undertakers, while fishing a crumpled tissue from her hideous, faux-leather bucket-bag. Bill and Frank, in top hat and tails, with long, sorrowful faces, are opening the hearse door and starting to lift out the flowers. Please, there has to be someone.

Richard

He waited uneasily, sandwiched between Claire and his mother in a pew just inside the door. The crematorium chapel was too small for the murmuring crowd, packed bum to bum, shoulder to shoulder, all the seats taken and many standing now at the back. Amidst extravagant floral arrangements up front, a live string quartet was playing. If his mother planned some disruption, she would have to climb over him and Claire to get out and run up the aisle. For the moment at least she was quiet, sizing up the other mourners, while Claire twisted in her seat, awed by the celebrity faces.

'I thought the press would be here,' Claire said.

'I told you – Mr Foyle's kept this one quiet. There'll be a big memorial service in Westminster Abbey.'

'Still,' she said, peering anxiously at the door, 'I thought there'd be at least one or two journalists.'

He couldn't help smiling, she was so keen to be photographed at Lord Whittaker's funeral. As well as a new dress – a long, slinky thing in dark green – she'd splashed out on a head-hugging hat and borrowed a rope of jet beads from a fellow care-worker. He squeezed her hand.

His mother's tactic so far had been to blank Claire completely. Emerging regally among the stray cats sunning themselves on her doorstep, she had ignored his introduction and Claire's greeting: 'Lovely to meet you at last, Deborah.' Then all the way here – on the bus to the Old Steine, on the second bus crammed with chattering students heading off to the campus at Falmer, and on his arm up the cemetery drive – she had channelled her displeasure that this gate-crashing strumpet was tailing along with them into a haughty pretence that she wasn't. Claire's efforts to engage her in conversation, his appeals to her not to be silly, all fell on deaf ears.

'Richard, look,' whispered Claire, pointing out yet another film actor who meant nothing to him. 'I can't believe I'm breathing the same air.'

His mother craned forward to see the chief mourners. He'd twice had to dissuade her from standing on the pew to get a better look. She tugged at his sleeve now. 'Look, Richard, the nerve of it. Bold as brass.'

'Who?'

'Her.' She pointed. A smartly dressed black woman had just taken a seat at the front.

'What about her?'

'A reserved seat – I ask you. His latest fancy piece, I don't doubt. Claiming right of place. Hogging the limelight.'

'Come off it. You've no idea who she is.'

The woman seemed to be on her own. She was shifting impatiently and kept glancing at her watch.

The scent of lilies itched the back of Richard's nose. The quartet's mournful strains insisted that he should be sad. He wasn't sad, he was hemmed in and apprehensive. He wanted to shake off the two women, vault into the aisle, and stride away through the sunshine, his suit jacket over his shoulder, his tie stuffed in his pocket. He would head home to Worthing: to the café where Tiffany, bless her, was supervising the installation of Wi-Fi today, or, better still, to his flat for his bicycle and off for a ride across the Downs, plotting a more conclusive escape. Peru had looked amazing over his cornflakes this morning. Rainbows and mist, mountains, rivers and jungles, Inca ruins. He would learn Spanish, earn his living somehow, go trekking.

'Hey, babes.' Claire leaned in close, smiling up from under the brim of the hat. 'Can we go to the big memorial service? Will your nice Mr Foyle get us in to that too?'

Richard coughed, hoping his mother hadn't heard. Nice Mr Foyle would almost certainly get them in if he asked, but the last thing he wanted was to have to go through this again, only worse, with banks of cameras and microphones.

His mother had tuned Claire out completely, thank

69

goodness. She was still tutting about the woman in the front pew. 'She'll be no one important,' he soothed her. 'Just paying respects. A producer or something.'

'A Hollywood producer maybe,' Claire said eagerly, reaching across him to touch his mother, who shrank like a snail from salt.

'Mum, be civil,' he snapped – but at last something was happening. The string quartet paused, then launched into another, more sorrowful, piece, and the congregation rose to its feet. Here came four undertakers bearing a casket laden with cream and yellow hothouse flowers around an incongruous little wreath of red carnations. A paunchy man followed behind, openly weeping, and a down-at-heel elderly woman brought up the rear, dabbing her dry eyes with a tissue.

'It's her, Richard, look,' hissed his mother. 'That cow who rang the police and slammed Harry's door in our faces.'

'Mum, shush.'

She was right, though. Déjà vu. A younger version of this person had blocked the doorway of Marine Parade when he was eleven.

'Ha!' said his mother. 'I can't wait to see her face when Mr Foyle welcomes us in for champagne and smoked salmon.'

The weeping man was presumably Foyle. His tears had Richard wondering suddenly, scanning the pews for more signs of male grief. There was an old guy near the front who looked very sorrowful. He was wearing a plum-coloured velvet jacket, and that was surely a toupée.

Could it be that Harry was gay?

There was no doubting paternity – ample proof of that in the mirror – but his mother's account of her seduction was untrustworthy. He wouldn't put it past her to have been the one who'd backed Harry into a corner.

He liked the idea. It had him softening towards his father. All those media photographs of the handsome old goat coming on to women: were they one of his masks, a marketing angle, a persona he'd hidden behind? He tried to re-imagine him as half of a devoted gay couple, faithful for decades to Simon Foyle.

It didn't quite gel. 'Quite a rogue by all accounts,' Foyle had said on the phone, which didn't seem like something a gay partner would say, and wouldn't Harry have confided to a partner that he had a son? Maybe all would be made clear in the eulogies or at the wake.

Richard glanced at his mother. Her eyes were as dry as the housekeeper's. The love she never tired of proclaiming was no more than self-pity, and even that wasn't genuine. It was a role she had played until it became her existence. As far as he could see no one here but Foyle and possibly the man in the toupée felt any genuine grief. The thought provoked a twinge of compassion. Whatever the self-serving truth of his father, it saddened Richard that someone so illustrious, with back-to-back retrospectives running on television and a day of public mourning in the offing, had barely anyone to shed genuine tears for him.

He put an arm around his mother's furiously quivering shoulders. 'The housekeeper's not worth bothering about,' he murmured. 'No one here cared for Harry except Mr Foyle.'

Harry

I am tearing from one end of the coffin to the other, leaping at each person I see – stranger, friend, enemy. There has to be someone here who will save me. How about these three at the back – two ill-dressed women, a young man with curly hair – my son, is it possible? – *oh help me, please*. But I'm dragged away.

Rows of solemn faces turn to watch the coffin go by. Most of them known to me, actors, directors, girlfriends. It's wonderful to see their bright eyes, their warm, living flesh, and I fling myself at them – *please help me – I love you*. I'm fired by the sudden, astonishing truth of this sentiment, but the universe presumes to know better. You loved not a one of them, it tells me, yanking me back. You felt contempt or indifference for most of them. The coffin, swaying on the undertakers' shoulders, tows me past them and on.

Good God, an ex-wife is here – the Danish one, Birgit. She and two cronies are hunched in a row, sawing chunks off my character, no doubt, as her lawyer once sawed chunks off my earnings. There's little point hurling myself at them, but I do just the same. And at Julian, my agent, misty-eyed, biting his lip. *Ah please, Julian, let's forgive all our differences*. No use, back I bounce to the coffin. The best in the business Julian may be, but I never liked the bastard and there's no undoing it now. He's not sad on my account. More likely he's pondering his own mortality or the decline in income my departure will mean for him. Or else he's just playing to the gallery. He has seen fit to wear a purple jacket and to sport his best hairpiece and a flamboyant silk cravat around his scraggy neck.

They are sliding the coffin onto the dais now, from where I can see the whole congregation. The sweet child who has the part of Cordelia is here, three rows back. She had me infatuated for a day or two – pray God that counts as emotional investment – she is less than ten metres away. But no, no, it doesn't. Next to her are Regan and Goneril and the assistant producer I've been bedding. Sweetly short-sighted behind those horn-rimmed spectacles, stacks of books by her bed, reverential towards me. I make frenzied attempts to transfer to her, but it seems I loved her not.

In a smug, healthy row to the left are the men: the producer, the idiot director, the director's assistant, Edgar, Edmund and Gloucester, and the fool, poor Lear's shadow.

Thou shouldst not have been old till thou hadst been wise.

Unfair, unfair. Who knew the rules of this game? Not you, fool, any more than I. He's not even looking up, too busy texting.

A handful of rubbernecking neighbours has turned out. None of them liked me and I liked none of them. I dare say the prospect of free alcohol and a nosey around inside my house helped Simon to round them up. On the front row is the solicitor – Pearl something – who drafted my will. I fly at her but run out of rope yet again. In our few meetings at her Western Road office, it barely crossed my mind to seduce this attractive Jamaican or to show any interest at all, engrossed as I was in the fine detail of distributing my largesse.

Is that it, is that everyone? I don't know the vicar or the four hired musicians in white tie and tails who are gravely bowing their instruments. My hopes lurch back to Mrs Butley and Simon. I strain with all my might to conjure affection for them, to satisfy the universe that this cantankerous, chain-smoking cleaner and pestiferous neighbour succeeded in worming their way into my heart. I propel myself through the air towards one, then the other. It just isn't true. There is no one I cared about, no one to rescue me.

The final horror is upon me. Time slows as it would in a movie, but I'm not in a movie. I am damned and defeated, about to lose this real world full of colour, sound, movement forever. The chapel, the flowers, the upturned faces. The lips, and the hands, and the eyelashes. The shuffle of feet and the clearing of throats. The motes of dust adrift in the summer light that dazzles in through the window-tracery. The perfection of Schubert, the poignant violin cadence, the cello's unhappy searching. The last chord dies away. I am frozen, unable to think or to act. Only a few eulogies stand between me and the flames. Between this transient world and time without end in an urn.

The vicar steps up beside me and clears his throat. 'We brought nothing into the world, and we take nothing out. The Lord gave, and the Lord hath taken away. Blessed be the name of the Lord.'

He knows nothing about it. His words show me no hope, give me no consolation. I can't bear to listen to him. I need a woman's pity and kindness.

'Mother.' The entreaty suggests itself. The last appeal of each dying man, no matter how brave. But my mother is decades dead, long forgotten. If her spirit ever lingered with me, I never felt it. I can't summon it now.

The vicar has given way to Julian, whose praise of me is so polished and practised, I know it almost by heart. Mrs Butley stifles a yawn. The solicitor looks sad. What was her name? Pearl something, some man's name for a surname.

Julian has stepped down and now Simon is speaking, choking with grief at the loss of his only claim to distinction – to have rubbed shoulders with the living legend that was me, occasionally being asked to feed my cat, take in a parcel or deal with my tradesmen. He launches, ill-advisedly, into a halting rendition of a Shakespeare sonnet:

'*Like as the waves make towards the pebbled shore,*
So do our minutes hasten to their end...'

Despite his amateur delivery, I should be concentrating

on the beauty of these words, drawing comfort from this sliver of Shakespeare, but I'm distracted by Pearl. There is something very lovely about her as she gazes at Simon. There is almost, I might say, an aura around her. Amidst all the heartrending, ephemeral loveliness of my last glimpse of creation, she's in high definition. Her broad cheekbones, her kissable lips, her sassy behind. Suddenly she's the best woman ever, enchanting. I want to dive beneath the lapels of her tailored black jacket, slide inside her blouse and her brassière and find refuge between her brown breasts. If only I'd felt this when I met her before. Oh powers that be, have pity. I loved this woman – I promise I did. I just didn't have enough time to realise it. You have to believe me. Let me go home with Pearl.

I reach for her again, go halfway towards her, urging myself on with hope and conviction. But my prayer is unheard or denied. I'm pulled up cruelly short, so near yet so far. My last minutes are racing past me like a river in flood. Forgive me, forgive me. Whatever I've done or left undone, I repent.

My gaze clings to Pearl, who still glows with come-hither gorgeousness. What draws me isn't her face so much or her breasts. She stands in a sphere of sharp focus, whose centre seems to be the curve of her right hip in the black pencil skirt. All at once I am concentrated and alert. The come-hither is not from Pearl, as I thought, but from her shoulder bag.

The vicar is winding up, and at his suggestion all present are lowering their eyes in silent remembrance. I hardly know what I am doing or why. I'm reaching again, but for Pearl's bag this time, not for Pearl, and – surely not? can it be true? – I am gliding towards it as easily as a snowflake to the ground.

The bag rests on her hip. I sail into the snug gap above and look fearfully back. The hateful box and its wretched contents will surely compel me to follow them. The quartet have taken up their bows, offering drawn out, desolate notes of Beethoven as the curtains glide across. I brace myself to resist the pull of the coffin, aim all the emotion I can muster at my inscrutable new home.

My luck holds. No malign force drags me away. I daren't stray an inch from where I quiver, tucked up against Pearl's nipped-in, tailored, feminine midriff. Thank you, thank you, whoever has let this happen. I am still in the world!

Black leather. A fold-over flap. Something inside the bag draws me in – what can it be? I peep beneath the flap, and I see it. The familiar A4 pages in their clear plastic folder. The black, ornate lettering. It's the will that I keep in my bureau! My last will and testament!

My relief is exquisite. I can't remember ever knowing such joy. Not a second too soon. As I dive under the flap and embrace this miraculous document, the congregation is exhaling wistfully at the sight of my earthly remains disappearing backstage. Sweet Jesus, that could have been me.

Richard

There was some kind of problem in the doorway where the crush of mourners waited to exit into the afternoon sunshine. 'Let me through, I'm gasping,' grumbled the housekeeper, shoving her way forward, cigarettes and lighter in hand.

Richard hung back in the pew with Claire and his mother, experiencing a lightness he hadn't expected. The scent of lilies no longer oppressed him; the claustrophobia had gone. Compassion had lifted the weight. The words said over the coffin hadn't clarified Harry's sexuality, but it hardly mattered. The old charlatan wasn't loved, not at the last, and Richard felt sorry for him.

A man in jeans and a denim jacket seemed to be blocking the door. Richard couldn't see him properly past the string quartet, who stood in line, calmly clutching their instrument cases. It must be a pain lugging that cello around. Between himself and the musicians was the black woman, who fished in her shoulder bag and brought a mobile phone to her ear. 'Hi... Yes, I've got it. Mr Foyle found it in a drawer at the house.'

Richard wasn't listening. His mother looked dazed. Was she sharing his sense of release? He hoped so. He put an arm round her. 'I'm really glad we came. Thank you, Mum.'

'What's going on?' said Claire, standing on tiptoe.

Simon Foyle was arguing with the man in jeans. The housekeeper was chipping in too.

'Haven't had a chance,' said the black woman into her mobile. 'I expect it matches our copy... No... look, I'll skip the reception. Be with you in half an hour, tops.'

Now that would be good, Richard thought. To skip the reception. To build on this sense of release and forgiveness instead of picking over Harry's bones at some awkward do. 'Hey, Mum,' he said hopefully, 'how about we go straight on home? Light those candles? Watch Hamlet?'

'Don't be silly,' said Claire. 'We wouldn't miss champagne at Harry's for the world, would we, Debbie?'

His mother frowned as though puzzled by the sound of Claire's voice. She squeezed past Richard and Claire into the aisle.

'Debbie?' said Claire, flashing her bleached teeth.

His mother straightened her back and took a breath from her diaphragm. 'We're going to Harry's,' she proclaimed.

People turned to stare.

'That house should have been my *home*. And yours too, Richard.' Her voice drew an echo from the chapel walls. 'We're going in through that door at last, and they're going to treat me like a *lady*.'

Claire put an arm round her shoulder. 'Like family, Debbie, because that's what you are.'

She threw off the embrace.

'Mum, please. Claire's trying to be friendly.'

He grinned at Claire to show solidarity, but then someone said, 'It's a reporter.' All eyes swung back to the doorway, and Claire's hand shot to her mouth.

'What?' said his mother. 'What's happening?'

'Clear off. You're not welcome.' Foyle looked beside himself, red in the face.

The man in jeans wasn't listening. He was dodging now through the knot of people towards them, squeezing past the cello case into the chapel. He glanced at the flowers and the closed curtains, then turned back, scanning faces. 'I'm hoping to have a word with Deborah Lawton?'

What on earth? Richard stepped in front of his mother, but too late, she must have nodded or something, because the man had spotted her. 'That's you, is it, love?' he said, producing an oily smile. He was recording all this on his mobile.

His mother stepped forward.

'No.' Richard pushed between them, making a grab for the mobile and knocking it flying. The reporter flailed backwards, trying to catch it, lost his footing and landed hard.

'Ouch! Watch it, mate.'

'Sorry, but she has nothing to say to you.'

'Don't interfere, Richard. I can say what I like.'

'Quite right, love. Freedom of speech.'

Claire, looking flustered, had run forward, pulled the man to his feet, and was attempting to tug him towards the door. 'You shouldn't have come,' she said.

Did she know him? Richard couldn't make sense of this.

'No, you shouldn't,' said Foyle, seizing the man's other arm. 'You're not wanted here.'

Richard lowered his voice to plead with his mother. 'Don't talk. He'll destroy you. No comment, okay?'

'You're the son, I'm guessing.' The reporter had shaken off Foyle and Claire and was back. 'No hard feelings – although if my phone's broken...'

The old man in the toupée retrieved it from the floor and held it out to him. 'Take it and go,' he growled, 'because I'll be suing your editor, chum, if you write a word about this private occasion.' His face was a near match for his jacket.

'Keep your hair on,' said the reporter. 'I'm not here for Lord Harry, I'm here for his lady.' He bowed low to Richard's mother, who fluttered and beamed. 'Because Harry let you down, isn't that right?'

'Back off,' said Richard. 'Leave her alone.'

'Thirty years ago? Left you high and dry like Miss Havisham?'

'Miss Havisham?' said Richard. The penny dropped. Claire had tipped this man off.

Claire shook her head helplessly, but there wasn't time to explode at her, because—

'Miss Havisham?' said his mother.

'I mean no offence, love. It's understandable how you would feel. A man like Harry.'

She was opening her mouth to spill all. Richard's life, decked out in her melodrama, would be spread across the tabloids. The press would camp on their doorsteps, peer in through their windows, pursue them down the street. 'Don't, Mum, please.'

'But, Richard...'

The answer came to him, the one thing that would deter her. 'It was Claire,' he whispered. 'Claire who tipped this man off to come here and make an idiot of you.'

'No,' Claire yelped.

His mother's face clouded. Her mouth shut and then opened.

'Please, no comment,' he begged her.

Her expression cleared and focused. She drew herself to full height. Turning her back on the reporter, she faced her audience across the footlights, filling her lungs again as Claire shrank behind the cellist.

'This was *her* doing, Mr Foyle. This woman's the culprit.'

They had to leave. No more talk. 'Come along, Mum. Enough said. Let's go now.'

There was no stopping her. 'And this one's no better than she should be.' Her finger swung to the black woman, who held up bemused, innocent palms.

Claire came out from hiding to put an arm around her. 'You're confused, Debbie love. You need to calm down.'

'*Don't you dare speak to me.*' His mother's shriek threatened their eardrums.

'Yikes,' said the reporter. 'You said she was batty, but—'

'Claire!' Richard bit back his fury. He grabbed her arm and his mother's. 'Come on. We're leaving.'

'I never said that,' Claire pleaded.

Foyle had Claire by the other wrist, pulling her to a standstill. 'Who are you exactly?'

'I'm... I'm Richard's girlfriend.'

'And let me get this clear. You invited the press?'

'No, honestly, I didn't. I was chatting to one of the old people I work with, that's all. I was telling him how exciting, the funeral of such an amazing man, and then before I could stop him he'd phoned his grandson, who turned out to be this reporter, and—'

'How dare you?'

'I told him not to come.'

'I'm so sorry. She knew it was private,' said Richard.

A throat cleared, and the crowd turned to look. An undertaker stood in the doorway, bowing slightly. 'Excuse me, Mr Foyle, sir, but they're needing the chapel. Do the mourners wish to view the floral tributes?'

Richard saw Foyle's eyes fill once more with tears. He was flapping his hands at the crowd, speaking in a hoarse voice. 'Please... everyone... make your way to the house. Let's rescue some dignity for Harry with a glass of champagne.'

As the chapel emptied, he swung back to Richard. 'Not you, though, or your mother or girlfriend. Invitation withdrawn.'

'No, please, Mr Foyle,' wailed his mother. 'You can't *do* that to me.'

'Be quiet,' the housekeeper snarled in her face. 'I remember you. You've been after his money for years.'

No one wanted to view the floral tributes. Most climbed into their cars and accelerated away down the cemetery drive. The cello went in the back of a Volkswagen estate. Only the reporter remained, and the black woman, wriggling out of her jacket, hanging it in a red hatchback.

His mother was distraught, Claire was making imploring faces at him, but there was no time to speak to them because the reporter's mobile was back in his face. 'It's true though, you are Harold Whittaker's son?'

'No comment' would sound like an admission. 'Absolutely not,' he said. 'That's a lie and a fantasy.' He looked hard at the women.

'How come Claire said you were?'

'She made a mistake.'

'Yes, that's it, I must have done.'

'A mistake, are you kidding?'

'You can think what you like, but he isn't my father.'

'Oh yeah? Why are you here, then?'

'Curious, that's all. No more comment.'

It didn't hold water, but he wasn't going to elaborate. He locked eyes with the reporter and made his gaze steely. He was no son of Harold Whittaker. It felt good to assert it. A father who wasn't worth having was easy to disown.

The reporter gave up on him. 'But you, love?' Moved close to his weeping mother. 'You've a tale to tell, isn't that right? Old Harry seduced you, eh, got you pregnant, then ran out on you – that's how it was, wasn't it?'

Her lip trembled; her breath came in sobs. She was opening her mouth to answer, and Richard was powerless to stop her.

'No,' she whispered. 'No. That's a wicked untruth.'

'Which part?

'All of it.' Her voice took on volume and certainty. 'I never even *met* Mr Whittaker.' She spoke clearly into the mobile. 'Not once in my life.'

Richard could have kissed her. His eyes misted with gratitude.

'So you made up the story?'

'Other people made it up. Like *she* made it up.' She jabbed her finger at Claire. 'My son looks a bit like him, that's all.

Always has done, from a boy. Just a coincidence, but people joke about it, and now it's got out of hand.'

A car door slammed. The black woman was driving away.

Richard did his best to sign off. 'Your time's wasted here. Really. It's been a misunderstanding – a muddle, that's all. There's nothing to know.'

Doubt dawned at last in the reporter's eyes. 'Effing wild-goose chase.'

'I'm afraid so,' said Richard.

The man glared at Claire. 'Get your facts straight next time. Okay?'

Finally he was going. He kick-started the motorbike that was parked by the porch and took off in a cloud of exhaust.

His mother was erupting at Claire now. 'Look what your meddling has—'

'Yes,' Richard jumped in, 'but listen – there's something important I need to say.'

Claire mustn't hear his mother recant. He was no son of Harry: that was the story now, and he was damn well sticking to it.

'I didn't mean it to happen,' Claire said. 'Old Mr Moly-neux got so excited. He said, "My grandson's a reporter," and—'

'Stop,' Richard told her. 'I don't want to hear it.' He put his face close to hers. 'Because, Claire, listen. Whatever you may think you know about me, think again. You heard what Mum said, and she's telling the truth – isn't that right, Mum?'

She nodded emphatically.

'I shouldn't have told you that story. It's a joke that I play, looking the way I do. So, I'm sorry, but if you spread the rumour and I get to hear about it, I'll be hopping mad, is that clear? I want you to tell Mr Molyneux and anyone else you've been blabbing to that you got it wrong.'

It wasn't enough. He needed to break with her.

'And actually, there's no easy way to say this, but it's over – we're done, Claire.'

'Ah no, babes, please.'

'It wasn't really working, and now this.'

She carried on protesting, but he found it was true: he was glad to step free of her.

Cars were beginning to arrive for the next funeral. He turned his back on Claire and hurried his mother away down the drive. The more distance he put between the two of them the better.

'Are you cross with me, Richard?'

'No, Mum, you were bloody wonderful. Truly.'

She hung on tight to his arm, half-running to keep up. 'I can't *bear* it. We were going to Harry's house and now Mr Foyle *hates* us.'

'Yes. I'm so sorry.'

'How *could* you have trusted that woman?'

'I don't know. Big mistake.'

'She dyes her hair, for a start,' she panted beside him. 'And those teeth aren't her own.'

Friday

Lily

The man with a van – *Call me all hours, no job too small, daft, humdrum or crazy* – had seen it all; nothing fazed him. Moonlight flits, stolen goods, passion and violence. Last week, with his bespectacled lady customer quivering with alarm in the passenger seat and her few sticks of furniture thrown in the back, the van was pursued to the traffic lights by a stark-naked man shouting, 'Come back, Georgina. I love you.'

This job was tame by comparison. He and the bloke were out on the pavement, filling the van with the bloke's stuff, which the woman was ferrying in armloads out through the front door. She was throwing him out, and he wasn't ready to go, but tough titty. He'd been nabbed doing the dirty, and that kind of lost him his rights. The man with a van had developed a point of view on these matters: he respected the disrespected birds who called time.

The bloke was still wearing his office suit – she must have sprung this surprise on him when he got home. She came to the gate with a cardboard box full of socks. 'I don't care if I never see another red sock in my life.' The man with a van was warming to her in spite of her livid left cheek. It was hard not to stare – it took some getting used to.

The bloke grunted morosely, offering the man with a van a look that said, 'Women, eh?'

'Do you need any help, love?' The man with a van followed her to the porch and peered into the hall. Posh place. Nice pictures. Nice tits on the woman too under that dust-smeared shirt. Dark hair sneaking free of the plait, curling damp on her neck from the humid July heat. Pity about the birthmark.

She swung on a heel to look at him. 'Not right now I don't, but next week I may well do. Anything he doesn't collect by Monday, I'll want taking to the tip.'

'Great. Here's my card.'

She read the slogan, then looked up with a smile in her eyes. 'Do you mean what it says here – no job too crazy?'

'Sure thing, love. I'll do anything, me, provided it don't get me arrested.'

'Right... okay... Look, on second thoughts, come in and help me carry some stuff. No, not you, Martin,' she snapped at the bloke. 'You're staying right where you are.'

She shut the door on Martin and led the man with a van through to the kitchen. Smart new worktops and units. Flowers on the table. Floor-to-ceiling window onto designer back-garden. She glanced back down the hall and lowered her voice. 'This very much comes under "crazy".' Her smile was a bit wicked. 'I've a proposition for you. I'll make it worth your while. What's *he* paying you?'

'Fifty quid.'

'How about I double that? Another fifty.'

'For next week's run to the tip?'

'Better than that. For putting on an act for him now, making him think we're getting off with each other.'

Forget the face, she was sexy, with her smell of fresh sweat. 'Tell me more,' said the man with a van.

Back out with the next load, and blimey, hey up, the craziness was starting. She was coming on fast to him, moving in close, smiling up at him coyly, bumping him with her hip.

Well, why not, and getting paid for it into the bargain. He slid an arm round her waist, dropped his hand to her bum, then instinctively jumped away as Martin straightened up from arranging a blanket over his music centre.

'Oi,' said Martin.

'Oi what?' she snapped back.

Martin swore under his breath, then said crisply, 'Okay, Lily, I get it. You're just winding me up.'

'Why would I bother? You're so gone, I can hardly see you.' She turned her back on him and shot a wink at the man with a van. 'You're a cheeky sod, aren't you? I like your eyes, though. Wait there. One more lot to go.'

While she was inside, the two men stood awkwardly waiting. Martin offered a packet of fags. Their heads bent over the lighter. 'Thanks,' said the man with a van.

'Take no notice,' Martin confided between savage drags of low tar. 'She's in a paddy, that's all, using you to get back at me.'

'Yeah, mate. You could be right.'

They blew smoke and stared down the line of privet hedges to where the traffic whizzed by.

She staggered out with a pile of coats and scarves and dumped them on the front path. Martin nearly fell flat trying to catch them, and she laughed.

'You vindictive bitch.'

'That's your lot for today. I'll have the books and music

sorted tomorrow. Pick it all up by Monday night or it's gone.'

As Martin straightened up with his armful of coats, Lily grabbed the hand of the man with a van, and this time he didn't jump away.

'Oi,' said Martin again, but she ignored him.

'Are you married?' she said.

'Not yet,' said the man with a van.

'Girlfriend?'

'Not as such, no,' he lied.

'Okay. So do you fancy coming back here when you've taken this pillock wherever he's going? Share a bottle of wine?'

'You're making an idiot of yourself,' said Martin.

'Takes one to know one,' said Lily. 'So, what do you say?'

'Well, I'm not sure...'

He was having doubts about this crazy job on the side. The bloke might not cough up the money he owed, might even get violent. But a glance into Martin's cowardly eyes had him smiling again. 'Yeah, why not, if you're offering.'

'You were joking, right?' said Martin, as the van turned the corner.

'About what, mate?'

'About what do you think, *mate*?' Martin said, in a voice you could have cut yourself on. 'You were joking about going back there?'

'No comment,' said the man with a van.

'You bastard,' said Martin.

He muttered and snorted a bit, then kept quiet the rest of the way.

The address was a crap street in some no-man's-land suburb. The landlady stood, arms folded, frowning – 'This had better be all of it' – as the two of them carried stuff up three flights to a pokey room under the eaves.

Back out on the pavement, Martin handed over the dosh. It was all there.

'Thanks, and no hard feelings, eh?' said the man with a van. 'Will you be wanting more bringing tomorrow?'

'Not by you,' Martin said.

'Fair enough,' said the man with a van.

She met him at the door with fifty quid in her hand. 'Thanks,' she said. 'Nice job. You should go on the stage.'

Her brown hair was down round her shoulders, still wet from the shower. She had on a fresh white T-shirt and a long wrap-around skirt.

'It wasn't difficult,' he said. 'You could've had me for free.'

She shook her head, smiling. 'Don't be daft.'

The birthmark hardly bothered him now. 'Nah, you're a stunner. You've got me all hot and bothered.'

Her smile faded. Her hand went to her cheek. 'Enough with the gift of the gab.'

He reached out, moved the hand away. 'Seriously,' he said. Gave her fingers a squeeze.

She looked at him, her head tilted, her eyes kind of narrow.

'How about it?' he said. 'Shall we open that bottle?' He gave her his best cheeky grin.

'I don't think so,' she said.

'Come on, love. Bit of fun. Bit of company, like you said.'

'No thanks.' She began closing the door.

'Okay, so next week then – you'll be wanting the stuff he leaves shifted?'

'Not by you,' she said. 'Sorry.' The door closed in his face.

'Fair enough,' said the man with a van.

Sunday

Harry

Ye gods, hear me. Take pity upon a poor wretch. Will I never find peace or a haven of safety? I've jumped out of the frying pan into a pending tray. In a deserted office in the small hours of Sunday morning, I'm still shackled to the will. Hours of concentrated beseeching have brought no mocking angel; I'm beginning to think Scotty & Co. don't work at the weekends.

Being a ghost is horrendous. Whatever I might have imagined, the reality is an infinity worse. Brief intervals of mind-curdling terror are succeeded by long days and nights of more boredom than I know how to bear. I yearn from the roots of my soul for unconsciousness. I never properly appreciated that sleep was a way to fast-forward the dull bits, to evade the grinding indifference of time.

I stare at the calendar, with its relentless enumeration of the days of July and its insipid image of Monet's poppy field. The second hand on the wall clock couldn't possibly tick round more slowly. Would to heaven I were somewhere lively and bitchy: a Hollywood party or Broadway on opening night. Or had some intellectual stimulation: a concert, a film, a TV drama, a play. Or, if I must be quiet and alone, let it be somewhere serene and beautiful: a sundrenched beach with gentle waves lapping, or my sitting room with its view of the Channel. Ah God, how I wish I were home.

Anxiety seizes me again. Because this may be it, I may be stuck here forever. I put immense care and feeling into my will – *a medium for an idea or a message*, said Scotty – but what help is that to me now? Have I traded my chances of escape on a molecule of an incinerated corpse for a solicitor's filing system: locked in a box or a drawer, a wakeful eternity with not even a calendar to look at or the uncertainty of what happens next to help the time pass?

I try to concentrate on the mice. At least they are moving with purpose. There's one nibbling a crumb by this pending tray and another nosing its way into an open packet of ginger nuts. I rarely saw a mouse while I lived. I would cheerfully have murdered any I found in my beautiful home if Henry V – sweet cat, how I miss you – hadn't got to them first; but right now I'm glad of their company, thankful to be distracted by their scurrying and rustling, their black eyes alert as they clean their quivering whiskers and fragile pink ears. *Boo!* I say, *Boo!* but they carry on, untroubled, oblivious. I have lost all power to command an audience, even of mice.

How horribly great is that loss. In my imagination I am poised in the wings again, impatient for my cue. Stepping forward, smelling the excitement out there, speaking the first line, feeling the love rush towards me across the footlights like a great warm breath. The camera adored me no less – I knew how to play subtle. Barely a twitch of an eyebrow – my mind shone out through my eyes. Countless times in the darkness of a movie premiere, watching such a moment, I have felt the sigh move through the room. It's obscene and deplorable what I have come to.

Count your blessings, I tell myself for the ninety-ninth time. The horror of those minutes between Scotty's abandoning me and my leap for the shoulder bag make even this ignominious cul-de-sac seem cosy and kind. But oh, the powerlessness. I've no fingers to switch on the radio that sits right beside me, or to open Friday's newspaper, whose second headline, trumped only by some twaddle about television nonentities, shouts *HARRY'S LAST SHOW – see page 3*. How immensely frustrating.

Why the deuce didn't Ms Pearl Allen LLB – says her brass-and-wood nameplate – have the decency, or greed, or curiosity, or plain laziness to pop in for a drink and a canapé at Marine Parade, just for five minutes? I would have been home and dry. Instead, huddled close against the will in the shadowy confines of her bag, after a muffled fuss of raised voices, I endured the cruelty of hearing everyone head off there without me. While they drank champagne to my memory, trampled my Persian carpets and smiled out at the bright turquoise sea, she brought me here through the bad-tempered afternoon rush hour. She dumped the will unceremoniously in this tray before spending the rest of the afternoon with a couple who'd been gazumped in Saltdean. That was Thursday, she was scarcely in the office on Friday, and the only person I've seen since is a gum-chewing woman who was here for all of three minutes, emptying the waste-paper bin, scratching her behind and making a few passes with a vacuum cleaner and duster.

The grey light is softening and gathering colour. Dawn is breaking at last. The herring gulls on the rooftops outside start up their aching lament. Only a mile away, my house calls to me. How I long to be among my familiar, beloved possessions. I wish to God I'd never answered the door to my chauffeur that last morning of my life. If I'd died in Marine Parade among my belongings and memories, I'd have slipped away from the corpse with no trouble and been at home all this time, safe and sound.

Have mercy on me, I beg you, Ms Pearl Allen LLB. Bring me something on Monday I care about, something that will carry me home.

Richard

Turning off the front, fishing for his keys, Richard was startled to see that the café was already open. Sunday was supposed to be Tiffany's day off. Not just open, it was crowded with mums, dads and children. A buzz of chatter hit him as he squeezed through the door. The place smelled of aftershave and warm cake and freshly ground coffee.

The woman beside him looked vaguely familiar. She was clutching a sandcastle bucket, half full of money. 'What's happening?' he asked her.

'Book launch,' she said with an air of great pride. 'My friend is a children's author. Well on her way to being famous.' She held out a copy of the book and rattled the bucket. 'You just missed the reading. Pirates, monsters and mermaids.'

Across the room Richard could see Tiffany's pink hair, sculpted into Lisa Simpson spikes. She was serving a queue of customers at the counter.

'The books are a bargain today,' the woman persisted. 'Only eight pounds, and my friend will be delighted to sign one for you.'

'I don't have children,' he said.

'Humpf.'

It came back to him that this was the soup woman, the irritable customer who'd announced Harry's death to him. 'You were here once before,' he ventured.

'Where?'

'Here, in this café.'

'What?' She seemed affronted. 'I've been lots of times.'

'Apologies. I've only seen you the once.'

Recognition dawned. 'It's you! You're the owner. The man who ran away.'

'Not exactly,' he said.

'Well, exactly and precisely, that is what you did. Most inconsiderate. God only knows what you thought you were up to.'

'Well, I—'

'Tiffany was in a terrible fluster. She barely knew where to begin, what to do for the best. So I offered my help, of course. We packed Maurice off and put the cakes in containers and figured out how to lock up. I told her, "Take the till money home with you. You don't want his nibs blaming you if there's a break-in."'

'No. Yes. Thank you.'

'She's a good girl, is Tiffany. Once she finds her feet, she doesn't need help dancing on them. Heaps of initiative.'

'I didn't realise you knew her.'

'Come again?'

'Forgive me, I'm confused. You seem to know Tiffany.'

The soup woman stared at him, then snorted. 'I get it. Gosh, you *are* out of the loop. I didn't know her – I met her that day. As I say, I've been several times since to make sure that she's coping, and surprise, surprise, it's you that's never here.' Her expression was fiercely censorious.

'I'm here most days, but—'

'Whatever. And then last week my friend was looking for somewhere to hold her Worthing launch, somewhere informal, so—'

'Omigod, Richard, I'm sorry.' Tiffany arrived at his elbow, grinning up at him, flashing a bejewelled skull and crossbones in her navel between peacock-blue shorts and an artfully ripped crop-top. 'Went completely out of my head to tell you. Hope you're cool with it.' She didn't pause for an answer. 'We're doing ice-cream sodas. And muffins, too – special order this morning, but don't worry, they're selling. Can't stop – there's a queue. Good thing you went to the wholesaler's.'

'Cool, yes, great,' he called after her. His voice died to a mumble. 'Well done.'

His feelings were uncomfortably mixed. Of course it was great, the espresso machine was going full pelt, but this felt like someone else's café, not his. He eased through the crowd to the library corner, where a miniscule woman with enormous costume jewellery had usurped Maurice's armchair to sign books for a swarm of kids. Maurice was backed up against the bookcase, clutching Tolstoy to his chest. Richard offered him a comradely scowl.

It fell flat. He saw now that Maurice was deep in conversation, holding forth to three ten-year-olds. 'Still no Ruskies to parley with, city burned to ashes and his supply line under attack. Boney had no option but to turn tail, head back to Paris, fifteen hundred miles. Then the winter came down, thick and heavy on all those soldiers and horses and guns. More snow than you can imagine. And the freezing, bastard cold—'

Richard pushed on towards the till, where Tiffany must be in dire need of help. But she was fine too, taking orders and payments. She shot him an anxious smile, still with her crush on him, wanting him to be pleased with her. Which he was – yes, of course he was – he'd be churlish not to be pleased.

She wasn't alone behind the counter, he realised. A young woman with a ponytail shouted, 'Yes, chef!' She was working the espresso machine like a pro and dishing up muffins. Then, 'Excuse me, sir,' a middle-aged guy in pink rubber gloves manoeuvred past Richard with a tray of used plates and mugs, which he unloaded into the sink and set about washing up.

'My husband. My daughter,' came a voice in his ear. He swung round to see the soup woman's barbed smile. 'And my own job today, you'll have noticed, is greeter and bookseller. All in all, considering the free help and the boost to your takings, I think you should buy one.' She indicated a pile of her friend's books on the counter and held up the bucket. 'I'm sure you know a child who would enjoy it.'

He didn't welcome her help, free or otherwise, but Tiffany was watching. This was Tiffany's friend. What on earth was the matter with him? The money was flooding in. His business was booming. He pulled a tenner from his pocket. He wasn't needed, that was the problem.

Not a problem – the answer! He didn't want to be needed, here or by his mother or by anyone he knew. In a flash, it was done. He'd decided. Because if not now, when?

'Keep the change.' He ducked past the soup woman, who said, 'Take a book.'

'Thanks,' he said, grabbing one from the pile, flapping a hand to get Tiffany's attention. 'I need a word. Spare a minute?'

He was through the counter flap, beckoning her into the

back room, eager to announce his impulsive decision. 'You're doing brilliantly,' he said.

'Ooh, thank you.' Pleased as a puppy-dog. 'I'm really enjoying it.'

He felt rotten to be bursting her bubble. 'But there's something you need to know. I'm about to sell up.'

Her hand shot to her mouth and her face fell a mile. 'You're kidding me?'

'I'm so sorry, Tiff. I was going to leave it to the end of the season, but, well, what with one thing and another, I can't wait that long. I have to leave Worthing at once.'

'No,' she said, crestfallen. 'Why?'

'I'm thirty. I'm stuck here. I need to move on.'

'Worthing's lovely,' she said. 'And I'll miss you.'

'For five minutes, maybe. Thing is, it'll happen quite fast. I just have to give notice on the shop lease and my flat, flog the espresso machine and any other stuff anyone wants to buy, and I'm free to go. I thought I should tell you, because you're—'

'Hang on a minute,' she said. 'Can I buy it?'

'What?' Was she crazy?

'Buy the stuff, take over the lease?'

He stood back against the shelves of tins and boxes and took in her eager face, the ripped crop top, the spiked hair. 'You don't understand,' he said slowly. 'The espresso machine's worth a couple of thousand. The rent's pretty steep, and then there are other bills, lots of them. I've been making a loss.'

'Yes,' she said. 'Scary. Two hundred a month. More in winter.'

He stared at her. 'How did you... did I tell you?'

'I shouldn't have looked.' She ran a blue sparkly fingernail down the spine of his accounts book, propped on a shelf between two cake containers. 'But it's really interesting, isn't it, running a café?'

'I suppose.'

'My dad can lend me the money.'

'He'd be daft to.'

'I'll make a business case to him, like on *Tomorrow's Tycoon*.'

'But Tiffany, it's not a good business.'

She said nothing, just smiled and put a hand to her ear. The café noise was her answer. Richard opened his mouth and shut it again. He was a crap businessman, that was the truth of it.

'We can have a proper contract drawn up and everything,' she said.

'Tiffany?' The soup woman's head came round the door, glaring at Richard. 'You're needed on the counter.'

'Two ticks,' she said.

When the door closed again, Richard slumped against the shelves. Inept. A failure. 'Okay,' he conceded, 'but sleep on it. Talk to your dad.' Sounding hollow and forced. 'And your mum as well. Make sure this is what you want to do with your life.'

'Hey, Richard,' said Tiffany, peering up at his face. 'I promise to do all that, but honestly,' all concern, 'I really, really wish you weren't going.'

'That's nice of you, but I have to. So it's yours if you want it. You have first refusal. See what your parents say and we'll talk more tomorrow.' He shook her hand solemnly, then reached for the door. 'I'm sorry I can't stay to help, but there's someone else I have to tell.'

He pushed back past the soup woman's daughter, through

the counter flap and the queue at the till and the crowd at the library corner, heading for the door. Maurice's voice followed him. 'Ambushed daily. Dying in droves. Eating the horses.'

He was going be free, that was what mattered: free of the café, its keys, debts, stock, float and furniture, but more than that, free of his mother. Her denial of Harry to that reporter was nothing short of amazing. She was over Harry, breaking free herself at long last. He would go straight to her now to make one final offer – take it or leave it – a month tops to help her dejunk her house and smarten her life up before he was out of here.

'Running away again?' called the soup woman after him, but he took no notice. Out into the street, the café door shutting behind him. In his head it was done. Back to the flat for the bike, then fast-pedal the ten miles to Brighton for the showdown with Mum. Next stop Thailand or Togo. Tibet. Timbuktu. Not running away, not at all. Putting a decade of failure behind him. Starting anew.

There was a book in his hand about pirates, monsters and mermaids. He gave it to a child on the front. 'Travelling light,' he told the child's mother.

Monday

Harry

What unimaginable relief, after days of solitary confinement, to be a fly on the wall, eavesdropping on a human conversation. The luscious Pearl Allen is here at last, and she has brought with her my good friend Simon Foyle, ushering him in and requesting him to sit down. She settles herself with her back to the view of bricks and downpipes, he with his back to the door. She offers him coffee. He declines but accepts a ginger nut. She bites into one herself before jumping up to unlock a drawer and fetch a folder.

Just look at the two of them, how splendidly alive they are. Pearl's supple, generous lips enunciating pleasantries and occasionally my name. Simon's moisturised jowls quivering as he smiles. Her brown fingers, tipped with glossy red varnish, searching among papers in the folder she has opened. His, pale and unmanicured, tugging at his earlobe.

He clears his throat tentatively. 'I should mention,' he says, 'Mrs Butley is still popping in every day, to feed Harry's cat and check on the place. I hope it won't seem penny-pinching of me, but I'm more than a little financially embarrassed, just at present, so I wondered—'

'Of course,' Pearl interrupts, 'the estate will pay her wages. Keep a note of any expenses you have on Lord Whittaker's behalf and I'll reimburse you immediately.'

I yearn to share the happy state they are hardly aware of. Breathing, touching, smelling, tasting. Living. It's excruciating to have lost it. Beyond this room, beyond the reception area, out on the street below, in the Monday morning bustle of Brighton's Western Road stretches a multitude of these incredible, brilliant creatures, of whom so recently I was one.

My fervent thoughts trigger hope. Before death, said Scotty, that's when the emotional investment has to be made, but surely repentance must count for something? I redouble the affection I'm beaming at this delectable duo, drawing on the deepest reserves of my training and talent to get into character, building to a flood of unconditional love. The outward rush of emotion is powerful: it has me spinning in the air above the will and the pending tray, lifting me upwards, certain at last I am free. I love humanity, and today I will go out among them.

I rise so far and no further, brought to a sharp halt inches short of the ceiling. The laws of the universe are not to be fooled: there is no one I truly love, and my freedom is bounded and useless. I drift disconsolately down to where Pearl's searching has finally located the will. 'How careless of me,' she says. 'I should have locked it away.' She's passing the plastic folder and me across the desk into Simon's eager hands.

'Something for me?'

I'm filled abruptly with shame. I can't bear to watch. My bequest snubs and demeans him. I should have been kinder.

'But how generous,' he's saying. 'I didn't presume to expect, not for a moment. Harry knew I had money troubles

– I have a small antiques business, and the market is not what it was – but I never once asked him for help.'

Pearl shifts uneasily. 'I should have explained better,' she says. 'There is something for you, but that isn't why I asked you to come. I take it you know that you're also an executor?'

Simon's jaw drops. Then he beams. 'I am? But how flattering.'

I'd forgotten this detail myself. When drafting the will, Pearl prompted me to involve someone acquainted with the house and its contents. Who better than a neighbour who dabbles in antiques?

He shakes his head now in wonderment as he slides the will out of the folder. Don't read it, Simon. I don't want you to read it.

'Most people check with their executors to make sure they're willing,' Pearl says. 'It can be an onerous task. You aren't sole executor. The other's myself, representing Walker, Macpherson & Allen, so if you'd rather take a back seat, that's fine – you'll hardly need to do a thing except sign a few papers, though I'd be grateful if you could bring me any financial documents he kept in the house.'

Simon isn't listening. To Pearl's evident discomfort, he's scanning the pages of the will for his name. She pushes on, covering her embarrassment with talk. 'The more I do, the greater our charges will be of course, but the estate looks to be huge – legal charges won't dent it. I'll give you a schedule of our rates – hold on.' She taps away at her keyboard, and the printer starts chugging.

Then Simon says, 'Oh,' and his hand with the will in it drops to his lap, jerking me after it. Unprepared for the movement, I shoot on past to the floor, where I linger in an agony of remorse. *One thousand pounds with thanks for his services*. Did I intend to insult him? I fear that I did. The sum stands as recompense for the pains he took as helpful neighbour, that he will doubtless take now as executor, but beyond that the message is 'get lost, you bothersome idiot', words I swallowed in life because of his usefulness to me.

His suede lace-ups have seen better days. There are mouse droppings on the plush green carpet. But my efforts to distract myself with these trifles are useless. I drift reluctantly upwards and peer over the edge of the desk.

'Mr Foyle, I'm so sorry,' Pearl is saying. 'He wasn't a nice man.'

The wall-clock shows 6.30. The day is slipping away. The edge of the will remains visible, poking out of the folder on top of this filing cabinet by the door. I hover on the brink of calamity. I'm going to be shut up in the dark any minute, there's no knowing for how long, it could be weeks, months, even years. Pearl rarely consults papers, does the bulk of her work on computer. This could be my last glimpse of the world before eventually what – a shredder, an archive?

Simon left hours ago. My mood rallied, cheered by their telephone conversations with the Royal Shakespeare Company. The head bean-counter came to the phone, then a couple of big cheeses who were clearly knocked sideways by my colossal bequest. But in a moment of horror to match that at the crematorium, the first thing Pearl did after she saw Simon out was to put the will in the folder and take the folder to the filing cabinets that stand in a row by the door. She parked it on top of them and slid open a drawer, while I shrieked unheard at the end of my tether.

The moment passed. She fished out a wodge of company letterhead and some pre-franked envelopes and returned to her desk, leaving me here, reeling with shock. The stay of execution can only be temporary. Before she goes home for the evening, she'll be back, opening another drawer, dropping the folder in, closing it, locking it.

6.35. I can't think straight for anxiety. Pickles 64123, do you read me? Please answer. I strain to conjure you from the air, imagine you perched beside me, dangling your feet, wriggling your toes, or else practising your lotus position on the green carpet. Please Scotty, hear me. I need you.

A receptionist looks in. 'I'm off now.'

'Okay, goodnight, Chloe,' says Pearl. 'See you tomorrow.'

6.43. There's no word from Scotty, no shimmer of golden curls or insouciant smile. Pearl paces between desk and window, phone to ear, trying to soothe the couple in Saltdean, pausing to make yackety-yack faces at herself in the small mirror that hangs on the wall. Earlier there were several calls from the media before she instructed reception to say yes, the firm was dealing with Lord Whittaker's estate but had no comment to make at this stage – there would be a press release in due course.

6.58. She finishes the call and returns to her computer. I don't know what she's been working on – my leash is too short to see. She's printing off sheets of letterhead, the envelopes too, checking them, signing them, sealing them, and – no, stop! – she's tidying her desk, throwing notes and scraps in the waste bin, brushing the crumbs of her lunchtime sandwich to the floor. Half-standing, she waits as a last letter prints. She signs it, seals it, and then it's happening, she's ready to leave. Briefly, she examines her reflection, smoothing her straightened hair behind her ears and practising her smile. Then she picks up the letters, shoves them into her shoulder bag, and heads straight towards me.

No escape, here she is, there's no stopping her. She parks her bag on the cabinet next to me and stoops to open a drawer.

Her hand rises through the air for the folder. The open drawer yawns below me like the gateway to hell. I dive for the remembered safety of the shoulder bag that lies here beside me. I'm in under its flap, burrowing amongst its contents, but it's useless. The will has me hog-tied. There's no way to save myself. I'll be dragged from this sanctuary and into the metal drawer that even now I hear sliding shut.

Shut, did I say? Yes, there's the sound of the key turning, but the bag lurches and steadies, bumping along and away, and somehow I'm here, still inside it, not filed, back on Pearl Allen's hip, saved again – can it be? But of course! – by *a medium for an idea or a message*, by these letters that must carry news of my bequests. In the dim light inside the bag I can make out the aura around them. I was too panicked to see it before: everything I was about to lose sight of was so sharp and so bright.

A door opens and closes, and another key turns. The flap of the bag lifts and a bunch of keys drops past me into the clutter. I'm hearing the tap of Pearl's heels on the stairs. Bright daylight seeps in around the flap of the bag, and all at once I'm revelling in the fabulous sounds of traffic and bustle and the chatter of strangers' voices as she strides along Western Road. I turn somersaults of glee among the throat sweets and tampons.

Before long she halts, lifts the flap, and here comes her hand again, closing on the bundle of letters. Out they go, into the evening sunlight, and out I go too. Wonderful! The startling vastness of outside. The infinite sky busy with gulls riding the wind. A red and white bus flashes past.

The vision is brief. There is no time to savour it. I'm plunged into shadow again, shooting with the letters through the slot of a pillar box, tumbling to the pile of post below, where I hover – dazed, reprieved, apprehensive – peering eagerly through the darkness, trying to decipher the addresses on this scatter of envelopes, praying that one of them will be to the Royal Shakespeare Company.

Damn it, they have landed face down.

Tuesday

Lily

On the echoing upper concourse of St Pancras Station, the man scanning the crowd from a stool in the champagne bar was charming, affable, well-dressed, well-educated, well-travelled, articulate, outgoing, talented, independent and attentive. At least that was what his online profile said, and here he was at a bar-table for two waiting for tonight's lucky lady to show. The barman was primed to breeze over the moment she arrived with two glasses of their cheapest bubbles, a smallish invest-ment while he sized up whether to move her on to the Grand Brasserie, or to a pizza house, or to apologise that he couldn't stay long after all, he had a last-minute work commitment.

He refreshed her mugshot on his phone. She should be easy to spot. Lots of brown hair swept off a smooth forehead above an elegant profile, her chin confidently raised. When she appeared, he would lock eyes with her and smile in delighted recognition, sliding from his stool and throwing his arms wide, offering a bear-hug before she knew what had hit her. It worked nine times out of ten. He wasn't tall or particularly attractive, but his ad didn't lay claim to either, and his online image was recognisably him, even if flatteringly enhanced by a fedora. The women were never as fit as their photographs either, and the secret of pulling them, he'd found, was to greet them like long-lost best friends.

He had high hopes of this one. Her emails were spirited and witty, and her voice on the phone was enticing, with none of the vamping or inane giggles that some of them seemed to think were alluring. The two or three restaurant meals needed to bed her could be a canny investment. Lily Caruthers could well see him through the summer. Who knew, he might even get serious.

Here she came. The same hair. The same profile. Young and fresh-looking, her face averted as if she expected to find him over there, not over here. He waited, poised to spring the smile and offer the hug.

Then she turned and met his eyes, and he saw what she'd been hiding, what her online image concealed. She was ten yards away, walking fast towards him, and he was on auto-pilot, down from the stool, arms wide, thinking, shit, there was no way he was taking this one to a restaurant.

She had the cheek – no, rephrase that, the gall – to refuse the hug. 'We don't know each other,' she said smoothly, 'and I can see you're a bit taken aback.' She extended her hand to be shaken.

'No, no, not at all.'

She was wriggling up onto a stool, and the drinks were here, twenty quid down the drain, the waiter pretending not to notice his date's hideous disfigurement.

'This is nice of you. Thanks so much. Cheers,' she said.

He hoisted himself onto his own stool, pulled out his cigarettes and spun the packet on the table. 'No smoking, sir,' said the waiter.

'I've upset you,' she said.

He couldn't look at her, didn't want to. He watched the

waiter to the bar, made a meal of returning the cigarettes to his pocket, then frowned up at the great, airy span of the glass-and-iron train shed.

'I promise you, it's only skin deep.'

He snatched a glance at her. Eugh, what a nerve. Enough with the stiff upper lip. She kept on about it, she was asking for it, she needed telling. He leaned in, lowering his voice. 'Upset hardly covers it. Pissed off more like, because you're bang out of order, not mentioning something so gross.'

'Excuse me?' Her eyebrows shot up. 'Well, that's friendly, I must say.'

What did she expect? He glanced towards the stairs that led down to the lower concourse and the Underground. She twisted to follow his gaze, then turned back. 'I could say the same thing,' she said. 'I don't remember you telling me that you're wider than you're tall and follicly challenged.'

His hand shot to his head. He pulled in his stomach. 'Totally different,' he said.

She smiled and said nothing.

'Not the same thing at all.'

'Quite different things, I agree.' Her smile became a grin, dimpling one cheek, crumpling the other. 'Look,' she said, 'I can cover my shame with one hand. Can you?'

'Not funny.'

'You're right, I shouldn't mock, but "gross" had me riled. Look. Stop. Rewind.' She held the hand out to him. 'Neither of us wanted to be pre-judged, that's all.'

He wasn't going to engage with this. It was time to cut his losses. He bent to grab his laptop bag from under the stool.

'Oh,' she said. 'Brilliant. I see.'

He shouldered the bag. Stood for a second, taking a good, long look at her. Half woman, half aubergine.

'What happened to the non-smoker with the great sense of humour?' she said.

He shook his head. 'The drinks are paid for. Have them on me.' He was away, heading fast for the stairs, pulling out the cigarettes and fishing for his lighter.

'Are you all right, madam?'

The waiter was back. Nosy or kind, it amounted to the same thing. She hated the presumption of strangers. 'Fine, thanks.'

She took a swallow of champagne and shifted the stool so her back was to the waiter and the bar. No escape: in the middle of the concourse a young man and woman stood hand in hand, gawping at her like kids at the zoo.

She took another gulp of fizz, all set to slip off the stool and leave. But wait. Let a few minutes pass. If she bolted now for the Underground, just her rotten luck she would overtake Mr Bald Ego, find herself on the same platform as him and have to endure his disgust once again. She pushed the empty glass aside and picked up the second. What a creep. She'd assumed all those adjectives in his ad were ironic, but he was just a humourless fart.

Calm down, she told herself. This was just as much her fault. She'd been half-crazy this week: throwing Martin out, playing dangerous games with that wide-boy removal man, defying insomnia by cruising dating sites at three in the morning. She had no business dating so soon, so impetuously. She'd forgotten what a minefield it was, and the bastard was right: she should have come clean on the phone.

She took deep breaths of station air, the smell of elsewhere: Nottingham, Sheffield, Brussels and Paris. Feet echoed on the concourse. None of it mattered.

It was a mistake swallowing champagne so fast – the bubbles massed painfully beneath her ribs – but the alcohol was taking the edge off. Her head spun slightly. She hadn't done the little shit justice. If he were still here, she'd be tearing strips off him.

'Bugger the lot of them, eh?' said the waiter, collecting the first empty glass.

She drained the second and held it out to him. His eyes were on her cheek. Then they dropped to her breasts.

She half-twisted her ankle as she slid off the stool. She swallowed the pain and kept walking.

The curious glances on the Underground were harder than usual to ignore. She met them belligerently, forcing one person after another to look away. 'No offence meant,' said a young man. 'You need to get over yourself.'

What she needed was to be alone. She sprinted up the escalator and power-walked the streets towards home. Turning the last corner, she played step-right-step-left with a woman holding a large dog on a lead, who blurted out, 'Hi!' before, 'Sorry, not thinking. We're neighbours. I'm across your back fence.'

The woman's eyes were glued to her cheek. The dog shoved its nose in her groin. 'Sorry. No time. In a rush,' she said and pushed past, blundering on up the street, digging for her keys, breaking into a run, her eyes blinded by tears, muttering, 'Fuck off and leave me alone.'

Inside, she paced the hall, throwing her bag on the stairs and yelling obscenities. At the nosy neighbour. At her horrible date and that chancer of a waiter. At her arsehole of a husband. At herself for her misery.

Gradually she calmed down and picked up the mail, most of it junk advertising, but there was one that looked interesting. High-grade white envelope. Brighton postmark.

Thursday

Harry

My, some bits of that journey were exhilarating. I wouldn't say no to a repeat. I even enjoyed the rough-handling into the mail sack and being thrown onto and dragged out of the post office van. I was bidding goodbye to Death and his minions, back in the world and finally on my way somewhere interesting. Not a hope in hell as it turned out, but the optimism was good while it lasted.

As Pearl's face-down letters sank in the growing pile awaiting collection, I relished the music of traffic and chattering shoppers that filtered in through the pillar-box slot. I imagined the possibilities that lay ahead. At some point in the bowels of the postal system I was going to be faced with a split-second choice of which letter to follow. What luxury to have options at last! Much as it was tempting to fly to the Royal Shakespeare Company, more filing cabinets lurked there, so I decided against it. Better to land on the doormat of some trivial person who would make much of the letter, finger it, re-read it, show it to others. I reviewed my beneficiaries accordingly.

With an upsurge of elation it hit me – one of them was my

sourpuss of a domestic! Was it possible that, in a magnificent stroke of fate, Mrs Butley would be my saviour? She'd been keeping an eye on my house, Simon said, feeding Henry V every day. It just needed the satisfying spite of *One thousand pounds with thanks for her services* to count as emotional investment, and I could attach myself to her letter. She would curse me and slander me, but I would relish the spectacle, and with luck she would cart Pearl's missive around in her ugly great handbag to flap indignantly in the face of anyone who would listen. She would carry it, and me along with it, over the threshold next time she fed Henry! I was dancing with joy in the dark pillar box at the prospect of being home safe.

The envelopes saw the light all too briefly between pillar box and sack – there was no chance to read the names on them. From the van, the sack was trundled into what sounded like a vast warehouse of busy machinery. It was untied and upended, and the contents cascaded from it in a jumble that buried me. Then packages were chucked one way, letters another, until Pearl's smart envelopes were grabbed and packed tightly, together with others, edge up, into a tray that inched me nearer and nearer to the flash of a conveyor belt.

Heavens, the speed and the racket. At first I was petrified, but the next moment I found my bravado. 'Do your worst,' I challenged the fearsome machine. 'I am of nothing made, so how can you harm me?' Nearer, nearer, nearer – then away I shot, as if in a pinball machine, whipped and whirled through the innards, to be stacked, packed and fired off again.

What a ride! Hairpin bends, loop the loops, you name it, at lightning speed through the infernal din. No chance to choose between letters, two snatched away from me, faster than thought, then another. It was just the throw of the dice that I ended up, giddy and elated, with the last, packed tightly into a bin for – damn and blast it – BN3, the Hove delivery office. Mrs Butley's address is BN1. My hopes of seeing home crumbled.

Thank my stars, though, I wasn't in an urn or a filing cabinet, and things might yet turn out well. Hove meant Deborah Lawton and her bastard child. It was years since the boy turned twenty-one and I put a stop to my payments. For all they knew I'd forgotten them, but here I was, winging their way with news of a fair-sized bequest, unearned, unexpected, to bring smiles to their faces. In my mind's eye I saw Deborah as she first appeared to me three decades ago. An ethereal beauty who turned out to be a pestiferous lunatic, yet as I waited in that post-office bin I found myself hoping that time had been kind to her. Was she at the funeral? Was hers one of the raised voices I heard from inside Pearl's handbag? I should have paid more attention.

There was a fair bit of waiting in the bin, but the hours didn't drag. For a while I danced on my leash, reliving all that delirious zipping and spinning, and when I quietened, the mix of hope and anxiety kept me alert. The lights stayed on in the warehouse and there were people about. A few took their coffee break near me, so I heard how someone's mother had run off with a tree surgeon half her age, how the new series of *Upton Manor* isn't a patch on the last one, and endless nonsense about *The Reality Channel*. Not a word about me. How fast I'm forgotten. I long to be among actors and people who value the arts, who must surely be mourning the passing of a theatrical superstar and debating his legacy.

As dawn broke the bin was loaded onto another van and driven off for local sorting. Sadly no more machines, just a whistling postie in front of a frame full of pigeonholes. Very soon, here was the letter, clutched in the same postie's hand as, still whistling, he pushed his red trolley the length of a rundown Hove backstreet. Here was I, bobbing along after it, eager to dive through a letterbox into Deborah Lawton's fair hand.

My expectations fell as flat as the letter did in this chaotic hallway. I'm at Deborah's all right, but I've been here two nights and the best part of three days, and she hasn't bothered to pick her mail off the floor or even to glance at it. Yes, that was her at the funeral, decked out in black at the back. Now, clad in an eccentric variety of draperies and adornments, she squeezes in and out across the heaped doormat with barely a glance at what might have newly arrived on it.

She has lost her figure with age, but not in the usual way. The slim waist is still there, but the welcoming curves above and below it have vanished. Desiccated, brittle, she offers barely a glimmer of her former sexiness. And dear me, the state of this place. The young beauty I remembered has become one of those pathetic creatures featured on television freak shows, who pack their homes floor-to-ceiling with so much jumble and rubbish they barely have room to move, sit or sleep. Her son – my son, I suppose – has come by a couple of times, making the case for a clear-out before he goes off somewhere. Does she listen? Not a chance. *That she is mad, 'tis true; 'tis true 'tis pity; and pity 'tis 'tis true – a foolish figure.*

Almost no light reaches this hallway, which is stacked either side with boxes and heaps of nonsense, on which she continually dumps more bulging carrier bags, while through the letterbox falls a steady stream of free magazines, fast-food menus and charity-collection appeals. I jig in frustration, willing the impossible woman, please, to bend down and sort through her mail. Because the situation is critical. Only a corner of Pearl's letter now remains visible. At any moment it will vanish beneath the avalanche, and I will go with it. It could take years to resurface; I might as well have been filed.

Scotty, damn it, where are you? Is there no way we can make this blessed envelope emit come-hither signals? I'm doing my level best here. It's high time the laws of the universe cut me some slack.

Richard

'Are you going to let go, Mum?'

She didn't reply, just hung on to the plastic sack, not meeting his eyes.

'Enough.' He let go himself. 'I give up. Have it your own way.'

She clutched at the banister to keep her balance. When he reached to steady her, she retreated further up the stairs, huddled over the sack as though it were a kitten he wanted to drown. 'You see what you're like,' she accused him. 'Pushing me, rushing me, bossing me.'

'For fuck's sake.' He slammed into the kitchen and leaned his head on a cupboard door.

'Language,' she called after him.

He gritted his teeth so hard his jaw hurt. This place stank. There must be food rotting somewhere. She probably had rats.

Calm down. He was leaving, remember. There was no point any more in being angry or worried about her. If she wouldn't cooperate, he was done. On Sunday, he'd pedalled straight here from the café book-signing, full of new energy, and she'd seemed to catch on to his plans, to go with his enthusiasm, to agree she shouldn't stand in his way. Yes, she'd prevented him from having a life. Yes, she should get her own friends. Yes, her hoarding was out of control, she wasn't eating properly, she needed to change. She'd thanked him for offering help before he took off round the world, and solemnly promised she wouldn't relapse into shoplifting. But today when he'd arrived to make a start, nothing doing. He'd seen immediately that she meant to be awkward. She was got up as a bag lady: the unravelling cardigan misbuttoned, the hem of the skirt falling down. Some Pinter play probably, or Beckett. She had on her self-pitying, querulous voice and kept repeating herself.

Same old, same old, one more phony performance, but things were moving fast: he wasn't bluffing or fantasising this time. Tiffany was excited about buying the café. Her dad and mum were coming round to the idea. They were busy consulting the bank and the soup woman and whomever, and soon the deal would be done. They were getting the business valued, debt free. Any debt above that would stay with Richard, but it wouldn't be much and he would be out of here, not a backward glance. Today's search of the world was for Ws. Warm Springs sounded nice, but probably wasn't. The pictures of Wagga Wagga were disappointing, but he fancied it just for the name. Almost anywhere but Worthing would be fine to begin with. Winnipeg, Warsaw, wherever. Somewhere to clear his head and see his way forward. Seriously, practically, he could do worse than start off in Wimbledon. 'Come stay with us,' Joe offered last night on the phone. 'The wife adores you. You're tidy and helpful, unlike myself. And I'm up for being your guide to the pubs of London.'

His mother sidled into the kitchen, keeping her distance,

her grip tight on the plastic sack, her voice full of reproach. 'I need *time* to sort things through *properly*,' she declaimed, sounding her consonants nicely so the back row could hear. The director in her head would be pleased with her.

'It's all right,' he said. 'I'm not arguing. You've won. If we're not going to do this, then I'm leaving this minute. I've plenty to get on with.'

She blocked his way to the hall. 'You just grabbed things,' she pleaded. 'You didn't give me a chance.'

Her crumble into panic drew the familiar pang of sympathy from him. It wasn't her stuff that she cared about. *Don't leave me* was the message she was too frightened to speak aloud. She had never once said it, unless perhaps over his cradle, but it had kept him here as surely as if she'd sobbed it every day of his life.

He hardened his heart. She wouldn't get to him, not this time, not ever again. She might be horribly lonely and vulnerable, but she'd no right to make that his problem. Thirty was way past the age when any self-respecting man should cut loose from his mother.

'Didn't you hear me?' he said, trying to squeeze past her. 'You can keep all your stuff. It's your choice. I asked you about every single thing in that sack, but—'

'No, Richard, you *told* me about everything in it. You said, "This is broken, this is useless, this is ridiculous."'

'Stop it,' he shouted, but she was in full flow, still blocking his exit from the kitchen.

'What you never will *grasp*,' she proclaimed to her invisible audience, 'is that *nothing* is useless to a props department, that every day, somewhere, there's a production in need of a dial telephone.' She pulled one from the sack with a flourish and held it up, right and left, to the cobwebbed ceiling.

Richard grabbed the receiver and put it to his ear. 'Hello. What? No, sorry, this isn't a theatre. My cloud-cuckoo-land mother just thinks that it is.'

'Of course I don't. I'm not stupid.'

He banged the receiver down. 'There won't be any production. Mum. No one is ever going to come looking for this useless phone.'

'Did I say that they would? My point is—'

'To hell with your point. The real point is that this should be your home, not a props department.'

'Exactly. *My* home. *My* collection. People collect things. *I* collect props.'

She made him so furious. 'Instead of eating?' he shouted. 'Instead of having friends? Instead of answering the door to people trying to help you? And it's not only props. Look at it.' He gestured in exasperation. 'It's scripts... programmes...'

'They're *valuable*.'

'Bloody well sell them, then!'

'I don't *want* to bloody well sell them.'

'Sunday review sections dating back decades. They're valuable too, I suppose?' He shoved past her into the hall. 'And this rubbish that falls through the door. You'll be stuck in here before long, walled up starving behind a mountain of pizza offers.'

He was bellowing. It felt good to let rip, to tear another sack from the roll, shake it out, start to fill it. 'You're impossible. Just look at the state of this place.' He squatted behind the front door and began shovelling great handfuls into the sack.

'Richard, you have to *listen* to me. What you *never* understand is that tidiness isn't a matter of right and wrong.'

'Please Mum, not that blather again!'

'It's not blather. Some people are far *too* tidy. You see them on television, washing their hands every five minutes, jittery if things aren't in straight rows. Which is fine for them – live and let live, I say – because that's how *they* are, but this is how *I* am, and—'

He wasn't listening. He was ramming circulars and magazines and junk mail into the sack. He was hurling it out on the step. He was marching back down the hall to the staircase to grab his pannier. He was leaving.

She was crying, or pretending to, but he refused to be touched by it. 'I would have been inside Harry's house,' she sobbed, 'if it wasn't for you. I'd have been welcomed like royalty.'

He turned and looked her straight in the eye. It helped to be angry. 'I'll let you know when I leave,' he said. 'I'll pop in before I set off. I'll ring when I arrive somewhere – so you know where I am. But otherwise, listen carefully, Mum, you're on your own now, okay.'

He charged out, banging the front door behind him. He swung the pannier to his shoulder and leapt down the steps to the street.

'Shit.' He'd caught his foot on the sack of junk mail, and it was spilling its contents across the pavement.

Ignore it. He would strap the pannier on the bike and speed off into the sunset. Just watch him go. He had one foot on the pedal.

It was no use. Joe's wife was right. He was tidy and helpful. Mess made him uncomfortable. The neighbours didn't deserve all this junk mail in the breeze. It wouldn't take him a minute. He was picking it up, stuffing it back in. Why the hell did he want to cry too? Dimly he knew that it wasn't his mother's chaos that trapped and enraged him; it was his childhood he was forever trying to clear out and slam the door on. It was high time he was happy. He would tie the sack off properly this time.

What was this? One for him? Richard Lawton Esq, c/o Ms Deborah Lawton. It didn't look like a circular. He ripped open the envelope.

The door creaked open above him. His mother's face was a picture of woe. 'What have you got there?' she whimpered, but he was too gobsmacked by what he was reading to answer.

Dear Mr Lawton

I am writing to inform you of a bequest made to you by Baron Whittaker of Dorchester. Please contact me at your earliest convenience to take the matter forward. The terms of Lord Whittaker's Will are as follows.

"I give to Richard Lawton the sum of £25,000 free of all duty and his receipt shall be a complete discharge to my Executors. The said gift shall be void unless

(i) witnessed by a warranted representative of Walker Macpherson and Allen Solicitors Limited the said person submits a sample of his DNA.

(ii) the said sample when analysed and compared by an accredited laboratory with the notarised profile of the DNA of Lord Whittaker that is held for safekeeping by Walker Macpherson and Allen Solicitors Limited shows beyond reasonable doubt that the said person was fathered by Lord Whittaker.

Any gift to a person who does not survive me by two calendar months shall be void as also shall any gift which

using all reasonable endeavours cannot be paid before the
second anniversary of my death."

I look forward to hearing from you.

Yours sincerely, Pearl Allen LLB

'What is it?' his mother repeated.

Richard shook his head in disgust, thrusting it furiously at
her as she came down the steps.

Harry

Twenty-five thousand pounds. You'd think the lout would
have the grace to be thankful. Instead, out of everyone's
earshot but mine, pedalling as though the Furies are after
him, he's bellowing the whole tedious range of gutter banali-
ties into the wind, telling me where I can stuff my money, and
threatening to tear up the letter and chuck it off the end of
Worthing Pier. I don't think he will follow through, but the
sentiment is discomforting. He's unlikely to frame it in gold
on his wall. Heaven knows what will become of me. He has
shoved it for now into the back pocket of his jeans, where
an inch or so remains visible, so I'm towed in his wake like a
water-skier.

We're speeding west along the promenade below Kingsway.
To my left, beyond the storm-massed heaps of pebbles,
stretches the English Channel in glorious panorama, the
glittering, blue-green field of white-crested waves that in
my life I never grew tired of beholding. I marvelled at its
beauty daily from my sitting-room window. The water is so
luminous today, horizon to horizon, that I'm reminded of
the aura that drew me to Pearl Allen, that shone around first

the will, then the letters, in the semi-dark of her bag. Is it possible, I'm suddenly wondering, that this spectacular sea is a qualifying host? Might I attach myself to these countless gallons of salt water if I were carried within ten metres of them?

The notion excites me even as it daunts me. Perhaps it would not be so terrible to be thrown off the pier. I imagine lapping in perpetuity at the beaches of Brighton and Hove, ducking and diving on the rosy horizon. Might I even be free to explore the whole of the world's oceans?

Through the wind's bluster I'm hearing the thunderous crash of the breakers, the cold rattle of churning stones, and no, the prospect is chilling. Such a wild and lonely existence it would be, forever roaming the coast or drifting in lightless depths among wrecked ships and downed Spitfires.

The view of the sea is receding now, obscured by stretches of grass and ugly, view-hogging houses. I may not want to dive into the waves, but I'm heartened to have seen their power and glory. Speed agrees with me, cheers me, whips my brooding thoughts from me and throws them to the wind. Though I can't feel the rush of salt air, or smell it or taste it, there's a thrill to be had flying through the world in its infinite variety, watching the tarmac flash beneath the bicycle wheels, the scatter of people, so remarkably alive, driving their cars, pushing their child buggies, chatting in shops and on pavements, tilting their faces to the evening sun. The afterlife has precious few pleasures, but this has to be one of them. Look at me, Scotty. In the face of your unfair, pettifogging rules, thrown from one near-disaster to another, this spirit is doing his best to keep his spirits up.

Well I never! Think of the devil, here Scotty is, materialising blithely upon the handlebars, craning his neck to watch a herring gull career in flight above the road, then waving to me across the back of our energetic companion, who, buttocks high, head low, pedals on as if no youth in a T-shirt and pinstriped trousers were blocking his view.

The thought for today emblazoned in gold across Scotty's T-shirt is *It is better to travel well than to arrive*. 'Well I never, this is progress,' he says. 'Good for you.'

I'm overjoyed. I fly forward to greet him. Perch on Richard's shoulder to beam at him. If I had arms I would hug him. 'Oh, Scotty, hello!'

'And hello to you,' he says. 'I thought I'd pop by, see how you're getting on. I'm so happy today – I've just been to visit my wife – and here you are, too, with someone you care about. I'm so glad you bumped into him. Did he come to the funeral?'

It surpasses wonderful to be seen and spoken to, even by an ill-informed, useless sprite. 'The laws of the universe are no better than random,' I tell him. 'Don't try convincing me there's any justice in them, poetic or otherwise. I'm not attached to this young man. He may be my son, but that has yet to be proved. I'm attached to a letter he's carrying. I could just as easily have gone up the crematorium chimney or into a filing system, and who knows where I'm going next. Recycling or landfill are strong possibilities.'

'Oh dear,' Scotty says. 'I am sorry to hear that, but I never said death was fair. At least it's a challenge. Keeps you awake and on your toes, if you'll pardon the bodily metaphors.' He leans to the left as we veer around a parked lorry, his arms outstretched either side of him like a child miming the flight of an aeroplane. His insouciance no longer annoys me, I am so pleased to see him.

'Although, to be honest,' he volunteers, straightening up,

'between you and me, I wish I could say the same for my own situation. Awake and on my toes, I mean.' His glance flits nervously to the sky. 'I shouldn't be sharing this, I could get into trouble, but between you and me,' he repeats in a low voice, 'I'm a bit disenchanted with my promotion. It's wonderful to be able to visit my wife, of course, but when it comes to the actual job, there's no scope for initiative at my level, and most of the time I'm just bored.'

'Bored?' I erupt. 'Don't talk to me about boredom. You wouldn't believe the stultifying hours and days I've endured. At least you can flit about, perch on handlebars, hitch rides in hearses.'

Our forward motion has paused. A foot on the ground, Richard waits at a pedestrian crossing. Calmer now, he pats his back pocket, checking the letter is there.

'When they let me,' grumbles Scotty, 'but then, when I am out in the world, what's the point? I'm getting better at explaining the rules to new spirits, you'll be glad to know, and there's some satisfaction in that, but it's not as if I can change anything.'

'No discretion?'

'Not that I can discern.'

'Or hotline to someone who has?'

'You must be joking. My supervisor's a real jobsworth, oiling her way up the ladder.'

'Well I never. Just more of the same then.'

One of life's – and death's – pleasures, I'm realising, is having someone to bitch with. Scotty's enjoying it too, grinning even as he complains. His disgruntlement heartens me: even an angel's world is imperfect. His pinstripes are less crisp than they were: a bit frayed around the pockets, no discernible crease.

'She's all by the book,' he says. 'Hasn't a clue what things are actually like out here.'

We're off again, cruising along into Worthing, where the buildings to our left give way to more stretches of grass, lines of beach huts and the wide, blue horizon. Richard straightens up and pedals hands-free for a while, the wind blowing his brown curls about. Possibly my son, possibly not – it hardly matters. 'I should have left more to Simon,' I tell Scotty.

'Simon?'

'Yes. Gay man with a crush on me. I left him an insultingly small sum of money. He took it ever so badly. I saw his face when he read the will.'

'Ah, yes, wills,' Scotty says. 'The people who make them,' he observes sanctimoniously, 'think they're about money, but the people who read them know they're about love.'

'I didn't love Simon, but—'

'Clearly,' he says.

'But does my remorse count for nothing? Why can't I attach to him now that I do care about him? It's unreasonable that the laws of the universe disallow posthumous emotional investment.'

'Hey,' Scotty grins, 'you're learning the lingo! Although...'

'Although what?' I say eagerly.

'I don't mean to doubt you,' he says, 'but it's in my job description to check. Are you sure you're remorseful?'

'Horribly so.'

'And emotionally invested in this man?'

'Absolutely,' I say fervently.

'Nuh-uh.' He shakes his head. 'I'm sorry, but I think you're kidding yourself. What I'm sensing is merely embarrassment. You're afraid he's revised his opinion of you.'

'Precisely, because he's the only person who's shown any sorrow or affection.'

'And you'll miss that, of course, but what affection do *you* have for *him*?'

Checkmate. Scotty has rumbled me. I still have no proper fondness for Simon. The thought of trundling through the world attached to the poor fool is scarcely uplifting. Into his bathroom for example, it doesn't bear thinking about. The problem is that the alternatives are abominably worse.

'I'd better go,' Scotty says. 'I've a couple more visits to make. Thanks for the update – I'll feed it into the system. Chin up. You never know.'

'I don't have a chin,' I say petulantly as he fades out, rippling his fingers at me in a wave of farewell. 'Or a pecker,' I add to thin air.

Richard is still pedalling along. Mine or not mine, a fat lot of difference it can make to me now. A cloud has come over the sun, which has sunk low in the sky. Ahead of us Worthing Pier stands in dreary silhouette against a choppy grey sea. The thought of all I so recently took for granted and no longer have sweeps through me in a great wave of loss.

What? Hey, be careful! Richard has slammed on the brakes, sending me flying forward past his ear then ricocheting back to his shoulder. An attractive young woman stands in the road, mouth open, staring for all the world as if she's seen a ghost. 'Hello!' I say, forgetting it's not me that she sees.

'For God's sake, Claire,' says Richard. 'You came out of nowhere.'

'I'm sorry. I didn't think. But you're here, and—'

'I could have killed you, you idiot.'

I've seen her somewhere before. She's pretty, she's flustered, she appears to be emotionally invested in this angry young man.

'Richard—'

'No, Claire. Really no. No hard feelings. Anyway, I'm going away soon.'

Her eyes widen. Lovely blue eyes. 'Away? Where to?'

'To Wales,' he says.

'Wales?'

He laughs. 'Or somewhere like that. I have to sort out the café and my mother— No, not my mother, she's sorted, and something else just cropped up – but then, forget it, I'm out of here.'

'For a holiday?'

'For good.'

'To Wales? You can't—'

'Or West Bromwich,' he says.

'Don't make fun of me, Richard. I need you to be serious. Listen, I'm really sorry about the funeral—'

Of course, that's where I've seen her. That was her, in the cloche hat, at the back, with Deborah and son.

'I was totally out of order,' she's saying. 'I completely get why you're pissed off with me, but Richard—'

'No, Claire.' He has his foot on the pedal. Passersby are turning to look.

'I need to talk to you. Alone, not in public like this. Come home with me, just for five minutes.'

He unpeels her fingers from the handlebar. 'I don't have five minutes. I've calls to make, planning to do, a mountain of things.'

'Tomorrow then?'

'Claire, it's over.'

He throws his weight on the pedal. He swerves around her, gains speed.

'Richard. Please.'

He's away.

I stare back at the young woman who stands in the road looking after him, and I'm seeing all the women I swerved around and away from. Then I'm looking at his face as he pedals and curses, and I'm realising that yes, just maybe, he bears some resemblance to me.

Friday

Richard

'Okay, I have to admit he is a bit full of himself,' said one of the receptionists, 'but he's got one of those faces you just can't stop watching, don't you find? At least I can't. If he's on the screen, I'm glued.'

'I suppose so,' said the other. 'I hate him, though, cos if he chatted me up, I know I'd be like ooh, yes please, when I ought to say, "Get lost, Quentin."'

'Get you! Like he would even ask you.'

'I'm just saying.'

'He's bound to win it though, isn't he?'

'Yeah, probably. The others are all a bit blah.'

They had phoned Richard's name through and asked him to wait. Ms Allen would be with him in a minute. He sat on a low sofa, behind a tired indoor palm, half an ear on their gossip about *Tomorrow's Tycoon*, half a mind on his mother.

Her latest delusion was that Harry's money changed everything: her son would no longer be abandoning her. Instead, newly solvent, he would want to make a success of the café at last, moving it to a better location. Hove, for example. There were lovely premises to let just round the corner from her. She'd been ringing him nonstop, last night and this morning, pressing him to invest in his future, refusing to take no for an answer. He imagined her dressed for the part as a small-business adviser, with shoulder pads and bossy spectacles.

'It's your chance to *establish* yourself, Richard,' she'd told him at six thirty this morning. 'This twenty-five thousand is what they call "seed-corn capital".'

He had hung up on her and stopped answering her calls. His phone was vibrating now, but he didn't even glance at it. His escape plan was intact – the windfall just made it more possible. He'd use Harry's money to settle the debts that Tiffany's valuation didn't take care of. He could relax about his finances, devote a year to exploring the world – Xanthi, Xiaoshan, Xique Xique – before deciding where to settle and how to earn some kind of living.

He was still smouldering, though, itching to march into this solicitor's office and tell her where she could shove her DNA test. He pulled the letter from its envelope and re-read its cold words. Twenty-five grand was less than peanuts to Harry, a stingy payout of conscience money, hurtful, humiliating. Kinder to have left nothing at all. Where were the millions from Hollywood going – to the Harold Whittaker Adulation Society?

Thirsty after miles of frenzied pedalling with the morning sun in his eyes, he took gulps from his bottle of water and tried hard to be calm. Pride was a fool's game, and no amount of railing at a solicitor would do a blind bit of good. He'd be an idiot to turn down the money; he was damn well going to have it; it was his quick ticket out of here.

Also, there was something this Brighton lawyer might be able to do for him. A complete long shot, probably out of the question, but worth a try nonetheless. A parting gift to his mother, and one in the eye for Harry if he pulled it off.

But yikes – what was this? He ducked behind the withered fronds of the palm. The black woman from the funeral was striding through reception, heading straight for him, her hand outstretched. 'Mr Lawton?'

Of course, it made sense. This witness to the crematorium fiasco wasn't some woman-friend, as his mother had supposed, but his father's solicitor, Pearl Allen LLB. He lurched to his feet, fumbling the handshake, dropping the letter and bending to retrieve it. His prepared words deserted him, and he found himself babbling. 'I only found this at my mother's last night, too late to call you. I've come straight here this morning. I ought to have rung first, but...'

He had no excuses. Of course he ought to have rung first. He was uncomfortably aware how sweaty he was from cycling. His face must be scarlet.

'It's not a problem,' she said. 'I've a space before an appointment. It's good of you to drop by. Please, this way.' She was leading him towards an open office door.

Courteous, inscrutable. She'd heard him lie through his teeth, denying Harry to that reporter, and now he was claiming Harry's money. What on earth must she think?

They were through the door. She was closing it.

'You're not going to believe this,' he gabbled, 'but whatever I said at the funeral, I really am Harry's son.'

She raised an eyebrow. 'I have to admit, I'm intrigued, but that's the point of the test. Please have a seat.'

He glanced round the businesslike, white-painted office. The window looked out on a wall. He hovered between the door and the chair she was offering.

'Tea? Coffee?' she said.

There was no way she would do him the favour he wanted to ask. 'No thanks. Can we just get it over with?'

She blinked at him, perplexed. 'The test, you mean? I'm sorry, we can't do that today. I needed to know that you'd like to proceed, before sending off for a test kit. When it arrives I'll be in touch about giving the sample.'

'How soon?'

'A few days. Please relax, Mr Lawton. Please sit down.'

The chair faced her desk. He perched on the edge of it, fidgeting with the letter she'd sent him. 'So, what does this test involve?'

'A swab inside your cheek, that's all. Saliva and cells. You'll need to bring photo ID – a passport or driving licence. All very straightforward. Witnessed by me, completely confidential, into an envelope and back to the company for analysis.'

'And then what? I'm sorry, I must seem impatient, but how long is this going to take?' He flattened her letter on the desk, pointing. 'You say two months, but the thing is I'm about to leave England.'

'Probate will be a while. It's a complex estate, so more than two months, I'm afraid.'

'More? Are you serious?' He half rose from the chair. 'Forget it. I'm not waiting that long.'

She leaned across the desk, offering a reassuring smile. 'Once you've given the sample, we won't need you in person. Assuming the result is positive, if you give me your details we can do a bank transfer.'

'Okay. Fine. Good.' He was back on his feet, heading for the door.

She rose too. 'So you're happy to go ahead with the test?'

'Happy?' His rage erupted. 'Are you serious?'

She frowned. 'But I thought...'

133

He was being unreasonable. She was just doing her job. He should agree with her that, yes, he was 'happy' and get out of here. His phone was vibrating again. His voice, too, was shaking, embarrassing him, but he needed to say this.

'My father could have met me anytime in thirty years, Ms Allen. He could have judged for himself or got his lousy test done when I was a kid. He could have taken me to the zoo and McDonald's like absent dads are supposed to do. He could have got to know me. So no, I'm not the slightest bit happy, and I hate jumping through hoops to get his miserable money, but I need it, so sod him, for twenty-five thousand pounds I'll take his insulting test.'

He drew breath. His phone stopped vibrating. Had he been shouting? He felt foolish. 'I'm sorry,' he said. 'None of this is your fault.'

She came round to his side of the desk. 'There's no need to apologise. I understand how you must be feeling.' She held his gaze. 'It's unprofessional of me to say this, please keep it to yourself, but off the record, my personal opinion for what it's worth...'

'Yes?'

'Well... this isn't a pleasant will. He wasn't a pleasant man.'

'Thank you. It means a lot to hear someone say that.'

She held out her hand, and he took it. 'I'll be in touch,' she said, 'as soon as the DNA kit arrives. What's the best way to contact you?'

As she wrote down his number, he remembered the other thing. It might be worth a shot after all. 'Actually,' he said, 'there is something else.'

'Yes?'

How to begin. 'It's my mother... No, look, it's probably

impossible, so before I go into all that, may I just check, is Harry's house empty right now?'

She looked puzzled.

'Don't worry. I'm not about to burgle it or demand to move in. I just wondered if maybe he shared it with Mr Foyle?'

'No, it's empty.'

'So, as I started to say... my mother... if she could somehow be shown inside, just a visit, it would mean so much to her. It sounds daft, but...' He stalled. It *was* daft. 'The thing is, she obsesses. After thirty years, it's not Harry she misses, it's more the acknowledgement she thinks is her due. The funeral might have helped, she was going to be welcomed across his threshold at last, but you saw what happened...'

The solicitor smiled.

'...and she's been fretting about it, bewailing that she was denied yet again, blaming me. Look, it's a huge ask, but it would mean the world to her to be inside his house. Pointless, but symbolic. It might help her let go.' He took a breath. 'To let go of me, not just Harry. I need her to let go of *me*.'

He shouldn't be saying this to a stranger. His face was still hot from cycling, but he felt it grow hotter. He pulled himself together. 'Really. Forget it. Say no. I'll quite understand.'

Ms Allen said nothing. Still smiling. Could it be possible?

'Not for long,' he said. 'Half an hour would be great – just to be let in and shown round with a smile. By an estate agent possibly? It wouldn't matter who, as long as they listened to her and treated her seriously.' He was trying to laugh, to make light of it. 'It's a cheek, I know, but if whoever it was could treat her like... well, like a VIP. That's what she needs. She wouldn't harm anything – I would make sure of that. Just to be invited in, shown around, kowtowed to – it would give her—'

'Validation. I understand.'

'Exactly. And then, who knows, she might sign off from the bastard, get on with her life at last...' He ground to a halt, conscious of jabbering.

'Leave it with me. I'll see what I can do.'

'Really?'

'Of course. Mr Foyle is joint executor, so he knows about the will, about you, and I'll explain to him that—'

'Mr Foyle?'

'Yes, we'll need his agreement.'

'Ah, no, bad idea. That's why I asked if he was living there. After the mess we made of the funeral, he's bound to say no.'

'I'll give it my best shot, I promise.'

'That's good of you, but—'

'No buts.' She held out her hand again. 'I'll let you know what he says and be in touch when the test kit arrives.'

'Thank you so much. I've been rude. You've been kind.'

She opened the door for him. Another quick grip of her hand, and he was away, through the outer office and down the stairs to Western Road, registering briefly that someone else was now waiting behind the tired potted palm: a young woman with a purple birthmark across half of her face.

Before unlocking his bike, Richard set his phone back to ringtone. The calls and messages he'd been ignoring weren't from his mother, it turned out – they were from Claire, for fuck's sake. He deleted them.

Harry

I don't believe it! You stupid, stupid boy! This goes beyond comic or tragic. Here I am, stranded on Pearl Allen's desk once again, all my adventures gone for nothing. The Post

Office, Deborah's desperate doormat, my bicycle tours to and from Worthing – where have they got me? Precisely nowhere, that's where, like the turn of some freakish merry-go-round. My son – if that's what he is – cares so little for me that he throws Pearl's letter down and me with it and flounces off without us. To top that, the brazen little bastard is bent on wheedling his irksome mother into my home, *my* home, where I long to be.

Then Pearl with her judgements! Talk about salt in the wound. All right, I grant you I wasn't a 'pleasant' man. I was an *artist*, goddammit – does that count for nothing? I should be respected and revered as an artist.

She has picked the letter up, realised what it is and – No! Jesus help me – she is feeding it into a shredder! The motor shrieks, the letter is sliced into strips, but thankfully I've come through unscathed. Now she is dumping the debris and me into her wastepaper bin, which the gum-chewing, bum-scratching cleaning woman will empty this evening into another blasted rubbish sack. I'm plagued by the wretched things, lurking about me like vultures.

Reception buzzes through that Pearl's next client has arrived, and she's off out to meet and greet, leaving me dithering between an uncertain, insecure fate with a tangle of waste paper and a certain, secure one with the will in the folder that lies open on the desk. On an impulse I transfer to the will – though is it better to take my chance in a paper-processing plant? I hop back to the wastepaper bin, except— What's this, I can't? Why can't I? Try again.

The 'can't' makes sudden sense. By no stretch of imagination did I ever invest emotion in some solicitor's letter. It was the bequests I invested in, the parcelling out of my wealth. The scrap of paper that brought Richard news of his share is no longer a qualifying host. I am once again stuck with the will.

I subside on the desk in despair. There's no earthly use in fretting and striving. Struggle gets me nowhere against the pitiless laws of the universe. Full circle, defeated, I may as well resign myself to my fate.

Pearl is back, showing in the new client, a young woman with a strawberry birthmark across her left cheek and jaw. Normally I would find her intriguing, but I'm past all worldly concerns. Just file me, Pearl, and have done.

'Take a seat,' she says. 'Tea or coffee?'

The client requests coffee, then twists abruptly in her seat, and Pearl jumps up too, because someone has barged in unannounced. Mrs Butley, guns blazing.

'Girl outside said I should wait, but unlike some who spend their time nattering and filing their nails, I don't have all day. I have to work for *my* living. I've had this since Tuesday,' she's waving what must be the letter Pearl sent her, 'but I've been too busy to come, and now I've no time to hang about.'

For all my gloom, her ridiculous fury is lifting my spirits. 'Disgusting is what it is,' she bellows. 'A thousand pounds? Bloody cheek. There must be a law against it, and I want it put right. I worked for that bastard for twenty-six years, put up with his airs and his nonsense, scrubbed his toilet, washed his unmentionables, and what does he leave me – a measly thousand pounds. It won't do. To think I paid good money for a wreath.'

Marvellous. I feel so much better, basking in schaden-freude as she carries on shouting the odds. Others are enjoying it too. A receptionist hovers in the doorway behind her, miming amused apology at Pearl. The purple-cheeked young woman's eyes dance with merriment. Pearl tries to slip a calming word in edgeways, but there's no stopping the ranting. On she goes.

Wait a minute, though. Pay attention. There's an aura around Mrs Butley. Not the stale-cigarette odour that after twenty-seven years I am thankfully spared, but a sphere of high-definition, exactly as there was around Pearl at the funeral. I know what this means. I have misunderstood the laws of the universe. Pearl's letter, clutched in this grudging red fist, must somehow still qualify. I'm not pausing to question or to dither between options. I'm flying to the letter like a lost child to its mother.

But I don't understand. Before I can land on it, the will tugs me back. Something else must be drawing me, some other centre within the luminosity that surrounds my enraged domestic. I launch myself again, homing in blindly, past the clenched fist and letter, down to the elbow hooked through the handle of the hideous bucket-bag, and I'm diving in, staring about me, at cigarettes and lighter, lottery tickets, purse, a used tissue, Polo mints, spectacle case, keys…

Keys! Of course! And oh Mrs Butley, I love you, I love you. Because here on this crowded ring must be the keys to Marine Parade, and all my strivings and hopes have been smiled on, because Mrs Butley, you wonderful, miraculous, fabulous woman, you are going to take me there.

Were these keys at the funeral? Did I transfer to the wrong handbag? Still, never mind, here I am, here I am.

The woman with the birthmark is speaking. Not that I'm interested – I'm too busy cosying up to my keys – but her voice is forceful and clear. 'Please. I'm in no hurry. I'm happy to let this lady go first.'

Mrs Butley growls above me, sensing an insult.

'Are you sure?' Pearl is asking. 'That's enormously kind of

you. Chloe, please would you look after Mrs Caruthers. Get her a proper coffee from over the road.'

The door is closing on Chloe and Mrs Caruthers. Pearl is soothing Mrs Butley, but I'm barely listening. I'm pogo-bouncing in and out of the bucket. Whee, look at me, look at me. Home safe, all bar the shouting.

'That effing man. That mean, bloody bugger.'

There's no calming or satisfying Mrs Butley, but equally nothing she can extract from Pearl Allen beyond the promise in due course of one thousand pounds. Soon enough, she is grumping and huffing her way out through reception, where Mrs Caruthers, and now Simon Foyle alongside her, stare from the sofa.

'The law is a donkey, Mr Foyle,' Mrs Butley informs him, 'and your precious Lord Harry was a pig. All those years I slaved, and for what?'

For me, Mrs Butley, my dear, I answer with relish. For me and a perfectly acceptable wage. So take your thousand pounds and spend it on tasteless nonsense for your philistine of a husband and your dozens of tedious grandchildren, and carry me, carry me, carry me home.

Richard

The call came when he'd pedalled halfway to Worthing under the scorching sun. 'For God's sake, Claire,' he muttered as he skidded to a halt. It was time to tell her in no uncertain terms to get lost. Pulling out his mobile, blinking the sweat from his eyes, he saw an unidentified number on the screen.

'Your request, Mr Lawton.' It was Pearl Allen. 'Mr Foyle popped in, so I've had a word, and he's happy for you and your mother to see the house.'

'He is?'

'No problem at all. The only thing is he'd like it to be this afternoon if possible.'

This was brilliant! Richard glanced at his watch. 'What sort of time?'

'Would three-thirty work for you? He'll meet you outside the house.'

'Mr Foyle will?'

'His flat is nearby.'

Richard called up an image of Harry's chief mourner, wreathed in smiles, shepherding him and his mother over the threshold. It didn't add up. Was Foyle planning some kind of revenge? 'But look,' he said warily, 'he's angry with us, which I quite understand, but this is pointless unless my mother feels welcome. Could someone else show us round?'

'Hold a moment,' said Pearl.

Her voice grew muffled. Foyle must be there – she must be consulting him. Richard stared back towards Brighton as the traffic sped past.

'Hello again. He'd like a word.'

Foyle's plummy voice came on the line. 'I'll be honoured to show you and your mother the house, Mr Lawton. The fuss at the crematorium doesn't matter, not in the slightest. I apologise for losing my temper.'

'But we wrecked it,' said Richard. 'I should have prevented it, not told Claire, kept the whole thing to myself.'

There was a pause. Then, 'How shall I put this?' Foyle said. 'One shouldn't speak ill of the dead, but I gather... I gather that Harry's will has rather offended you?'

'Yes, but—'

'It offended me too. He didn't care tuppence for anyone, did he? It's not the money so much, I wouldn't want you to

141

think that, but I was under the illusion that he had some respect for me.' Another pause. 'Anyhow, it turns out he didn't.' Foyle's voice was tight and clipped.

'He certainly knew how to put the boot in,' said Richard.

Foyle cleared his throat. His tone lightened. 'In my humble opinion, the funeral did our great thespian full justice.'

Richard laughed. 'You're right!' First the solicitor, now the neighbour – it was good not to be alone in disliking Harry.

'So, the house,' Foyle said. 'Rest assured, I will roll out the red carpet and give your ill-used mother the hospitality she fully deserves. Is three-thirty possible? It's short notice, I know, but I'd be much obliged.'

Richard checked his watch again. He would need to turn round, pedal back – no, first ring his mother. Please let her be in, not out shoplifting. He would break the news on the phone, then go there and take a shower and some deep breaths in her cluttered bathroom while she costumed and titivated herself. Only then could they set out for Marine Parade. 'Can we make it four o'clock?'

'Wonderful. That should be fine.'

'Thank you so much, Mr Foyle.'

'Not at all, don't mention it, and please, do call me Simon.'

It was gone ten past four when Richard and his mother got off a bus on Marine Parade and battled to make headway against the hot wind.

'He'll have given up and gone home,' his mother wailed. She'd chosen to come as a pre-Raphaelite Ophelia or possibly an angel. The long white dress, blown hard against her ankles, hobbled her progress. The fringed shawl flapped behind her like wings.

'No, I can see him,' said Richard. 'He's there on the steps.'

In the pillared porch of Harry's fine, three-storeyed Regency residence, Foyle, in grey linen jacket and pink cravat, was scanning the seafront in the other direction, so they were nearly upon him when he noticed them. His face exploded in beams. 'Ah, there you are. Richard and...?'

'Deborah,' his mother gushed breathlessly. 'It's so *kind* of you to do this for us. Simply *wonderful* of you after our *spoiling* everything.'

Foyle took her hand in both of his. 'All forgotten, I assure you. It's a pleasure and privilege to meet you properly at last, Deborah.' He turned to Richard. 'The young lady – Claire? – is she not with you today?'

'No longer with me, full stop.'

'Simon, you *are* wonderful.' His mother clung to Foyle, laughing gaily. 'Before we go in, there's something *important* that I really *must* say to you.'

Jesus, now what? She was standing way too close to the unfortunate man, fixing him with her dramatically made-up eyes. 'I know that Harry has been *terribly* unkind, but he needs us to *forgive* him.'

Foyle made a sour mouth.

'Because he's a *great* man...'

'Was,' Richard corrected.

'... a genius really, so the normal rules just *cannot* apply.'

'Rules like kindness and truth?' queried Foyle. Richard caught his eye. 'But let's not argue, dear lady,' he said. 'He meant a great deal to us all.'

'Exactly,' said Richard.

'Anyway, don't stand on ceremony. Come in. It's high time you were made welcome here, and there's someone I'd like you to meet.' Foyle pushed on the open front door.

The air inside was cool. There was a faint scent of

furniture polish. To Richard, it was like revisiting a dream. Here was the interior he had glimpsed past the bad-tempered housekeeper when he was eleven. From a chequerboard of black and white floor-tiles, a curved staircase with wrought-iron balustrade swept up towards the first floor.

Only one thing was new. The portrait of Harry on the wall beside the foot of the stairs, a full-size image of his father as 'grand old man': that wasn't here when he was eleven. Dressed in tapered green trousers and blue open-necked shirt, Harry stood on the same elegant staircase above the same expanse of chequerboard tiling, his hand on the banister rail, his eyes challenging the visitor, so convincing it was tempting to mistake the painting for reality, the real staircase for a painting. At his feet sat a large black-and-white cat with equally arresting green eyes.

'What a *wonderful* picture,' cried Richard's mother. 'It's him to the life!'

'A Hockney,' said Foyle. 'It's called *Harry and Henry V*.'

Richard hardly knew where to look. At his father's mesmeric eyes, at the black-and-white moggie, fat and breathing, that was ambling downstairs to greet them, or at the young woman rising from the Regency chair by the door. Smart jeans and white T-shirt, small rucksack, shy smile. He recognised her from this morning. Once seen, hard to forget. The left side of her face was all fiery birthmark.

'Richard, I'd like you to meet Lily. The will suggests you may be brother and sister.'

The cat wove back and forth round their ankles, mewing loudly. 'Sweet thing. He's hungry,' said Foyle.

'You're mistaken,' announced Richard's mother. 'I have only *one* child. May I see the house now?' She stalked past the young woman and started up the stairs.

Richard and Lily stared at each other.

'Of course,' Foyle said hurriedly, 'but what I mean is—'

'It's all right, we know what you mean,' Richard said. He couldn't stop looking. The twin plaits of brown hair. The candid, surprised, smiling eyes. The right cheek. The left cheek. His sister.

'You need time to yourselves. Don't worry, I'll take good care of Deborah.' Foyle caught up with Richard's mother, beaming and bowing. Richard began to like him, began to think of him as Simon.

His mother turned, playing the Empress Josephine possibly, and looked haughtily down to the hall. 'Richard, don't *linger*, dear. We've waited our whole *lives*. Come and see your father's house.'

A disconcertingly Biblical phrase. 'I'll be there in a minute,' he said.

'Let me show you the sitting room first, dear lady,' said Simon, cupping her elbow. 'Harry spent so much of his time there. The view of the Channel today is quite magical.'

'I need you with me, Richard,' she called, but the pull of Harry and her new role as his fêted widow was too strong. She let Simon guide her on up the stairs, and their voices grew faint.

'Richard Lawton,' said Richard.

'Lily Caruthers,' said Lily.

He searched her face for resemblance. 'I hardly know what to ask first.'

Her eyes shone, brown like his own. His heart thumped in his chest.

'Me neither,' she said. 'It's happened so fast. Tuesday, I didn't know who my father was, then suddenly he's Harold Whittaker of all people, leaving me money just when I could do with it. And now you – it's crazy. Crazy and amazing and wonderful.'

He nodded like a mad thing, lost for words.

'And this isn't the end of it – there are three of us – we've another brother, apparently.'

'You're kidding me?' His mind whirled. A sister. A brother. Out there, all the time, and he might never have known.

'He's called Jon Griffiths. Jon without an h. Not far from me in South London – Pearl's waiting to hear from him. But never mind him – today it's just us.' She gave a little jump of excitement. 'Bang, bang, bang. I get the letter on Tuesday, ring Pearl. She sends off for the DNA kit. I meet Simon when I'm giving my sample this morning. He asks, do I know you, and Pearl says about your mum wanting to see the house. So here I am.'

Richard's tongue was catching up with his thoughts. 'You only found out about Harry on Tuesday?'

'Yes, from Pearl's letter.'

'I mean, your mum didn't bang on about him all your life? Wow, I envy you.'

'Well, thanks.' She grinned. 'Not many people say that to me.'

'Sorry, I didn't mean—'

'I know what you meant. Hey, should we hug or something?' She came a step closer.

He found he wanted to laugh and cry at the same time. He chose laughter, hugging her, then holding her at arm's length.

'I'm thirty. How old are you?'

'Twenty-seven.'

For twenty-seven years he could have had a sister. This sister. Cruel Harry, what heartless tricks he had played. Richard frowned at the portrait. 'What does your mother think of all this?'

'Not a lot. She died when I was five.'

'Forgive me, I'm so sorry. Foot stuck in mouth.'

'No, really it's fine. I hardly knew her. She took one look when I was born and dumped me on her parents.'

'Because of this?' His hand hovered over her cheek.

Her nod outraged him.

'She made a mistake. You're beautiful.'

Lily grinned. Her brown eyes sparkled. 'Why thank you, dear brother, and so are you, by the way.'

He didn't want to stop looking, in case she might vanish. They sat side by side on the stairs. 'So you never knew who your dad was?'

'All my grandparents could get from my mother was that he was a shit.'

'Not a bad summary.'

'She was worse than him, though – at least he paid up. It turned out when she died that she'd been getting child support from him and keeping it for herself.'

'That's awful. Appalling.'

'We found out because the bank traced my grandparents and the money started coming to us. We never knew who sent it, and when I was twenty-one it stopped.'

'So, how come your mother died?'

Lily pulled a face. 'Fell off a hotel balcony on the Costa Brava, blind drunk.'

'When you were five? How traumatic.'

She shrugged. 'I was heartbroken, yes, but I didn't really know her, and my grandparents were lovely – best mum and dad I could have wanted. They kept the worst of it from me until I was older. Enough of me, though. What about *us*, eh?' She hugged him again.

Richard glanced upwards. 'I was forgetting the house. Do you want a look-see?'

'He showed me already. It's ever so grand. Like an old-fashioned stage set – one of those where the maid comes on first with a feather duster and answers the phone. But don't let me stop you – you need to take care of your mother.'

'No.' He felt reckless. 'What I need is to be in a pub with my sister, just the two of us. Simon's doing an excellent job. Give me a minute – I'll tell them I've been called away.'

He took the stairs two at a time, to find his mother, a radiant medieval queen, sipping champagne, charmed silly by Simon and fawned on by Henry V.

'What a splendid room,' he said, barely glancing. 'Hey, Mum, I've just had a call from the café. Bit of an emergency – I need to dash back to Worthing. Sorry and all that, but you'll have to make your own way home.' He shook Simon's hand warmly. 'Thank you ever so much.'

'Indeed, *dear* Simon,' his mother's voice followed him down the stairs, 'bless you for everything. Tell me, which chair did Harry usually sit in? This one, I'm guessing.'

Below in the hall, his astonishing sister was waiting. She smiled up at him, perfect in every way – he wouldn't change anything. He couldn't remember ever before feeling so happy.

'Kemptown is just back of here,' he said. 'I know a nice little pub – The Hand in Hand.'

The old Beatles' track played in his mind. The clash of guitars, John's nasal insistence, Paul's yodels. *I want to hold your hand*. He scooped Lily's hand from her side, swung it back and forth, kissed it. 'It's hard to believe that you're real.' They would walk to the pub, side by side, brother and sister.

Someone was turning a key in the door. It swung open, and there was the bad-tempered housekeeper, stubbing a cigarette out with her foot, clutching an enormous battered handbag and an armful of cat-food tins. Her jaw dropped at the sight of Richard. 'You? How did you get in?'

For a moment he shrank with the remembered shame of an eleven-year-old, but Lily squeezed his fingers. 'Mr Foyle invited us,' she said. 'He's upstairs.'

'Humpf.' The housekeeper shut the door with her hip and dumped the keys in her bag. 'There's no end to the liberties everyone's taking. He should have asked me first.'

Richard let go of Lily's hand to glance at his ringing mobile. For goodness sake. Claire needed to take no for an answer. He put the length of the hall between himself and Lily and huddled over the phone. 'Just stop this, do you hear? There's nothing to say. I don't want to talk, now or ever.'

'But listen,' she said.

'No, you listen—'

'Hear me out for two seconds.' She pushed on, raising her voice. 'Because, Richard, I'm pregnant.'

The air around him hummed as though something had just exploded. He heard himself speak calmly. 'Okay. Yes. Are you in your flat?... No, I'm in Brighton, but I'm on my way. I'll be with you as soon as I can.'

He ended the call and stood for a moment, staring at the mobile.

Raising his head, he saw Lily, and the same calm voice from his mouth said, 'I'm so sorry, but that was a real emergency. I do have to go.'

In less than an hour, he was on Claire's sofa in Worthing, staring at the blank TV screen. She had gone to fetch whisky.

'You shouldn't be drinking,' he called dismally after her.

'The whisky's for you,' she called back, 'and for me when you say I have to get rid of it.'

Her words shocked, then tempted him. She stood in the doorway with a bottle and two glasses. Vulnerable not predatory, gentle not harsh. All the way here he'd been angry, but anger was impossible now. 'You would do that?' he managed.

'Do what?'

It sounded crass to repeat it. 'Get rid of it?'

She lowered herself onto the other end of the squashy sofa, one of the three possible places this terrifying baby might have been conceived. She held the bottle and glasses to her chest. They stared at each other. 'I don't know,' she said.

'Harry told my mother to get rid of me.'

Claire blinked. 'You never said.'

'He refused to see her. Sent her money and the name of a doctor in Harley Street.'

'Very nice, I'm sure.' Claire set down the glasses. Unscrewed the bottle. 'Thank you for coming,' she whispered.

'I'm not Harry.'

'I know you're not.'

'And she didn't get rid of me.'

Claire smiled. 'Good decision.'

Shit, he was giving mixed messages. 'Sorry. I didn't mean...'

Her eyes searched his. 'Didn't mean?'

'To imply anything about what you should do.'

Her smile froze. She half-filled a glass and pushed it towards him. She put down the bottle. Then picked it up again and poured one for herself. 'So. It's true, then.'

'What?'

'About Harry. Not a story?'

He fingered the glass, lifted it and inhaled the fumes. 'Sorry. Yes. I only wish it weren't true.'

She stayed quiet. The silence grew longer. She huddled at the other end of the sofa, holding her glass in front of her, staring at it as though needing to hear his verdict before deciding to drink.

He didn't have a verdict. He couldn't possibly ask or expect her to do away with a baby. She had to make her own choice, which might be to keep it. And then a child – a person – a man or a woman would arrive in the world wanting a father, like he had always wanted a father.

He would never escape Worthing now.

He gulped whisky. 'How long have you known? Did you know at the funeral?'

'I was worried, but it could have been nothing. I thought I was probably just late. I didn't want to alarm you, but with… you know, with us breaking up, I thought I'd better take a test, and—'

'How did it happen, though? We've been careful, haven't we?'

She nodded, leaning towards him. 'Yes, every time. It's bad luck. Something slipped, something tore, foreplay, afterplay, who knows. I would never, I promise…'

She faded out and sat back, putting the untasted whisky on the table.

He couldn't meet her eyes any more. He looked down at his shoes on the yellow rug, remembering the good sex they'd had. He didn't love Claire, that was the truth of it. He didn't want to be with her. More than ever in his life before, he wanted to get out of Worthing and never come back. Today's letter was X, he remembered. Xanadu.

'So,' she said. 'I need to know, what do you want?'

'I want this not to be happening.'

'But it is,' she said quietly. 'Or it isn't. Your call.'

He tried to lift his eyes from his shoes, but he couldn't. In any case, he mustn't answer her; she had to speak first. 'No,

Claire.' He made himself say it. 'It's for you to decide. What do *you* want?'

She picked up her glass again. 'If I had it... the baby... would we be together?'

The question hung like a pall in the air. Tomorrow it would be places beginning with Y, and then would come Z, the end of the line.

'I would stay here in Worthing.' There, he had given it to her, the death of his dreams. 'I would help you with money. I would be a dad to my son or my daughter. But you and me, Claire,' he managed to look up, 'I'm sorry, but no.'

The colour drained from her face. He wished he could help her, but he couldn't unsay or qualify.

'Okay.' She swallowed a mouthful of whisky and shuddered.

He made himself keep looking at her.

'I'll need to do a bit of thinking,' she said.

'Yes, of course.'

'And shit. Of all the times for this to happen. I've only got three weeks to get out of this flat.'

'I'll help you to look.'

'No!' A fierce shake of her head. 'No, you're all right. I'll find somewhere.'

'Of course, and good luck with it. So... let me know what you—'

'Yes. Thank you.' She put down the whisky and got to her feet. 'That's what I'll do, then. I'll let you know.'

He drained his glass and stood too. There was nowhere the conversation could go. He took her hand, drew her close to him and put his arms round her, but she remained rigid, face averted, her own arms at her sides. 'It's best that you leave now,' she said.

He let himself out and walked home through the sunshine, barely able to think, hearing instead the tumble of the waves on the pebbles and the shrieks of small children having fun at the seaside.

Harry

Finally! Oh, the joy and relief! My bliss is barely dented by discovering my house full of unwanted guests. Whom do I find in the hall but that ungrateful boy, Richard? Then, after he rushes off for some reason, leaving Mrs Butley and the woman with the strawberry birthmark staring at each other, whom do I then discover upstairs but desiccated Deborah? She is fingering my photographs and disporting herself on my silk upholstery, champagne flute in hand, while Simon coos at her – but these annoyances scarcely matter, because at last I am safe!

As if this weren't delight enough, I am no longer tethered or constrained in the slightest. Every object and surface here oozes my emotional investment, and I can flit from one thing to another as a ghost ought to do, caressing the damask wallpaper, the luxuriantly carved picture-frames, the fine collectibles and leather book spines. I can hover over crystal lamps and voluptuous tasselled pillows, and roll in ecstasy across the antique, hand-woven carpets. Home at last!

The aura I've seen around my qualifying hosts is now everywhere; the house throbs and pulses with brilliance. I realise I haven't felt easy for a single moment of my banishment from this beautiful place. I've barely known who I am. The framed photographs, the Hockney portrait downstairs – precious, precious, these images of myself that I have been starved of – each one floods me with so much recognition that I feel almost embodied and have to check in a mirror.

No eyes meet my own from the glass. There's no strong, proud jaw or head of white curls, only a reflection of the room with its trio of interlopers, from whose lips my name falls with such pleasing regularity while Mrs Butley grunts and grumbles backstage.

Undeflated, I glide to the window and marvel briefly at the expanse of azure sea roiling in from the horizon beyond the promenade railings. Then I spin and pirouette towards Henry V, my gorgeous, great, green-eyed feline with his white boots and ridiculous white splash across his haughty pink nose. I land square on his back.

Did he twitch? Dare I hope? He growls softly and shivers his tail. Can it possibly be that he senses me? Mrs Butley is banging a tin, and I'm riding him piggyback into the kitchen. He runs, purring like a football rattle, to the bowl she slaps down, but he doesn't tuck in. Instead he's squirming as if he has fleas. When I glide to the black granite worktop, he calms and begins to gobble his meal. When I land on his nose, he lets out a squeal, leaps six inches into the air, wild-eyed and fluffed out to double his size.

What a brilliant discovery! Why didn't I think to tickle the whiskers of a passing mouse in Pearl's office? It's been so long since I had any effect on the world.

'What the heck's up with you, Tommy?' grumbles Mrs Butley. She takes pride in calling every cat she has dealings with 'Tommy'. She says there's no point in remembering their names. 'The stupid animal's having a fit or something,' she calls through to the sitting room.

By the time Simon puts his head round the door, I'm weaving figures-of-eight through the handles of my giant, stainless-steel, American fridge-freezer, Henry has his nose in his food bowl, and Mrs Butley looks like a fool. I have power, I have power. I am making things happen.

It's addictive. With apologies to poor Henry, I tease him and Mrs Butley some more, until she says, 'Pesky animal. Do you need the vet?'

Bad idea. I don't want to risk losing him. So I leave well alone, watching until I'm sure that he's calm and she's mollified before I head back to the sitting room, to find that the young woman with the birthmark is no longer here and Simon is in the process of saying goodbye to Deborah too. About time. Shoo. Away with you, woman.

'Feel free to ring me if you'd like to come again.' He leads the way to the stairs, but Deborah lingers behind, touching breakable things that are best left untouched. *No. Put that down.* She has hold of the fragile little porcelain bowl from the mantelpiece. She's smearing fingerprints across its hand-painted surface, and— What? *Hold on. Stop thief!* Her back is to the door and her fingers move fast. She has it wrapped in a lace handkerchief and slipped into her imitation Regency reticule.

Simon is back. *Did you see that? How dare she? Make her empty her bag out. Call the police.*

The damn fool has missed it. 'Things may move quickly,' he's saying. 'If you'd like to visit again, I mean. Sotheby's are coming on Monday to look at the contents. It'll all be packed up and gone soon. And the house itself – the agent reckons it will sell fast. He expects a bidding war – foreign plutocrats, luxury letting companies, that kind of buyer. It's ultra high-end, and when you add in the association with Harry – well, there's bound to be a blue plaque eventually, and—'

I've stopped listening. I've plummeted from the space the little bowl has left on the mantelpiece down into the grate.

Please not! This can't be. I've been so anxious to find my way home, but for what? My home will most probably be converted to flats. Henry V will be palmed off on a stranger. My beloved possessions will be scattered to the four winds.

The awful truth hits me. I'll have to stay in a house that is no longer recognisable or choose just one thing to follow. Already it's starting, the torture of choice and of loss, because my cherished, exquisite little hand-painted bowl is at this very moment on its way out of the door.

Saturday

Richard

He had abandoned her yesterday, thrusting his business card at her and blurting something about an emergency. He had pushed past the housekeeper, sprinted to the bus stop, fretted through the halting bus-ride to Hove, wrestled his bicycle from the D-lock on his mother's railing and pedalled furiously towards Worthing and Claire and her baby, almost forgetting that he had a sister, barely giving her a thought.

But Lily, wonderful Lily, hadn't forgotten him or taken offence. She'd booked into a bed and breakfast for the night and turned up here in the café this morning, shaking the rain from her red umbrella in the doorway and smiling hello. 'What a great place you have.'

He loved her spontaneity. As soon as she'd seen what was going on – a local artist's exhibition of watercolour vistas of Sussex – she had set about making herself useful: waitressing for Tiffany, charming the soup woman and chatting knowledgeably with the painter about his techniques.

Richard was impatient to have her to himself, to discover more about her, but he was needed to man the espresso machine, as Tiffany, radiating happiness, passed the orders along. The artist's friends and the Saturday strangers enticed in from the rain were ordering complicated coffees and chomping their way through a stack of fancy cakes.

Tiffany's pink hair was whisked up like candyfloss. Her minidress, white with black polka-dots, scarcely covered the bum of her Union-Jack leggings. Her elation gnawed at his conscience. He should be telling her that he couldn't sign over the café after all, that he might be staying in Worthing with a child to support. He should be deciding how to tell his mother as well. She was still ringing him every few hours to wheedle and whimper, demanding to know what his plans were. The good news, Mum, is I'm staying in Worthing. The bad news is that Claire, whom you hate and detest, is...

No, not yet. Claire hadn't decided yet, and he was exhausted from agonising, so − taking care not to scald himself with espresso steam − it was time to concentrate instead on the mind-boggling fact of having a sister. Wow! Each time he looked at Lily, astonishment thudded into him, making him grin despite his dilemmas. They would soon have a brother as well. The solicitor had promised to let Lily know when Jon Griffiths made contact, and then, Lily said, they must meet up, the three of them, like some kind of family. Richard, Lily and Jon. Completely amazing.

Something was spoiling his enjoyment of Lily, though. He'd begun to notice how the customers were rubbernecking her when they thought she wasn't looking. Some stared blatantly, some surreptitiously. He wanted to tell them, for goodness sake, stop. What a nightmare her life must be, never going unnoticed, never able to melt into a crowd. And for what? Celebrities traded their privacy for adulation and cash, but Lily had no compensation.

He beamed admiration at her, received a broad smile in

return and felt the warmth of it. She was wiping a table, saying something to the couple who were sitting there. Cheerful, outgoing, natural – how hard it must be to keep that up, instead of hiding herself away or yelling 'Fuck off' at each open-mouthed bastard. His fury was growing. He had to restrain himself from telling that child in the striped T-shirt to stop gawping. Nothing would change: the next child through the door would gawp just the same.

For some reason, his mother's excuses for Harry rose to his mind. What was it she'd said in her obstinate present tense that refused to admit he was dead? *Everyday happiness frightens him. He doesn't know how to do it. It feels like forgetting his lines.* What complete self-indulgence. Harry made an art out of not being himself, whereas brave Lily, here she was, staunchly herself despite being cast on life's stage as a freak.

Maurice presented himself at the counter, *War and Peace* tucked under an arm, his face a grimy picture of disdain. 'Noise pollution,' he complained above the hubbub of voices and the sound of a mobile phone going off. 'It's not good enough.'

'Sorry, Maurice.'

The customers queuing for coffee were catching a whiff of him and edging away. 'Fine words butter no parsnips,' he said, eyeing the cakes.

Richard slipped him an almond croissant. 'Just the one, mind.'

'I hear the woman with the face is your sister.'

Bloody hell. He would have snatched the croissant back if Maurice hadn't already sunk his yellow teeth into it. He opened his mouth to tell him to watch himself, but Maurice got in ahead of him. 'She's fucking gorgeous,' he said, spitting flakes. 'Tolstoy would have fucking adored her.'

Before Richard could answer, Lily arrived at Maurice's side, waving her mobile. Maurice shuffled backwards, contemplating her as though she were a Hawaiian sunset. She smiled at him, and he bowed.

'I just had Pearl on the phone,' Lily told Richard. 'Pearl Allen. She's in the office completing a house sale. It's bad news. The letter to Jon Griffiths has come back unopened, marked "gone away".'

'Who's Jon Griffiths?' Maurice wanted to know.

'Enjoy the croissant,' said Richard.

'It's a bummer,' said Lily when Maurice at last shambled off.

'So what happens next? Did Pearl say?'

'I told her I'd have a go. The address is South London, near where I live. I'll drop by – see what I can find out. Someone may know where he's gone, or give me a clue at least.'

'Good thinking.'

'And so, I was wondering.' She smiled across the counter at him. 'He's important to both of us, and we never got to the pub yesterday, and today's lovely, but no time to talk. We could get to know each other on the train, have supper and a bottle at my place. My spare room is nice. Any chance you could get away for the rest of the weekend, big brother? Come back this evening with me?'

Lily

Mrs Jones's daughter was out with her mates for the evening. Her son and husband were watching the doubles finals. 'I'll be upstairs reading,' she told them. If they bothered to come looking, she had the perfect excuse for being in her daughter's bedroom: it was flooded with the end of another lovely day's sunshine. She pushed up the sash and leaned out to look along the row of small gardens. No one in sight, just a cat sunning itself among next door's geraniums.

Soon, feet up on the bed, head propped by pillows, she opened her book. It was some literary thing chosen by her reading group. All right, she supposed. She tried to think of intelligent things to say about it at the meeting next week. The main thing was to finish it. Trouble was she kept dozing off.

Sitting up with a jolt, she found the light fading. Some noise had woken her. She peered from the window, and there they were across the fence, on the smart Yorkstone patio, laughing and clinking their glasses together. The young woman with the birthmark, and a young man who wasn't her husband. Good heavens, they looked really chummy. What was going on?

Sunday

Harry

I can't help it, I'm fretting again. Since Friday afternoon, through a long night and day and another long night, the elation of homecoming sadly has faded. I've done my best to prolong that first, insane happiness, but relief is an emotion that resists extension. Sotheby's are coming tomorrow, said Simon. My home will soon be dismantled, and every beautiful feature and facet of it now fills me with grief and disquiet.

I am too much in my own company. The only flesh-and-blood human who comes through the door is Mrs Butley. Powered by wrath, she pops in once a day to feed Henry V, drop cigarette ash on the floor and loot drawers for spare cash and small valuables. I try not to begrudge these losses, to see them as payment for the entertainment of hearing her curse me. I have heard all she has to say on the subject – she has the habit of repetition, as if to assert something twenty-nine times to thin air makes it truer or more worthy of indignation – but it's nevertheless cheering to hear my name still in her mouth. Even when she falls silent or chunters to herself about people unknown to me, her fleeting presence here passes the time. People-watching is my only alternative to stultification, and I'd rather watch Mrs Butley than no one. She's my one-woman soap opera.

Henry V himself mostly sleeps. His few waking hours are spent roaming free beyond the flap in the garden room downstairs. I've been tempted to go out with him, hunting for mice in the shrubbery, but so far can't bring myself to risk the adventure. I'm not ready to let this place out of my sight.

I no longer tease Henry because the last time I managed to spook him he bolted through the flap and stayed out for so long that I worried he wouldn't return. It was getting harder to alarm him in any case, requiring more effort and ambush each time. It seems that an invisible spirit tickling his nose and bouncing around in his whiskers has become unremarkable to him, almost beneath his notice. Like the abrupt hum of the fridge-freezer, the washing machine's spin-cycle, the sound of the flushing lavatory and the large cat that lurks behind the mirror on the top-floor landing, like all these things and more that once sent him into paroxysms of fight-or-flight, the resident ghost is now barely worth a blink or a pause in his grooming.

So, I'm running out of ways to distract myself or help the time pass. Sometimes I gaze from a window, wishing there were more people to see. The summer crowds on the lower road and the beach are obscured from my view, even from the bedrooms. Beyond the green railings on the far side of Marine Parade, opalescent water stretches towards the blue sky. A few take a stroll at this upper level, walking their dogs, licking their ice-creams, leading their children by the hand, but my house is set back and the road and far pavement are broad, so it's hard to make out their faces.

I've whiled away several hours in contemplation of

Hockney's fine portrait of me, examining the detail of his brushstrokes, the audacity of his colours, trying to conjure the echo of his dry, Yorkshire tones as he peered owlishly at me around his huge canvas and nattered on about painting northern trees in all seasons.

The nights are the worst. There's little light to see by and time slows to a stop. No wonder some old ruins fair shriek with suffering spirits. No soul in Brighton watched today's rosy dawn break upon the Channel with more abject gratitude than mine, but the sunrise brings only another promise of sunset. I'm interminably weary.

This morning I lingered a while with the photograph of Larry and me that hangs on the wall of my study. How handsome and easy we were, arm in arm, Larry and Harry, he in his sixties, I in my thirties already tipped to outshine him, alive and full of tomorrow, tingling, nerve-ends excited, eyes open, ravenous for fame. Smiling proudly, dazzled by flashbulbs, holding our BAFTAs aloft.

'The effort to carve yourself into different shapes,' I remember Larry asking me shortly before he died, 'to be successful, to be famous – what's the alternative?'

He was afflicted with stage fright, poor Larry, unlike myself. I never made the trip from the dressing room feeling less than utter conviction in the character I was about to embody. Never happier or more at ease, no room for nerves or self-consciousness.

'There isn't an alternative,' I told him. 'We are the lucky ones, who outshone the rest.'

'Yes,' he said, thumping his chest. 'The future will be looking back at us giants straddling the theatrical world. We are the best bulls in the ring.'

But even fine memories pall. Because he breathes, dreams

and twitches, the nearest I can get to contentment today is to watch Henry V sleeping. This last hour it is all I have done. He lies on his side on the deep-pile Persian carpet, his tail extended behind him and his front and back legs arranged so that he seems frozen in mid-leap among the stylised flowers and trees. His white muzzle gives the illusion of a smile as he quivers at private visions. Oh sleep, the time out of time that humanity begrudges itself, how I long for you. How I miss the dreams you might bring me, the strange, illogical power they would have to ease my fears.

'Do *you* sleep?' I asked Scotty last night. 'One level up from me, do you close your eyes, put your angelic head on some celestial pillow and tune out for a few hours?'

'Not as such,' he said, 'but I can't say I miss it. Between assignments and visits to the wife, I meditate. Want me to teach you?'

'I know how to meditate,' I snapped. 'It didn't work in the mortuary fridge, but I'll give it another try if you say so.'

He'd dropped by just after sunset, filling the sitting room with his golden glow and me with a storm of delight at the postponement of the terrible hours of darkness. 'Scotty darling,' I greeted him. 'How immensely glad I am to see you.'

He was squeezing me in between induction visits to newer ghosts. 'I'm not supposed to be here at all,' he said, glancing furtively around. 'Your case has been signed off for annual review.'

When I asked how his job was going, he launched into a tirade. 'Don't get me started. Talk about top-down management, it's monolithic – not a shred of respect for local knowledge. I'm the caring end of the operation, and I care very much, but what earthly good does it do?'

He didn't pause for an answer. 'I'm supposed to be in awe,

but if you ask me the higher echelons are clueless. They have their smug fixed ideas and refuse to see past them. Only one right way of doing things, no initiative expected or tolerated. They don't consult – you can't tell them anything. They're all ego, no commonsense.'

Working himself into a fury, he began throwing his arms about. 'Middle management are just as bad, busy parroting top management's nonsense, wilfully blind to how stupid it is, kowtowing up the line. The whole enterprise is a good idea gone wrong.'

'Well I never,' I said when at last he subsided. 'You certainly needed to get that off your chest.'

He looked abashed. Settling himself slowly on a tapestry footstool, he regarded his gilded toenails. 'You're quite right. I'm letting it get to me. I should rise above it – channel it into positive thinking.'

He wasn't impressed by my own fretfulness. 'You're doing better each time I see you,' he told me. *A jug fills drop by drop* said his T-shirt. 'But you haven't the first clue how to meditate,' was his parting shot as he shimmered away into nothing.

So I've been trying to do it, if only to prove him wrong. It used to be all about watching my breathing, but I've no breath to watch, so I try 'om' again, as I did in the fridge – om, om, om – but I can't get the hang of it: my thoughts refuse to switch off. Okay, you were right. I give in. Come back and show me how, Scotty.

Breathing.

The cat breathes.

I may as well watch the cat breathing. He has rolled on his back to keep his head in the sun. His front paws dangle either side of his chest. His chest rises and falls, rises and falls.

Yes... my thoughts are settling... I think I'm feeling it... maybe...

No, stop thinking. Stop trying. Empty the mind.

Rises. Falls.

Rises. Falls.

Rises.

Falls.

Richard

South London might not be Bali or Goa, but strolling through it with his new sister was giving Richard a taste of freedom. His troubles were far away. This was what it would be like to take off into the world. His vision would clear. New places and people would engage him.

Lily was leading him on a mile-and-a-half-long zigzag between her house and Jon Griffiths' last known address. The backstreets were quietly busy with Sunday hedge-trimming and car-washing. Each corner they turned, the hedges stretched away to a new suburban horizon, golden privet, green privet, all clipped to within a millimetre of their lives. The houses were clones of the basic Victorian model, their porches and doors painted a variety of hues, their bay windows offering kaleidoscopic glimpses of interior worlds.

The miles between Brighton and London were making it easy for Richard to smile at his mother, and even at Claire and her baby. If he never went back, they would sort themselves out somehow without him. He had just made Lily laugh with the story of his mother's seduction, including every embellishment – Harry's bare chest and iridescent eye-makeup, the smell of his greasepaint and sweat, the Barbican full to capacity eager for his next entrance.

'How romantic,' said Lily. 'No wonder your mum was swept off her feet. What a rogue Harry was. I'd give anything to know how my own mother met him. She had all sorts of jobs, but I've an idea she once worked as a film extra. Maybe that's when it happened.'

'Rogue' was a word Simon had used: an old-fashioned term, not altogether masculine. 'I've been wondering if Harry was bisexual,' said Richard.

'Surely not?'

'Yes, I know, but Simon was in tears at the funeral, so I thought...'

She grinned up at him. 'You're half right. Simon confided in me when he was showing me round the house. His passion was all unrequited. Harry was as hetero as they come. All the same, he fooled Simon into thinking they were friends, and the poor man was mortified by the will. One thousand pounds with thanks for his services. Did he tell you?'

Chatting with Lily was easy – no subject felt awkward. It was as if he had known her forever. On the train up from Worthing last night he'd even told her about the baby. 'I'm in shock, trying to pretend it's not happening. But it is happening, or it could be. I had plans, dreams, but now my life's on hold until I know what Claire decides.'

Despite Lily's sympathy, he hadn't wanted to say more about it – 'I'm determined to put it out of my mind for a couple of days' – and she'd been correspondingly brief about the husband she'd just kicked out. 'Least said, soonest mended. I think I was some kind of weird trophy to Martin. I met him at uni, where I stood out from the crowd in what seemed like a good way for once. I felt confident there, a bit special. I think that attracted him. I'm sure he believed that he loved me, and I thought I loved him. But since uni it's not

168

been the same. He's done so well in his job, which is fine, of course, but work takes all his time and, well, I've realised we never had much in common. Marry in haste, eh? He's a cheat and a liar. I'm sure he's not giving me a thought, and I'm trying to pay him the same compliment.'

'Feel free to have a proper rant if you want one,' Richard had told her. 'You're entitled.'

'Nuh-uh. I've done all that. I was in a real state at first. I did some silly, rash things.'

'Like what?'

'Oh... well... nothing serious. Kicking him out was a good one. Getting angry in public, drinking too much, going on a crappy blind date, that kind of nonsense. I was letting it get to me, only making myself more unhappy. So enough wallowing. Stop it. Forget it. Plans and dreams, you said. Let's forget all our problems, darling brother. What are your dreams?'

Darling brother. He had really liked that.

Travel, he'd told her. Exploring the amazing places out there that aren't Worthing or Brighton. He slipped his arm through hers as they turned another corner. 'Here I am at last, eh, sis? Living my dream. On the run for two whole days to South London.' He waved a hand at the hedges. 'How long have you lived in these exotic surroundings?'

'All my life. I inherited the house from my grandparents five years ago. Martin and I only just finished spending a fortune on it, though actually it turns out it was me spent the fortune. I'm left with the bank loan, which is why Harry's bequest is so handy.'

'Do *you* fancy travelling?' he asked her. 'Does the wide world ever call to you too?'

'Maybe one day. Who knows,' she said, 'but for now home

suits me fine. I know it's dull, but it's gentle – if that's the right word. Polite? Civilised? Hell, I'm sounding snobby, small-minded. What am I trying to say?'

'I don't know. You tell me.'

She thought for a moment, running her hand along more neat, green privet. Then, 'I've got it. It's anonymous, that's what I like. They say suburbia is all twitching net-curtains, but I haven't noticed. I get stared at less here than anywhere.'

A man looked up from hosing his tubs of geraniums as they went by. 'Lovely day,' he said, smiling.

'Yes, isn't it,' she replied. Twenty yards further on, she murmured to Richard, 'See what I mean. He didn't even blink. Round here I'm mostly free to be me.'

He wasn't sure he believed her. Did she believe it herself? These suburbanites might disguise their curiosity, but it was there just the same. He turned to look back and saw the man staring after them. Lily turned to look back and the man became intent on his hose.

'Brighton was okay,' she said. 'People mostly accepted me in Brighton on Friday, no trouble.'

'That's good,' Richard said. 'It's a town full of odd bods – maybe that's why. How about Worthing?'

'Not too bad.'

'I was furious at the stares you got in the café.'

She smiled. 'People always look – they can't help it. It's the way they look that matters.'

Last night, as they ate pizza and salad on her patio, he'd spotted a woman spying from a neighbouring bedroom. He might feel trapped by Claire and his mother, but Lily was trapped by her face. She dealt with it bravely, but it must hurt. He didn't ask her about it except when she spoke of it herself. That seemed the best way. Everyone else in the world homed in on her birthmark. He wanted to make plain by his lack of curiosity how little it mattered to him.

She had a desk job dealing with government statistics and surveys. 'Meetings and emails and figures on screens,' was her answer last night to what filled her time. 'I get glazed looks when I say how much I enjoy it. I've always loved numbers, that's the thing.'

It fitted the pattern, he thought now. Gentle, civilised, anonymous: numbers took no special notice of her.

'We're here. That's the house,' Lily said.

They had turned one more corner without his noticing, and she was pointing across the road. No one was clipping or hosing at Jon Griffiths' last known address. Its hedge was a heap of rebellious ivy, unkempt, overgrown. The glass in the bay window was dirty and the torn curtains were drawn.

'It looks empty,' she said, but crossing the road they could tell that it wasn't. From inside came the clamour of heavy-metal music. They paused by the gate. *No junk mail*, said a door sticker. *No hawkers, bleeding hearts or God-botherers*, another. *Beware of the dog*. 'Oh blimey,' said Richard.

All at once he was less keen to track down his mystery brother. Lily was wonderful, but there was no guarantee Jon would be too. Rather the opposite: Harry's son, after all.

'Deep breath,' Lily said. 'It feels like knocking on a door for one of our surveys.'

'What? I thought you worked in the office.'

'I went out with an interviewer a few times as part of my training. She was calm, nothing fazed her. Smiled for England. That was how she lulled people into agreeing to answer her questions.' Lily put a hand to her cheek. 'Oddly enough, this face of mine helped – the interviewer's hit-rate went up. I guess people felt awkward telling the afflicted to get lost.'

'Or maybe they loved you at first sight, like I did,' said Richard.

She grinned. 'Fingers crossed for this one.' She closed the gate behind them, stepped up to the door and rang the bell.

It opened on a chain. Out-of-control barking and a strong smell of dog exploded through the narrow gap. A man with mean eyes and a week's worth of grey stubble glowered at them.

Lily spoke quickly, smiling and with a warm voice. 'Not Jehovah's Witnesses. Not selling anything. We're looking for someone who used to live here.'

'You the police?' It was hard to hear him over the barking. The dog seriously wanted to kill them.

'Not at all,' Lily said. 'Just me and my brother. It's our other brother we're after – Jon Griffiths. Our father just died, and Jon doesn't know yet.'

Richard beamed corroboration.

The door slammed shut in their faces, then opened without the chain. The dog, standard issue pit-bull, lunged and scrabbled, desperate to get at them, held back by the man's grip on its spiked collar. The man was wearing a dirty vest and track-suit bottoms over his muscles and tattoos. He scowled at Lily. 'What the fuck happened to your face, love?'

'Nothing,' she said pleasantly. 'It's how I was born.'

'Jesus. Can't they do something about it?'

Still she smiled. 'No. It's complicated.'

Controlling his temper, Richard offered a hand and shouted above the racket, 'It's Jon Griffiths we're looking for. Used to live here.'

The man didn't take his hand. He was dragging his dog away, shoving it through a door towards the rear of the house, shutting it in. 'Griffiths, you say? Are you from the papers?'

'What?' An uneasy sense of déjà vu seized Richard. He glanced over his shoulder, half expecting to find Claire's journalist at the gate.

'God, Keith, you're slow.' A woman emerged from the heavy-metal din of the front room. Lank grey hair, a man's shirt over balcony-bra cleavage, a cigarette in her hand. Eyeing them suspiciously. 'What's it worth, that's what they're not saying.'

'Yeah.' Keith squared up to Richard. 'What's it worth, pal?'

'A fiver?' offered Lily.

'Try harder, love.'

'A tenner then.'

'Nope,' said Keith. 'What's your boyfriend got to say for himself? Fifty, and we might be talking.'

'A hundred, more like,' said the woman.

'What?' Lily gasped. 'We're just looking for our brother.'

The woman held Richard's gaze. Took the cigarette from her mouth. 'Tell that dog to shut the fuck up, Keith,' she said.

Her stare was unflinching. 'Griffiths didn't have no brother nor sister.'

'Half-brother,' said Richard.

'Is that right? So how come you don't know where he is, when everyone else does?'

'Come again?' This woman knew something they didn't. There was information as well as greed in her eyes. 'Okay,' he said. 'Twenty quid.'

'A hundred,' she said.

'Twenty.'

'Fifty,' she said.

'Thirty, and that's final,' he said.

173

'Humpf. Okay.'

'It had better be good.' He pulled out his wallet. 'Twenty's all I've got on me.' Fished in his pocket. 'And some change. How about you, Lily?'

Together they rustled up thirty pounds and handed it over. Keith quit kicking the door to the dog and sidled back up the hall to watch.

'Okay,' said the woman. 'It was Griffiths upstairs when we moved in down here. Two of them, mother and son. Years back.'

'That's right,' said Keith. 'We knew him, no mistake.'

'Only to look at, mind,' said the woman. 'We didn't get cosy. She was a right superior cow.'

'We'd recognise him, that's what I'm saying,' growled Keith.

Richard let his impatience leak. 'Come on, what next? Where did they go?'

'Got behind with the rent. Did a runner.'

'But you have their address, right?'

'Are you joking? As if we bloody care where they buggered off to.' She paused, smirking, to stuff the cash into her bra, coins and all.

'Just a minute,' said Richard.

'Keep your hair on. There's more.'

'Better had be.'

'At least we know who he is,' sneered Keith. 'Unlike you, for all he's your brother.'

'Look, do you know where they went, or don't you?' said Lily.

'Nope,' said the woman. 'We don't know where they went, but we do know where Jon Griffiths is now. Come in here and I'll show you.' She disappeared into the front room.

'Go on. She won't bite,' said Keith above the frustrated howls of his man-eating dog.

Richard met Lily's eyes, and she nodded. They left the street door open behind them and edged into the darkened room.

The place was a wreck, not as full of junk as his mother's, but far gone in filth and stink, a heavy mix of sweat and burgers and dog. The television was on, sound drowned out by the distortion and beat of the music. The woman scooped up a trampled copy of *The Sun* from the floor and pointed at the TV. 'He's gone now, but he was just on the news. That's why Keith thought you must be the papers.' She shoved the newspaper at him, and Richard looked uncomprehendingly at the headline.

COOL WIN, QUENTIN!

'That's him,' said the woman. 'Same boy grown up. We'd know him anywhere.'

The photograph showed the curly-haired winner of *Tomorrow's Tycoon*. 'Drop-dead gorgeous heartthrob of the nation' ran the caption.

'Poncy little git changed his name,' said Keith.

Monday

Harry

As I watch, Henry V wakes abruptly, jumping me out of today's meditational trance. His ears twitch, angled to catch some sound I can't hear. Then he yawns and stretches before heading for the top of the stairs, where he waits, his eyes fixed on the street door below.

I hover next to him, watching too. Mrs Butley has already been today, so this must be Sotheby's. Sure enough, here's Simon, punching the code into the house alarm, a young fogey in tow. Expensive haircut, moleskins and Oxford shirt, a large carbon-receipt pad and a small tablet computer.

He stands in immediate awe of the Hockney. 'Wo-w,' he says slowly. 'Really wow. I had no idea there'd be anything like this. It'll stir up international interest. It could fetch – golly – I don't know how much. I hope it's insured. I trust the house is secure.'

I visualise my portrait hanging in the Met, and it dawns on me. Suppose I were to attach myself to it, cast my lot in with it. I could be there too, basking in the admiration of the crowds. I need to be careful, though – it might equally end up on the wall of some private collector, or worse still in storage.

Upstairs the auctioneer dryly disparages each piece of furniture, each treasured collectible, despite the receipts and other evidence of authenticity that Simon has unearthed from my files. 'The market's depressed,' he says. He takes record shots with his tablet and taps in notes to go with them. 'To be honest, there's little interest nowadays in this style of thing. We can sell it for you, of course, but none of it will fetch much. Guesstimate, Hockney apart, five or six thousand, less commission, for the lot.'

Little upstart! How dare he? Any discerning buyer will salivate over these wonderful objects. Simon protests too, turning pink around the collar and ears, until his anxiety begins to perplex me. It's no skin off his nose if the vulgar world doesn't share my good taste; it's the RSC's loss. 'I'm in the antiques business myself,' he asserts feebly.

The auctioneer nods and smiles. He doesn't enquire into Simon's profit-and-loss account, doesn't argue or snipe. The next time Simon challenges an estimate, he stares vacantly out at the sea. 'Great view,' he says. 'That and the Hockney will fetch a vast amount more than any of this stuff.'

I sulk in corners, hating both of them, adding my ghostly weight to Henry V's feline beams of disdain. The young man picks things up, puts them down again, queries their provenance, points out their defects and starts to draw up a list of the things he will take. Swiftly, methodically, he itemises the sitting room, the bedrooms, the study, the garden room. 'The personal memorabilia may well fetch a bit,' he says. 'The great man's clothes and private papers and so on.' At last some respect, and I warm to him slightly. 'We'll let the valuers have a look and see what they think.'

He's back on the landing, pausing before descending the

stairs. 'Hang on,' he says, brightening, 'how on earth did I miss these?'

My two hand-coloured, eighteenth-century folding maps of the American colonies hang here in gilt frames, well away from the sunlight.

He has come alive, as he did when he encountered the Hockney. 'If these two babies are genuine, they're worth a fair bit.'

Simon is all ears. 'A fair bit? Meaning what?'

'Hard to be exact.' The young man has them off their hooks, and out comes a magnifying glass.

'Ballpark figure?'

'Golly, that's beautiful. In such good condition. Off the top of my head, hmm... five thousand apiece, but that's minimum. Fifteen, maybe twenty thou the pair if we get telephone bids from the States, and why wouldn't we?'

Simon is beaming.

'They're genuine all right,' the auctioneer enthuses. 'Look, you can tell by the wear along the fold-lines. Impossible to imitate that in a reproduction.'

He straightens up, smiling broadly. 'Okay, I think that just about covers it. The van and the men are outside.' He's trotting downstairs, his tablet tucked under his arm. 'We'll start wrapping things and loading up, except for the Hockney of course. I'll arrange specialist packing and transport for that.'

As he reaches the hall, he spins on a heel to take another look at it. 'I can't tell you what an amazing find this is. Such a pity it has to be moved from this setting where it belongs.'

Simon lingers on the landing. I hover on the staircase halfway between them.

'I'll give you an itemised receipt now. What happens next is our valuers take a proper look and I email their reserve prices for your approval. Should only be a few days.'

'Fine,' Simon calls down the stairs. 'Although,' he adds abruptly, 'on second thoughts...'

The young man turns from the door. 'Yes?'

'These maps...'

Is Simon's voice trembling slightly? The young man's smile freezes.

'Yes.' Simon gathers certainty. 'Would you leave them, please? I think I can find them a private buyer.'

'A well-advertised auction will get you a much better price.'

Simon clears his throat. 'Thank you, but I'd rather...'

We wait in vain for the end of the sentence. A private buyer? Private to you, Simon? You bastard.

'Ah,' says the young man. He frowns, shakes his head, but then seems to decide that it's none of his business. 'Anyway, let us know if you change your mind. We'd love to handle them for you.'

Two hours later, after I've suffered the unutterable anguish of watching most of my home swaddled in blankets and bubble wrap and carried away, Simon bids the auctioneer and his scene-shifters adieu and returns to the landing, where Henry V paces, uttering small, pitiful cries.

Simon picks up one of the maps and plants his fat lips on the glass.

You unutterable arse, I tell him.

Tuesday

Richard

Alone in his flat Monday evening and into the small hours, Richard had drunk his way steadily through the remains of a bottle of whisky and a six-pack of strong lager and had watched back-to-back episodes of *Tomorrow's Tycoon* on catch-up TV. What he saw gave him the creeps, but he stayed the course, from the portentous start of the series to the razzmatazz finale. Then he began again from the start, muttering curses through Quentin Griffiths' big scenes and fast-forwarding between them.

The sequence in which Quentin was declared winner obsessed him. He paused and replayed, paused and replayed, unable to stop. He stabbed at the buttons on the remote, examining freeze-frames of this monstrous brother, curly-headed, hypnotically charming, that Harry had foisted on him. 'Thank you,' Quentin repeated, over and over, smiling frankly into the eyes of the viewer. 'Thank you so much if you voted for me.' Richard jabbed the remote again and swallowed more alcohol.

When Tiffany had first shown him the magazine photographs, he'd acknowledged the resemblance but thought little of it. Now that this man was his brother, he saw something far worse. As he drained the fifth can and cracked open the sixth, he was recognising someone he knew all too well. Here was the same self-assured egoism as Harry's, the same mesmeric gaze, the same compelling voice that, shout or whisper, the world couldn't help listening to and half of it couldn't help falling in love with. 'You so, so deserve to win,' enthused the series presenter, a shrill bimbo called Mariella Dukakis, who never stopped pawing the man and thrusting her silicone breasts in his face.

Tiffany wasn't the only one with a crush: the whole female population seemed to be smitten with Quentin. Pearl Allen's receptionists fantasised about him, and even Pearl herself received the news on the phone with an audible intake of breath, followed by, 'Well, I never.' She was now busy making contact via *The Reality Channel*.

Most galling of all, even Lily was thrilled by the idea that this vile individual was her brother. In that squalid front room in South London, Richard had turned to her, assuming she would share his dismay, and had immediately seen that she didn't. Her hand was to her mouth, but her eyes were full of laughter and excitement. He did his best to hide his own feelings, because he could find no way to explain them that didn't sound churlish or jealous, as if he were miffed at being upstaged.

It wouldn't do. He had to call a halt to this resentment, he told himself. Mustn't let it come between him and his wonderful new sister. He *was* jealous. He couldn't deny it. It galled him to hear Lily enthuse about how much she liked this guy and how amazing it was that he was their brother.

Sibling rivalry wasn't the half of it, though. Quentin might be better looking than he was, more charismatic and clever and successful than he was, about to launch a business with half-a-million-quid's-worth of prize money in his pocket, but none of that really mattered. No, the truly appalling thing was that this brother was famous, his name on everyone's lips. Just when Richard had hoped finally to step out from under Harry's shadow, here loomed another. He gulped down more lager.

Everywhere this man's face was on screens and hoardings, his name in the mouths of strangers. He'd been mentioned at least three times in the café today. The nightmare was happening all over again. The king was dead; long live the king. From A-list to Z-list, Richard's life would yet again be hijacked and derailed and curtailed and – damn Quentin to hell, he hated Harry and he detested this obnoxious brother.

One scrap of comfort was that his mother would detest Quentin too. She'd been oddly silent since Friday, when he'd rung to say, 'No time to explain, got to run, visiting a friend for the weekend.' He'd gritted his teeth for a deluge of questions and worries, but instead she'd said, 'Fine, dear – have a nice time,' and since then hadn't called him, not once. He ought to check up on her, but he was too drunk right now – what was the time? – and, oh shit – he lurched to his feet – he'd forgotten about Claire, who hadn't called him either, and Claire's baby. His mother would hate Quentin, but Claire would be thrilled. Richard stumbled around the room, spilling lager and four-letter words. First her child's grandfather was Harold Whittaker; now its uncle was the heartthrob winner of *Tomorrow's Tycoon*. She'd tell everyone – there'd be no stopping her – she was the expectant mother of celebrity royalty. Soon there'd be flashbulbs and microphones and interviews, and Richard's kid, just an ordinary kid, would end up embarrassed by his pretentious connections or else insufferably pretentious himself.

Richard dropped back into the armchair. The alcohol wasn't working. His mind was in overdrive. He needed to talk to Lily. She would understand how he felt.

He brought the watch on his wrist into focus. It was what – four in the morning? But Lily was his sister. A sister wouldn't mind being woken. A sister would forgive him. That was what sisters were for.

He reached for his mobile – damn, not here – lumbered upright and into the bedroom – nowhere to be seen – and collapsed across the bed on his stomach, groping for the blessed thing on the floor, playing in his mind how the conversation would go, how she would completely understand and accept that they should neither of them ever have anything ever, ever to do with…

Somewhere his mobile was buzzing. His eyes opened to blinding sunlight falling in through the undrawn curtains. He'd been talking to Lily. Lily must be calling him back. Where was the phone?

He set off through the flat in pursuit of it. His head hurt. His mouth was parched. He'd been talking to Lily on the bed five minutes ago. How had the phone got into the kitchen?

Here it was by the breadbin. He picked up. 'Hello, Lily.'

'Who's Lily?' said Claire.

His head buzzed and his sight grew foggy as sweat broke all over him. Sagging to his knees, feeling queasy, holding on to the sink, he croaked, 'What day is it?'

'Tuesday. Are you all right?'

'Hung over.'

'And Lily?'

'My half-sister. Long story. Harry spread it about a bit. How are you, Claire?'

'Still pregnant. I said I would let you know.'

'Yes?'

'I've decided to have the baby.'

'Right.' He pressed his head hard on the edge of the sink and stared down at the floor tiles.

'You said you would stay around? Be a dad?'

'Yes,' he said. 'I did. Will.'

'Thank you.' Oddly, she was laughing. 'Well, I guess that's it then for now. Drink lots of water.'

'What's so funny?' he said.

Silence. No answer.

'Damn it, Claire, what the hell is so funny?'

The line was dead, he discovered. He jabbed at the phone. It rang again in his hand.

'Claire?'

'Mr Lawton. Good morning.'

'Sorry, who?'

'It's Pearl, Mr Lawton. Pearl Allen. The DNA kit has arrived. When would you like to come in?'

The wall clock said five past ten.

He felt sick. He couldn't think straight about DNA tests. Not today. 'What day is it?' he said again.

'Tuesday.'

'Tomorrow?' he offered.

'Tomorrow it is. Would eleven suit you?'

'Fine. Okay.'

He dropped the phone and only just made it to the bathroom, where he vomited once, retched several times, then lay curled for a while on the floor, trying to come to terms with his life.

Harry

Another long afternoon takes forever to unwind itself before another interminable night. I don't know what time it is – the auctioneer took all the clocks – but I'm watching through the French window as the shadows creep, left to right, across the wall at the end of the garden. The grass is parched, the foliage droops, and out front the neighbours' car alarms keep going off. It must be a baking hot day.

Beside me Henry V snoozes time away in a wicker armchair lined with down cushions. Before the carpets were rolled up and carried off, he spent his afternoons stretched out upstairs in the sitting-room sunlight, but bare boards are not to his liking.

I follow him constantly around the house now, much preferring his company to my own. The bedrooms and study are shut to him, and although I can slip beneath doors in my restless patrols of the house, there is little to hold me in those empty rooms, and soon I am out again, heading to wherever he is. When they find him a new home, I'll be sorely tempted to attach and go with him, but I absolutely must not. A cat's life is short, and he'll only end up dead in a ditch somewhere, or in an incinerator.

Whenever he's awake, I project myself into his skin, adopting the world view of a cat, sharing his frustration as he natters at birds flying free beyond the windows. When he sleeps, I contemplate his felinity and meditate on his breathing. Sometimes, as now, while I wait for his fathomless green eyes to open, I ponder the chances I have let slip away. So many opportunities I've squandered unthinkingly, and now my options are dwindling and each still holds its terrors.

I could have attached myself to one of the small treasures Mrs Butley has pilfered, followed it to whatever tasteless dump she inhabits, become acquainted with her husband and grandchildren and dog or whatever, before taking my chance in a car boot sale or a pawnshop. At least I would have been among people. I may care for no one, but I crave the fuss and eventfulness of humanity. When Henry goes, that will be the last I shall see of Mrs Butley's tin-opener and hear of her grumbles.

So many people I shall probably never see again: the whole of my acting acquaintance, my legions of fans, not even daft Deborah, or my solicitor, or my bicycling son. I could have escaped in Deborah's fake-Regency reticule with that little hand-painted bowl, could have been half-buried now in the tip she calls home. Or I could have followed the maps to Simon's failing antiques shop, enjoyed his doomed efforts to get their full value, gone on with them goodness knows where. I might have ended up with some dry-as-dust, dreary collector, but who knows? They could have been pounced on by a dealer, resold at auction, and any day now I would have been bound for the New World. Or else I could have gone in the Sotheby's van to London, played Russian roulette in the auction room between a life of adventure or some dead-end existence as one of my precious objects went under the hammer. As it is, there is only the Hockney to follow now or the house to remain in. The odd sticks of furniture that are left aren't worth risking an eternity on. I expect Simon will offer the lot to a clearance firm, but I've had a good look and a think and I shan't be going with any of them.

The Hockney, I keep telling myself, I must choose the Hockney. I love it dearly, and it will surely take me to some public place where not only the painting but I myself will continually be noticed and praised and admired. Yes, no doubt about it, it has to be the best option. And yet the house tugs at me, has me wondering should I let the picture go and stay here to haunt it. After all my struggles to return, it will be painful beyond words to leave. These rooms hold memories that even now soothe my distress. The parties of the great and the good I have hosted here. The beautiful women I have caressed. The calls from producers I have taken. The marvellous scripts I have read and got under the skin of. I have to keep reminding myself that my home will be invaded by strangers, rarely thinking or talking of me, who will gut the building, knock rooms through, erase all trace – no, no, I must go with the Hockney.

And yet, and yet. I stare out through the French window at the terrace, the parched grass and the shrubbery. The Hockney, the house – two last things – I love each of them so dreadfully much, yet can have only one. I must tour my sad, echoing home one more time, in search of whatever it is that I cannot bear to lose. I turn from Henry V and float towards the hall and the stairs—

And it hits me full force. But of course, it's so obvious. In a few short days it has become second nature, and I've forgotten to treasure it. What my house gives me is freedom of movement: the ability to glide upstairs and down, wearying of one scene, trying another. More even than this, it offers me views of the world beyond, from three levels, front and back, south over the sea and the promenade, north over streets, gardens and treetops. How can I relinquish these torturing glimpses of weather and season and seascape, of people and animals, flowers and green leaves? If I go with the painting, I'll be in some gallery. Will I ever know daylight again?

The choice is cruelly impossible. From the foot of the stairs, I drift back to the garden-room to gaze gloomily through the window, where darkness is falling. The sunlight no longer dapples in the breeze through the wisteria. Here comes night, when time slows to a halt and fear and loneliness threaten to swamp me.

Behind me, Henry V wakes, yawns and stretches, starts to lick a back leg, then thinks better of it and heads for the hall. I hurry after him, up to the kitchen, where he finds his bowls empty. As he laps water, my mood sinks in dejection because I know what comes next in his daily routine, and yes, he is on the move again, fast, with me close behind him, padding down the stairs, back through the garden room, making straight for the cat flap.

There's no time to hesitate. I'm going to risk it. As his tail slips through, I slip through with it, and the flap bangs behind us. It will be fine – nothing bad will happen to him or to me – he'll return as he always does – and the Hockney will be here – they won't come for the Hockney so late in the day – but it's too late for second thoughts anyway because here I go, towed by a speeding cat across the grass into bushes. For a moment it's glorious and I dance on the end of my leash.

Whichever I choose, house or Hockney, Hockney or house, for now it's pure joy to be out under the sky.

Henry pauses to squat by a clump of lavender. Can I transfer to the lavender, I wonder? Explore the garden without being dragged everywhere? Work my way back when I wish to, across shrubs, grass and terrace to the house?

Too hazardous, I decide. Safer to stick with the cat. Trees and plants are all very well, but my garden was only an occasional passion; I can't trust that anything in it is a qualifying object or be sure what does or doesn't have a welcoming aura.

Henry scratches over his doings, sniffs at them, takes a good look around, then heads off into the undergrowth at the end of the garden, with me very firmly attached.

Wednesday

Richard

He frowned at the cotton bud in his latex-gloved hand. There was no point in withholding his DNA. The gesture would cost him twenty-five thousand pounds, and Quentin Griffiths would still be his brother. Just do it.

He drew the swab firmly, once, twice, three times, across the inside of his cheek and handed it over. Pearl dropped it into the plastic container, screwed the lid shut and put it in a Jiffy bag. She stripped off her gloves and tossed them with his own pair into the wastepaper bin.

'Done,' she said.

'Done,' he echoed, lowering himself to the chair by her desk.

She was busy checking through papers now, signing things. She had to vouch that she'd witnessed the test, that this was his sample and nobody else's, that the passport he'd handed her belonged to the person who had given the sample.

Lily was his sister, he reminded himself as he watched. That was the good thing to hold on to. He must ring Lily soon. From being so desperate to speak to her when he was drunk, he'd swung the opposite way. Claire's decision had numbed him into turning his phone off and tuning his brain out. He had steered clear of the café too, unable to face telling Tiffany that he couldn't sell up after all. He felt such a heel snatching the business back from her. She was entitled to something – a share if she wanted one. He needed to think the café's future through properly. And his own. He could no longer dream of putting air-miles between himself and his troubles. He was staying in Worthing forever, becoming a father.

He supposed, in a way, that this was a second good thing to hold on to. A baby. He began to imagine it, a tiny hand gripping his finger, a little face looking up at him, a child, boy or girl, calling him 'Daddy'. He'd like that. But the Quentin connection would blight even this. The story would erupt in the tabloids, and reporters would come knocking.

'I'm surprised he hasn't already gone public,' he said aloud.

Pearl was watching the scanner hum its way over his passport. She looked up and smiled. 'Quentin? I've advised him to make certain of the DNA result first.'

'No need,' Richard said glumly. 'He's got Harry written all over him.'

'It won't take long to prove it. He's giving his sample tomorrow.'

Richard's breath caught in his throat. 'He is? Coming here?'

'The TV company is driving him down. We're expecting a Bentley or a limo or something. Shall I give him your number?'

Richard's thoughts wouldn't join up. 'Well... yes... I suppose so.'

Shit. He tried to imagine the conversation. He would

have to be friendly, at least to begin with. His viewings of *Tomorrow's Tycoon* had been paranoid drunk. The guy was charming, everyone said so. He shouldn't judge him in advance. Shit.

Pearl sealed the Jiffy bag. 'The company works fast. I should have the result in less than a week. I'll just give it to Chloe to post.' She went into the outer office, leaving the door standing open.

Richard contemplated the brick wall beyond the window, determined to look on the bright side. A third possibly good thing was his mother. She'd been suspiciously chirpy when he'd checked up on her before going incommunicado. She didn't know he was staying in Worthing, she still thought he was leaving, yet, 'I'm fine and dandy,' she'd asserted on the phone, with only a slight edge of Bette Davis. She hadn't pressed him to visit her and he hadn't offered. He'd no wish to be drawn into her latest machinations. Still her cheerfulness cheered him. It had to be an improvement on tears and pleading. No shoplifting – he reached to touch the wood of Pearl Allen's desk – no calls from flummoxed police officers. Simon's red-carpet welcome must have done the trick, straightened her out at last. Quentin's media circus had better not ruin that.

'By the way,' Pearl Allen was back in the room, 'Lily Caruthers tells me the estate owes you twenty-one pounds fifty-eight.'

He twisted to look at her. 'Pardon? What for?'

'Your share of the expenses to track Quentin down. Would you prefer cash or a cheque?'

While she went to fetch cash, he struggled not to feel snubbed. Such an impersonal way to refund him. Why hadn't Lily claimed the whole thirty and paid him herself next time she saw him? Good at numbers, his sister. Good at writing him off when a better brother turned up.

Stop that, he told himself sharply. He was being unreasonable.

Here came Pearl with the money. He signed the receipt mechanically, his mind still on Lily. Lily was lovely. She would never go cool on him. She'd probably been trying to ring him.

Pearl was speaking.

'Say again?'

'Is there anything else I can help you with today?'

He looked at her blankly. He needed to step out onto Western Road now and ring Lily. 'No. No, thank you.' He got up. Offered his hand.

There was something else though. Something niggling at him before the baby and all this Quentin kerfuffle. He pulled his mind back to the will and the money and Harry. 'Actually, I did have a question. Not that it matters, but—'

'Fire away,' said Pearl.

He didn't know how best to put it. 'I imagine my father was worth a mint. All those Hollywood movies.'

He ground to a halt. Was she frowning?

'I'm going through the papers,' she said. 'Contacting the bank and the stockbroker and so on. I'll need to verify the savings, price the assets, add it all up, deduct expenses and inheritance tax. It'll be a while before we—'

'No, I didn't mean – it's not the amount – my question is, who did he leave it to?'

'Ah,' she said. 'Ah, I see.'

She didn't see, not at all. She thought he was greedy.

'Don't get me wrong – I'd like to understand him, is all. He's given his flesh and blood almost nothing. You'll say it's none of my business.'

'On the contrary,' she said, 'beneficiaries have a general right to know the main points of a will. Once probate is granted it becomes a public document, and—'

'What?' he interrupted. Was he hearing right?

'Once probate is granted—'

'Our names and all this DNA nonsense will be public?'

'In the probate registry. Anyone interested would need to apply—'

'But some journalist is bound to do that!'

Pearl Allen looked steadily at him.

'If Harry was alive,' he muttered, 'I would personally kill him.'

'Yes... well,' she said. A second ticked by. 'The main legacy, though – I'd be happy to tell you. May I count on your discretion until there's a formal announcement?'

She brought up a file on her screen. Scrolled down. 'Here we are. The details are complex, but this is the bones of it.' She read: '*The residue of my estate subject to the payment thereout of my funeral and testamentary expenses and all debts due by me at the date of my death shall be held in trust by the Royal Shakespeare Company according to the terms set out below for the establishment and running of a new theatre in Dorchester, to be called The Whittaker Theatre.*'

She looked at Richard over the top of the will. 'I'm not sure if you knew, but Dorchester is where he was born.'

Richard suddenly saw the funny side. He got up from the chair, laughing. 'Well, of course. Doesn't that just take the biscuit? Keeping his name in lights – what else would he spend it on? Does The Whittaker Theatre need a props department, I wonder? No, don't answer that – just thinking aloud.'

He reached for the door handle. 'Forgive me. You've been so nice and so helpful, and I've been all over the place.'

She smiled. 'It's okay. You've been fine.'

Crowds of shoppers jostled him on the pavement. The sun bounced off the buses. Forget Harry, he thought. Forget Quentin. And stop fretting about foreign travel. There were worse places than the south coast of Sussex to be stuck, and tons of good things in his life, most of all Lily. He switched his phone on, and there they were: three missed calls from her, two of them this morning. He rang her number straightaway now with no plan of what he would say – it would be easy and natural to talk to his sister.

'Hello?'

Her voice made him smile. He'd got everything out of proportion. 'Lily, I'm so sorry. My phone's been off, and—'

'Hang on just a minute,' she said. 'I'll be right with you.'

And then she was talking past the phone, winding up her conversation with someone. 'I'll do the analysis and get back to you.'

She was in her backwater office, among her government statistics, doing the job she liked because it was anonymous. When Quentin and the will became public, Lily's life would be invaded by the media too. He'd been selfish, not realising, not thinking about all the cameras that would be thrust into her newsworthy face. He needed to warn her, tell her about the probate registry. She'd understand he had nothing personal against Quentin, it was just—

'Hello again, Richard. How are you?'

'I'm fine. So sorry I've been off radar. It was—'

'Richard, listen a mo. Have you just been with Pearl?'

'Yes.'

'And she told you?'

'About the money? Yes, thank you, she paid me—'

'No, Richard. Where are you?'

'Just outside her office. It's really hot here today. Smelling garlic from somewhere – I'm ravenous. Hearing your voice, wonderful Lily, but—'

'Is anyone with you?'

'No. Why?'

'Because I've something to tell you. I'm so disappointed. I thought Pearl might tell you. She rang me this morning and – Richard, I'm sorry, but my test came back negative. My mother, she got it all wrong, or maybe she lied to Harry. He wasn't my father.'

Harry

My! How enormously I'm enjoying my excursions with Henry V. I've been out with him three more times since I first chanced it yesterday. I had no idea that he roamed so far. I imagined we would spend the hours skulking under some bush, perhaps making the odd hop into next door's little courtyard, but the back gardens barely detain him. After a short sniff around, his routine is to scramble up the trellis and over the wall, zigzagging along the tops of numerous fences to the side street, where he loiters a while before deciding which direction to head off in.

Human company is what he is after, just as I am. He rolls shamelessly in the paths of strangers, getting his ears scratched and his tummy tickled, rewarding compliments with much mewing and purring. Most of his fans are women. There was one in the side street this morning – well into her fifties but prettily, comfortably so, cheeks rosy, eyes bright, decked out in caftan and beads and red-painted toenails – petting and praising him before he set off on his travels. 'Proud pussums,' she crooned, 'pussikins, puss of my heart,' scooping him up and pressing him, and me with him, to her generous bosom, burying her very kissable face in his fur. 'You're the best cat in all Brighton. How I wish you were mine.'

When finally she abandoned us, he turned inland and padded through half of Kemptown in the glorious July sunshine, sitting on front walls, having occasional stand-offs with rivals, staring through their cat flaps and sneaking in to polish off their leavings.

Tonight – Wednesday evening, I think, though I'm losing track of the calendar – he has trotted around to our own front doorstep to tuck in his paws and watch the world go by. So here I am, under the night sky, looking out past the parked cars and across the quiet two-way hum of traffic to the green sea-railing, contemplating the glimmering streetlamps that stretch away west towards the blazing wattage of the pier.

A minicab just dropped off a neighbour, and the driver is closing his boot. Henry untucks his paws and starts miaowing hello, rubbing up against the porch wall. I am growing a touch weary of his love-ins with strangers. This man is no more fascinating than a fish-and-chip wrapper. Time to practise my meditation, I think. I levitate serenely above the pair of them, gazing across at the elegant lampposts, tuning in to the faint sound of the breakers beyond. The sea's rate of breathing is a good deal slower than Henry's, a more suitable rhythm for emptying my mind.

After a while, glancing down, I find I have risen high above Henry, all the way to the ceiling of my fine Regency porch. That's odd. I try to ignore the oddness, empty my mind again, but it persists and begins to perplex me. I'm wondering have I somehow cut loose from my qualifying object. Is meditation the key to unchaining me? I float towards the road and the sea but am soon pulled up short. Frustrating, but so be it; let's try the other direction, and – well I never! – before I know it I'm passing effortlessly to the roof of the porch and from there to the wall of the house.

What a discovery! Why did I never think of it? My love affair with this building embraced the outside as much as the interior. It's a sublime piece of architecture. From the day I set eyes on it, it had to be mine. Way back then, burning a hole in my bank account were the proceeds of my racy portrayal of Rhett Butler in the hundred-million-dollar remake of *Gone with the Wind*. I brushed aside all financial advice and blew the lot on this period house, whose never-failing beauty I drank in each time I approached it.

Amazing. Incredible. I am rushing upwards, most wondrously, past the windows of the sitting room, and my study, and the top-floor bedroom, all the way to the roof, where I spin joyfully under the stars.

Far below, there's the clunk of a closing car door. Anxious that Henry will leave without me, I quit the roof and hurry back down to the porch. No panic: he's alone on the step, yawning and stretching, but before I reach him an idea knocks me sideways.

Could it be? I barely dare test it, but surely it has to be possible? And yes, yes, it is! I'm diving through the front-door keyhole into the hall, ricocheting ecstatically around the walls, and saluting my glorious portrait. I zoom to the first landing, then back down the banister and out through the keyhole again.

The full knowledge hits me: I can be outside whenever I want to be, with or without Henry V. It has never crossed my mind to imagine what is now so obvious. I whip back and forth through that keyhole – porch to hall, hall to porch – in a froth of exuberance, because at last I am clear in my mind: the house not the Hockney is the choice I will make. Whatever fine gallery it goes to, the painting will hang indoors and I will be tied to it, whereas the house stands in free air and I am unshackled. The painting may fall out of fashion, end up swathed in bubble wrap in some storeroom, forgotten, whereas this lovely old building is listed. It may suffer neglect, but it won't be demolished; it will always be sought after. The painting will be viewed by a succession of persons unknown to me who will stay only a few minutes. By contrast, I will get to know the strangers who invade my home, maybe even grow to care for some of them a little. I'll be able to watch television with them, and there will be mischief in tormenting their pets. They will boast to their friends that the great Harold Whittaker lived here. They will swap memories of my performances, and anecdotes of my life.

To celebrate the upturn in my fortune, I soar to the roof again, where to my utter delight I find Scotty on a chimney stack, twirling on one pin-striped leg like Eros in Piccadilly Circus. 'Blow me, this is quite something,' he says. *Happiness increases when shared* says his T-shirt.

Together we gaze out over the magnificent, 360-degree view. At the whole of Brighton spread like a shimmering quilt, the marina and cliffs to the east, the pier and floodlit Royal Pavilion to the west. At the dark bulk of the sea.

'Tons to do, boss on my back, can't linger,' Scotty grumbles, beginning to fade into the night, 'but I sensed something good was happening with you, so I thought I'd drop by.'

For once I see him vanish with equanimity. He'll come

again soon enough, I feel sure. Ever glad of his company, I fancy he is starting to take pleasure from mine. But tonight, I don't need him. Tonight, I shall watch the stars turn above me while the city sleeps beneath me, and look! here behind the chimneys is a nest: a roosting herring gull and two chicks. Can a bird sense me, I wonder. Let's see if I can put the wind up them.

Thursday

Richard

For the fourth time in ten minutes, Richard hovered at the ticket barrier before melting back into the crowd. A tannoy announcement echoed in the wide space above him. At any second the London train would be here, nosing around the long curve into Brighton. She was on it. Her last text: *Due in 18.10. See you soon x*

He'd come by train himself from Worthing, not wanting to turn up red-faced and sweaty from pedalling through this heat. The air was oppressive after another sweltering day. He felt ill at ease in unfamiliar chinos and a new shirt. Get a grip. When was he ever this nervous about meeting a woman?

She'd been genuinely upset on the phone yesterday. 'It's not the money,' she'd explained. 'It's you. I had a brother – two brothers nearly – and there we were, getting to know each other. Now I'm bereft, entirely without relatives again.'

Bereft? Poor Lily. But why? Standing there dumbstruck on the pavement outside Walker, Macpherson and Allen Solicitors Ltd, his mobile clamped to his ear, it had dawned on Richard that *he* wasn't bereft, not at all. On the contrary, the light pouring from the sky was redoubling its brightness.

Without pausing to think, he'd said, 'But nothing's changed, Lily. You and I won't lose touch, never ever. Come to Brighton. Let's have a meal or something.' And she'd sounded so happy. 'Richard, how nice. Are you sure? I'd love to.'

In that moment he'd understood his elation. Nothing had changed – that was true. Claire was having his baby. Quentin was about to drag him and his mother through the celebrity media. He still yearned to set sail for New Zealand or Mars. But Lily was in his life, and Lily wasn't his sister, so...

Except now, waiting for her train to come in, he felt stupid. She couldn't have been plainer. She wanted brothers, saw him still as a brother. Whereas he, ever since he'd put the phone back in his pocket yesterday and strode off along Western Road, grinning at strangers, had been asking himself what he wanted and getting the same answer. He wanted Lily.

'She'll never guess you've been playing away.'

'What?'

The bloke grinned, motioned at Richard's hands and walked on.

He'd forgotten the flowers he was clutching. The gift seemed absurd now, cheesy or worse, a nonsensical impulse-buy at Worthing station. Lily would feel awkward. She would have nowhere to put them. They would clutter up the whole evening. Brothers didn't give flowers.

He laid the bouquet on a bench and re-tied his shoe-lace. A quick glance around to check no one was watching and he was back at the barrier empty-handed.

The train had arrived. Already its doors were sliding open, disgorging passengers, a sea of bobbing faces heading his way. He could feel the adrenalin pumping. It was daft to be so on edge. The whole magic of Lily was how easy he felt around her, and he mustn't lose that just because he—

Oh God, here she was. Coming towards him, smiling and waving. Heart-stoppingly gorgeous in a pink sundress.

Just to be with her had him wanting to punch the air. Did she feel the bounce in his step? They were strolling down from the station towards the sea, close, side by side. He kept bumping against her.

There's no rush, he told himself. It was too soon to speak. 'I think I'm falling for you,' would be shocking from a brother. At best, blurted out, eager beaver, by a recent ex-brother, it would seem opportunistic and shallow. He lacked the words to convey the certainty he felt. Her elbow nudged against his waist; their strides were in synch. He imagined veering from this easy connection into awkward distances and misspeaks.

'Shall we go to that pub you mentioned, near Harry's?' she said. 'The Hand in Hand, wasn't it?'

'Good thinking!' On cue, the Beatles yodelled again in his head, segueing with a cymbal crash from Ringo into *She loves you*. He grabbed her hand and swung it. 'That's exactly where we should go.'

Yeah, yeah, yeah! His tongue would untie itself in the quirky little pub, or their eyes would do the talking. She would realise how glad she was that they weren't related, recognise him just as he had recognised her – it wouldn't need words. Years from now, they would speak of The Hand in Hand, saying, 'Do you remember that silliness about being brother and sister?'

Here they were at the clock tower. They turned left, down towards the Old Steine. 'It's a bit of a walk,' he said.

'That's fine. Got my flats on. I like walking with you.' She slipped her arm through his. 'So, what a story, eh? What a fine song and dance.'

'You can say that again.'

The people coming towards them were staring at Lily, and he had to remind himself why. He couldn't keep his eyes off her either. He wanted to lift her and spin her around.

Was her smile slightly awkward, not entirely at ease? But of course, what an idiot, how unfeeling of him, to be grinning gormlessly and leaping along when she'd told him that she was bereft. He straightened his face. 'Seriously though, how awful to have twenty-five thousand pounds offered, then snatched away.'

'I suppose,' she said, 'but the money was only a bonus. Easy come, easy go. Life's going to be a whole lot cheaper, I've realised, with Martin gone. He was forever splashing the cash. I'm lumbered with the building-works loan, but I'll manage. And poor Harry, think of all those years he paid child support and I wasn't his child.'

'Poor Harry, rubbish.' Richard was laughing again, he just couldn't help it. it was such a miracle that Lily existed.

She smiled up at him. Her eyes were amazing. 'It's losing my brother that pisses me off.'

'Not lost. Not at all,' he said.

Her smile broadened, and it was all he could do not to kiss it. Surely now she would realise, but her lovely eyes slid away. They had reached the Old Steine, and she was watching for a gap in the traffic.

Time enough. Time enough. In the pub would be better. A pint of real ale would help him find the right way to say it, to ask her.

Not far to go, they made it across and were following St James's Street into Kemptown. Straight on, arm in arm, five or ten minutes further and they would be there.

'So, how's your mum?' Lily said.

'Fine.' He must quench this ridiculous grin. 'Suspiciously so. I rang her last night, and she sounded happier than I've heard her in ages. Than I ever remember hearing her, actually. Didn't mention Harry, not once. I'm trying not to count chickens – there's no trusting her – but maybe, just maybe, she's finally over him.'

'That's great.' Lily gave his arm a squeeze. 'I'm so glad for her and for you. And the café and Tiffany?'

'Booming and blooming.' He had no idea if this was so – he still hadn't been in.

She met his eyes seriously. 'And Claire, have you heard from her yet? Has she made up her mind what to do?'

Shit. Richard blinked, mouth open. He wasn't free to love Lily, that was the truth of it. Or he was, but she wouldn't believe that he was, would be shocked that he thought that he was. He should have rehearsed this bit.

'Forgive me,' she said. 'I shouldn't be nosy. It's none of my business.'

Her gaze dropped to the pavement, her arm tensed in his. In the blink of an eye, here they were in awkward distance and misspeak.

Silence. This wouldn't do, he decided. He must be completely straight with Lily, and somehow things would work themselves out. He stopped walking, turned her towards him and took hold of her hands. 'She rang me on Tuesday. She's going ahead, having the baby.'

'Wow... ah... that's...'

She was clearly dismayed. Disappointment, he tried to persuade himself, but then reality kicked in again. Even if she had feelings for him, even if she didn't feel shocked or incestuous or both, what could he possibly offer her, stuck down here with a child to support, while she had her job and her life up in London? The dismay was just sisterly sympathy.

'Yes,' he said, 'it's a bummer.'

To be holding her hands felt awkward. He dropped one; she let go of the other. He twisted his head to look back along St James's Street, in the direction of Worthing and Claire and her baby. 'Upshot is I won't be selling up or setting off on my travels.'

They turned and walked on, side by side, no longer touching. 'Well I never. A baby,' she said.

He laughed uncomfortably. 'It takes a bit of getting used to.'

'It'll turn your life upside-down.'

'Yes,' he said. 'Still, a baby...'

'You're right. Can't be bad. Possibly wonderful when you get your head round it.'

She was being polite. Their closeness was slipping away.

'And there was I,' she said, 'wondering all the way from the station why you were so happy.'

He grinned hopelessly. No, you've misunderstood me, he wanted to say, but he couldn't. His happiness had crashed, and it would be tasteless or worse now to explain why.

Harry

Last night on the roof was quite something. I stayed until the lights of the city began to go out and dawn broke, pink and pearly, beyond Black Rock, above the eastern horizon. By first light I explored the back of the house and made the excellent discovery that the terrace and garden are also included in my fiefdom. The decision to remain with the house feels more and more right. Even when Henry V has gone, I shall be able to roam in the shrubbery, watching the birds and the insects, meditating on the progress of the shadows across the grass or the patter of rain on the leaves.

Returning up and over to the porch, I watched as this new day grew busy with human activity. Occupants of the neighbouring flats were leaving for work, and the postman came by. When I sailed in at last through the keyhole, I could almost say I was happy at the prospect of spending an eternity tied to this home that I love. What relief to have made up my mind, to be finally settled and safe.

Today though I'm sad because these are my last hours with Henry V. Mrs Butley was on the telephone to Cat Rescue about 'Tommy' this morning, and I gather they're coming to get him tomorrow. It will be heartbreaking to lose him; I've grown used to his company, his feline gift for solitude, his sweet personality. I hope the new occupants will bring me a cat, but no replacement will match up to Henry V.

Tonight – by my reckoning Thursday – I'm going to stick closely by him. I'm on his shoulder now, one last time, as he negotiates the back fences, surefooted in the dark, and drops to the side street. For a while he dawdles here, sniffing at the wall and the lamppost, perhaps hoping that the woman who made a fuss of him yesterday morning will arrive. I hope so too. I should like to be clasped to her generous breasts once again, to see her painted face softened by the lamplight as she croons, 'Best puss in all Brighton, how I wish you were mine.'

But the street remains empty, and Henry is setting off into Kemptown. I'm cheering him on, more than content to have one last tour of this charming locality. He turns right onto St James's Street and doubles his speed, bowling along as though on a mission, keeping close to the walls and the shop fronts. He's not on the look-out for prey; I've learned that about him. He may chatter at gulls through the house windows and leap at fluttering moths, but the only mouse he's paid attention to while I've been with him practically threw itself at his feet, and he wasn't much bothered when it ran off again. He shows little interest in fish-and-chip shops either. He's stuffed full of pet food. No, he's scouting for human adoration and territorial rivals.

I'm guessing it's around ten: the café we just passed was dishing up puddings and coffees to the tables outside, and from an alley comes the inebriated chatter of drinkers milling around a bar. A woman spots Henry and starts making a fuss of him. He rolls on his back and paddles his paws in the air, but her cat-tickling skills are not up to standard and he soon loses interest and sets off again.

Now he halts, hackles rising, sniffing the air and fine-tuning the angle of his ears. Where's the enemy? Ah, yes, I see. From a side passageway two eyes glow like little moons. We approach inch by inch, and the other cat begins to complain: a growl that slides up the scale to a descant. Henry pauses for thought before countering with a fine alto. For a while they duet peaceably until, as Henry edges nearer, his adversary ups the ante with a yowl of such savagery and outrage that Henry concedes, retreating as warily as he came, a slow-motion film sequence run in reverse. Before heading off, he recovers his dignity by sniffing then spraying a litter bin, staking his claim.

Forty yards further on, he slinks beneath a parked car as a gang of youths approach, shrieking and whooping. They don't see him, they're soon gone, and he's off again, more slowly now, pausing to sniff at a dropped take-away, miaowing at a woman who's putting out her wheelie bin. 'Shoo,' she says. 'Scram.'

She claps her hands and runs at him, hissing, sending him streaking to the next corner and round it into an alley that leads back to the seafront, and – dear me, what's the matter? – all at once he is freezing and hissing and doubling in size. I can't see it. Where's the danger? And then, oh save me, I see it and hear it, and it isn't a cat. A snarling fox, sideways on, fluffed up and on the tips of its toes just like Henry but double his size, advances crabwise towards us.

Run! Run! My afterlife flashes before me: all the dangers and disasters I've come through. The fox displays its sharp teeth and emits an unearthly shriek. They're circling each other, barely two feet apart, each hunch-backed with ears flattened, spitting and making their unsettling noises. Henry howls like a banshee; the fox repeats its ghoulish bark. I'm the only ghost here, and I'm the one who's spooked. In my terror I'm jumping about all over Henry. *Run*, I'm telling him, *run!*

When I hurl myself at his whiskers, he shakes his head, distracted, mewing, trying to throw me off – and then the world is a blur. The fox lunges for his throat, misses, but sinks its teeth into a back leg and hangs on. Henry screams and lashes out, until at last the fox lets go, and we're streaking away at astonishing speed, faster than the bicycle ride. I look back – the fox is hot on our heels – Henry is out between the buildings onto Marine Parade, and—

Wham! what happened? I'm hurtling along towards the pier because – Jesus! – Henry is on a car bonnet, sliding up to the windscreen, and I'm looking into the horrified eyes of the driver. Amid a squeal of brakes and tyre rubber, the car comes to a halt. Henry slithers back down the bonnet, hits the tarmac and lies still.

Oh no! Sweet cat! What have I done? *Don't be dead*, I

implore him, bombarding his whiskers, jumping up and down on his nose.

He shows no sign of life. His hind leg is bloody, ripped by the fox. He must have a smashed skull or internal injuries.

I look wildly around me, horrified for myself as well as for Henry. Far away to one side of us is sea, far away to the other white-stuccoed facades – and yes! there, just across the road, is my beautiful house, and I stretch out for it, but it's no use.

'Christ!' The driver is out of the car, peering at Henry. 'Lunatic cat,' he says. 'Sorry, mate, looks like you're a goner.'

He straightens up for a moment, peering across the road at the houses. Then he slides his hands beneath the limp body, lifts it at arm's length and carries it to the pavement.

No, I beseech him. *The other way. Please.*

It's useless. He's laying Henry down against the green seafront railing. He's sliding back into his car. He's driving away.

More cars zip by. Through the railings I can see people on the beach far below, bunched around the glow and smoke of barbecue fires. Others stroll in clusters along Madeira Drive, but no one walks after dark on this no-man's-land pavement high above them. Poor Henry can't help me, not any longer. Maybe his spirit is here, silent, invisible, but it's useless to me. I'm tethered to road kill, stranded midway between the home that I love and the sea that I love, unable to transfer to either.

As if on cue, my porch leaps into focus in LED light. A curly-headed young man leans carelessly against one of my pillars, a hand in his pocket. With the other he gestures at my front door, while smiling to camera and chatting into a microphone held by a woman with implausibly long, shapely legs. On a parked white van I can make out the lurid purple-and-orange eye of *The Reality Channel*.

They are speaking about me, making a programme about me. Oh please, young man, young woman, cameraman, turn your heads and look over here. This is Harold Whittaker's cat. This is Henry V. Help me, please help me.

Richard

'I don't imagine the fuss about Quentin will last,' Lily said. 'Reality stars are like Christmas lights. A whole lot of ooh-ah – then the plug's pulled and they're back in their boxes.'

Richard nodded. 'You're probably right. My friend Joe says pretty much the same thing.'

Actually, he was past caring about Quentin. The pub smelled of sweat and suntan oil, and it seemed a long time since he'd had sex. He watched Lily's mouth move and her fingers play with the beer-mat. It was hard not to imagine her body under the sundress. Slow down, he told himself. Don't blurt out how you feel. She saw him half as a brother, half-spoken for by Claire.

They had managed to find a small table in the tiny, crowded bar and were now on their third round of real ale. He was drinking too fast, the pub only served bar snacks, they ought to move on to a restaurant. She'd switched to halves after the first pint and this last time had asked for a shandy.

Her mouth moved. Her eyes smiled at him. The right one smiled more, but the left one, above the birthmark, was more perfectly shaped – very beautiful and solemn and kind.

'The Harry nostalgia will blow over too,' she was saying. 'He'll soon be a has-been, one of those twentieth-century pin-ups that no one mentions much and the teenagers haven't heard of. Head down, grit your teeth, you'll get through it.

Just think, ten, fifteen years from now, your baby will be proud to have vaguely famous relations.'

He wished she would stop mentioning the baby. He tried to focus and say something sensible. 'You must be relieved though – to be out of the limelight yourself.'

'Too right. I'd have hated it. I was telling myself to be brave. It was going to happen – I couldn't avoid it. Fame was just people, nothing I'm not already used to. I'd begun to wonder if it might work in my favour – help strangers to see past the state of my face. I might even have developed a taste for it.'

'Do you think?'

'Nuh-uh.' She laughed. 'I was dreading it, but it shouldn't be too bad for *you*. Or not for long anyway. Just be the straightforward, normal person you are, and my guess is they'll soon lose interest. That Quentin bloke's brother, that actor bloke's son – there'll be no story unless you give them one. People will forget why they recognise you – they'll think they saw you in a supermarket queue.'

He swallowed more beer, feeling slow-witted. Drink made her articulate, while his own mouth refused to move. Perhaps briefly she had found him attractive, but the easiness was gone, the sense of brother and sister was evaporating and nothing would come in its place. 'You're a straightforward, normal person' was probably code for 'Don't even think about it'.

He scoured his brain for a new topic. She was smiling at the antics of a bunch of students at the next table, but he felt overwhelmed by their noise. He'd told her already how Harry was using his millions to put his name on a theatre, and there was no more to be said about Quentin.

She seemed stuck too, tipped back on her stool, looking

round at the pub decor. Yellowed newspaper clippings in place of wallpaper, a Victorian penny-slot machine, snipped-off neckties hanging from a beam, and in the midst of it Lily, out of his league, out of his reach.

They both started speaking.

'Your eyes...'

'Maybe your café could...'

They stalled.

'What?' she said.

He was saved by his phone going off. 'Sorry.' He pulled it from his pocket. Unknown caller. 'Hello?'

'Is this Richard Lawton?'

He knew at once who it was. He was back, slumped on his sofa, necking a can of strong lager, gazing in mesmerised horror at his television screen. 'Quentin,' he heard himself say.

'You're kidding,' said Lily.

'Pearl Allen gave me your number because, blimey, we're brothers. Ain't that something?'

'Yes. Yes, it is.'

'Can't get my head round it. Can't wait to meet you. I meant to ring earlier – been one thing after another. Only just made it to Harry's solicitors before they closed, then more interviews and nonsense for the show, but long story short, I'm in Brighton, so I was wondering, any chance of a meet up?'

'Well,' Richard said, 'I don't know. You see—'

'Sorry to call so late. I would say tomorrow, but they've got me doing a whole heap of stuff in London first thing. Fuck knows when I can next get away. I have wheels tonight, so it's no problem that you're over in Worthing.'

'No, yes, I'm...' He hunched over the phone and lowered his voice. 'The thing is I'm with someone.'

Nicely vague, should put him off, and yes, it was working.

'Whoops. Shit. Sorry. Hope I'm not interrupting.'

Lily's voice in his other ear. 'It's fine. I'd love to meet him. That's if you don't mind? I was so nearly part of the story.'

He could see no way to refuse her. 'Still, can't be helped,' Quentin was saying. 'Give me a call when you're—'

'No, let's do it now.' Richard stared helplessly up at the line of snipped neckties. Tried to make his voice jolly. 'Because actually she knows all about it, and we're in Brighton ourselves.'

'That's great! Are you sure? Don't want to intru—'

'Really, it's fine. Whereabouts are you?'

'At our illustrious father's front door, just across from the seafront. What a brilliant house, eh? So, shall I come to you?'

'Okay. It's no distance. Cut inland to St James's Street, turn right and keep going a few hundred yards. It's a corner pub called The Hand in Hand.'

'Wicked. I'll find it. Don't go away.'

'Well I never,' Lily said as Richard ended the call. 'How exciting. Does he sound nice? When he's not on the telly, I mean?'

He nodded dumbly, staring at her shining eyes. The best and most beautiful eyes in the world. Yes, Quentin sounded nice. Very nice. Nice enough to see past the birthmark quite probably. A charismatic, nice heart-throb with half-a-million-quid's-worth of reality-show prize money burning a hole in his pocket was about to stand side by side with a straightforward, normal bloke with a café in Worthing and a baby on the way, and no prizes for guessing which brother Lily would fall for.

Harry

Henry V is breathing. Barely perceptibly his flank rises and falls. I rise and fall anxiously with it, as if I were capable of pushing air into him and drawing it out again. Oh please, cat, stay with me. I've had more than I can take of death and decay.

I battle to calm myself, to empty my mind of all but the slow sound of the waves far below us. Music and voices drift up from the beach, the tipsy shriek of a woman. A supermarket lorry thunders by, trailing hip-hop from the wound-down cab window.

It's no use, I can't meditate; my situation is too awful. Henry is dying and no one will find him. He'll be swept up as refuse and carted off for incineration or landfill, and I along with him, when meanwhile, in full, poignant view across the road stands my heaven and haven, the house I could spend eternity in, if only, if only. Please glance over here, TV crew. Please rescue my cat. Come on, Henry V, wake up and drag yourself home.

There is nothing and no one to pray to. Call on old comforts. Recite soliloquies to keep the anguish at bay. Hamlet was right – to be or not to be doesn't even begin to scratch at the question. And the poor, wretched Scottish king, he soon found out that the afterlife, too, is a tale told by an idiot. My several renderings of Lear while I lived were phenomenal, but I would surpass them all now if I could only be heard. Then let fall your horrible pleasure, laws of the universe. Here I am, tethered, your slave, a poor, invisible, weak, and despised old man!

'What's with the grand talk?' says Scotty.

I look up, and there he sits, emanating radiance, on the

sea-railing above me, the breeze ruffling his golden curls. *To understand everything is to forgive everything* says his T-shirt. 'Oh forgive *me*,' I cry.

'This really won't do,' he says. 'Everything was going so well, and now look at you.'

'Don't gloat.'

'I'm not gloating. You were my success story. I've been trying to explain to my unimaginative, stuck-in-the-mud supervisor how spirit aftercare needs more resources, a bit more discretion and empathy, and—'

'So please, you must help me.'

He looks at me, shaking his head.

'After all that I've been through.'

He draws his knees to his chin, rotates on the railing, lowers his feet again and stares out towards the barbecue fires and the sea. 'My powers are so limited.'

'What are they, though?' I remonstrate with the pinstriped seat of his pants. 'Discretion, you said. You must have some – what is it? Look, look – I think he's still breathing. Can you keep him alive?'

'Sadly not.' Scotty scissors his legs back over the railing, drops to the pavement and bends over Henry and me. 'A beautiful cat. I much prefer them to dogs. I always—'

'Or help me detach from him. Waft me back to the house with a wave of your angelic hand. A few yards, that's all, I'm begging you. No one will know. I won't tell tales, I promise.'

'I can't do that either.'

'Can't or won't?'

'I would if I could.' His face is so close. His golden skin glows; his eyes shine with compassion. 'I care about you,' he says. 'I don't think you deserve this. I'd like to see you okay.'

Gratitude and self-pity rob me of speech. He settles

himself, cross-legged, on the pavement, glances around him and lowers his voice. 'There *is* a power that I have. I'm supposed to put in for permission to use it, but that can take weeks.'

'Please, what is it?'

'They would probably deny the request anyway.' He leans back on his hands and contemplates the night sky. I follow his gaze, but there's nothing to see except the stars that the two of us celebrated on the rooftop, was it only last night? 'Time clearly is of the essence,' he says.

'Yes, yes it is.' Is he going to help me?

'That putative son of yours. The young man on the bicycle.'

'What about him?

'Does he know the cat?'

My mind whirls, then remembers. 'Yes, I think so. He came to the house with his mother, but—'

Scotty jumps up. 'He would be able to carry it!'

'What?' For a moment I'm stunned, then I explode with impatience. 'Brilliant. Now why didn't I think of that? Such a pity he isn't here.'

'There's no call for sarcasm.'

I fling myself at him. 'You're as much use as a snorkel in a tsunami. You talk about aftercare, but what have you ever done, actually done, to—'

'Shut up and listen to me. What's your son's name?'

'Richard... Richard Lawton, but what the hell does it—'

'Enough! Are you listening? I saw him that day on the bicycle. I would know him again. I could try to find him now and do what I can. Risk myself for you, is what I'm saying – an unauthorised use of my power. That's if you haven't just blown it and made me decide you're not worth it.'

'No please, I am worth it, I promise.' He's begun to fade

out. 'Where are you going? Are you going to look for him?'

No answer. Scotty's presence is thinning from gold to silver. Away to the west a desolate police siren wails.

'Please find him, don't leave me.'

The darkness presses down. A shrieking gull swoops over Henry. The blaze of LED light has gone out on my porch, and *The Reality Channel* van is driving away.

Risk himself for me: is that what he said? Suddenly I'm frightened for him as well as for myself. 'Dear Scotty,' I entreat the pitiless night. 'Albert, I should say, Mr Pickles, my friend, what is it you're risking for me?'

A mere glisten drifts in the air.

'Because I do care, Scotty lad. I don't want to harm you.'

There is no one to hear me. He's gone.

Richard

He looked up. Through the pub noise, had someone just spoken his name? The woman in the doorway, scanning the customers, he knew her from somewhere. Huge, amused eyes. Breasts like a Barbie doll. Legs a mile long disappearing into a microskirt.

The students on the next table quietened. A ripple of interest went round the bar.

'Richard Lawton?' the woman said, advancing towards him. 'It has to be.'

Comprehension hit him as he rose to his feet. She knew him because he looked like Quentin. She was the presenter from *Tomorrow's Tycoon*.

Someone wolf-whistled. Someone else shouted, 'Great to see you in the flesh, Mariella.'

He met Lily's terrified eyes. 'Oh no,' Lily said, but then

Mariella was beside them, folding her flamingo legs to crouch by their table on her unfeasibly high heels. There was fake-tan goo on her face. He'd disliked her on television; he hated her now. And so much for Quentin's being a nice guy.

Interest was growing. People were holding up phones. Shit, why hadn't he thought of that before telling Quentin to come here? He and Lily would be on YouTube in seconds. He did his best to shield her from the lenses. She was loosening her hair to cover her face and retrieving her bag from the floor. His balance was shaky, his thoughts blurred. He shouldn't have had the third pint.

In his face came the false smile that had infested his living room. 'Wonderful to meet you, Richard. I'm sorry about this.' She nodded at the onlookers. 'It happens wherever I go. I'm Mariella Dukakis from *The Reality Channel*.' She lowered her voice to a whisper, but the whole pub had hushed and was listening. 'I wanted a word before you meet Quentin.' Her hand on his arm. 'I knew at once it was you. You look so, so much like him.'

'Nonsense,' he said. Grab Lily's hand. Get out of here fast. Bodies and tables were blocking the way.

'And the totally brilliant thing is how much Quentin and you both look like your father.'

'No, you're mistaken.'

The TV smile slid over to Lily. 'And you? You are?'

'No one,' Lily mumbled. 'I was just leaving.'

He nodded. Yes, quickly, slip away, Lily. He would hang back, give her time to get clear. He squeezed her hand. 'I'll ring you.' She set off, finding a way through the crush and out of the door.

Mariella stared after her. 'The poor woman.'

'Meaning what?'

'Well, it can't be easy.'

Don't rise to it. Get the spotlight off Lily. 'You're recording this, aren't you?'

'Not yet. Not quite yet.' She flung her arms wide, revealing no hidden camera or microphone, only a scatter of tattooed stars across her silicone cleavage.

'But of course we simply have to record it.' She re-energised her smile. 'That's what I wanted to tell you. We're making a documentary, *Where Next for Quentin?* He's such a brilliant winner – viewers can't get enough of him.'

She was no longer whispering. She grinned at her audience, then flourished a hand at the doorway, through which came a man with a camcorder, taking a panning shot of them all.

'So we're following him, candid camera, through his post-show experiences and, totally amazing, it turns out that Quentin's father was Harry Whittaker. *The* world-famous Lord Harold Whittaker. How about that?'

A new buzz surged through the room. The blood thumped in Richard's ears.

'Quentin was going to keep schtum about it – can you believe that? But we were there when he got the message to ring Harry's solicitor. And then,' she swung back to Richard, 'today we discover about you!' She raised dramatic hands and widened her eyes. 'OMG, a surprise mystery half-brother.'

Someone said, 'Wow.'

'And now Quentin's here, just outside.'

A girl at the next table gave an obligatory shriek. All eyes went to the door.

'No,' Richard said.

'You must be so excited to meet him.'

'No. I refuse.'

He might as well not have spoken. To whistles and cheers, here came Quentin.

'Forget it, I'm leaving.' Richard shouldered his way to the door.

'Hey, wait,' Quentin said, but he was out on the pavement, clocking the TV van and starting to run through the dark.

Voices called after him, but he didn't look back. Lily was fifty yards up ahead, walking fast. In the light of the street-lamps he could see the pale sundress, the hair loose on her shoulders, the characteristic sway of her hips. He sprinted to catch her up. She turned at the sound of his running feet and waited, smiling. Here he was. Lily's hand was in his. 'I love you,' he said.

'What?' Her face lifted to his and he kissed her.

'I love you. But quickly, let's run.'

It was said, it was done, he had kissed her, and okay, he was tipsy, but he'd never been clearer about anything, and she didn't seem shocked or offended. 'You mad thing,' she said, but she was giggling and grinning as she raced back alongside him towards the Old Steine.

Somewhere behind them, Quentin was shouting, but Quentin could go screw himself. He had kissed Lily, was running with Lily.

'That was my fault entirely,' she panted. 'Telling you to invite him. How stupid of me. All those people with phones.'

She was laughing and saying he'd handled it brilliantly. Soon he would kiss her again and—

But wait. Something had changed in his head. He stopped running. Something made him stop running. Lily stopped too. 'What's the matter?'

'I don't know.'

He spun round, looking for whatever had halted him,

searching for the thought that had stalled him, rocking on his heels on the pavement, unsure what to do. The thing was important, that was all that he knew. Life and death, show-stoppingly important. He couldn't think what it could be or why it should matter. He must be more smashed than he'd realised. He peered down a side-street towards the seafront.

Lily grabbed his hand. 'They're coming after us. Please Richard, I really don't want to face them. Let's run.'

'I can't,' he said. 'I have to...'

It was there on the tip of his tongue, but he still didn't know what it was. Drink had never robbed him of thought before; this felt like the marijuana trips he'd been on in his teens. He held fiercely to Lily, trying to find the end of his sentence.

'You don't have to. You don't have to meet him,' she said. 'Not here, not now. Please, I don't want to. Richard, stop it, let go of me.'

He shifted his grip to her wrist. Was he losing his mind? He had no control of his thoughts, no power to speak or to move from the spot. He tried to start running with her again, but almost lost his balance, lurching sideways instead. The little street to the sea felt like the best way to go, although that made no sense whatsoever. It was too late to escape. Quentin was here, striding towards them. Mariella and the cameraman too.

Sudden light dazzled him. Before he could object he was enveloped in a bear hug, and warm in his ear came Quentin's murmur, 'Bloody Mariella. I'll sort her out later, I promise. Thanks for changing your mind.'

His mind hadn't changed. He wanted nothing to do with this man. Why on earth had he stopped?

Lily had the same question. 'Richard, what are you doing?'

Her expression was frantic. He still had tight hold of her. Any second now, he would understand and explain to her. He would get control of himself and all would be fine. He just needed to—

What? What was wrong with him? Why couldn't he move or speak?

Quentin released him from the hug and offered a hand to be shaken. Richard refused it, holding tight to Lily.

'It's incredible,' said Quentin. 'You'd think there'd be words for a moment like this, but there just aren't. Anyway, *I* don't have them. I'm pinching myself. After all these years, a brother, out of the blue, who'd have thought, it's just massive—'

Richard had no words, but the nation's heartthrob had plenty. The same easy stream of them that had poured from the television rose now around him until he was struggling to breathe. Beyond the glare of the cameraman's light-panel, he could see dark shapes of people and the flashes of their mobile phones.

'Omigod, folks,' Mariella told the crowd and the cameras, 'the poor guy is speechless. This is so, so emotional.'

'And Richard, who's this?' Quentin switched his enthusiasm to Lily. 'What a beautiful woman. Is it your wife? Could it be you're my sister-in-law?'

'No,' said Lily. 'It couldn't.'

In her eyes Richard saw fury. He had no excuses. He let go of her hand, and she ran.

For what felt like forever he was held there, assaulted by white light, devoured by pitiless lenses, listening to Quentin and Mariella jabber on, unable to speak or to think or to move. His feet and mind tugged him towards the side street, but the pack would only pursue him. He stood his ground silently, until eventually it began to be over. A woman in a yellow T-shirt put herself between him and the cameraman. 'He's not going to talk to you. Leave him alone,' and the mood of the mob changed. Soon they were all chipping in, 'Lay off him. He doesn't want to be filmed.'

'Hey, folks,' Mariella said winsomely, 'we're only wanting to say hi,' but the heckling continued and she finally told the cameraman, 'Cut.'

The light died, and in the relief of the darkness, Quentin's voice came again in Richard's ear. 'Abject apologies. You really do hate this stuff, don't you? I'll make sure they don't screen it. Let's wind it down and find somewhere private, okay?'

Richard looked stonily at him.

'You're right, I'm just making things worse. I'll call you and grovel. Now watch the Pied Piper.'

A quick grin and a squeeze of his shoulder, and Quentin was striding off the way he came. Sure enough nearly everyone followed him.

The woman in the yellow T-shirt peered into Richard's face. 'Do you want me to call a cab?'

He shook his head. 'No thanks. Please just go, everyone.'

'Good on you,' she said. 'Don't let them wear you down. We have a right not to be famous. And your wife really *is* beautiful. Come on,' she told the few who remained. 'Show's over. Nothing to see.' Back and forth like a sheepdog, she began moving them towards the pub.

'Thanks,' he called after her.

Lily was long gone. He pulled his phone out and called her.

'What do you want?' Was it tears he could hear in her voice?

'They've gone. It's all right now. I'm so sorry. Where are you? I'll catch you up.'

'No, you won't.' Definitely tears. 'I've had enough, and I need to go home.' Short of breath, walking fast. 'I can't believe that you did that. First you say you love me—'

'I do.'

'And then you do that. You say you don't want the attention, but you obviously do want it, and that's fine, up to you, but you had no business making me—'

'No,' Richard said. 'I mean yes. He promises they won't broadcast it.'

'It'll be out already,' she wailed. 'Video clips of us all over the internet. What possessed you?'

'I don't know. It was an accident.'

What was wrong with him? Still he had no explanation. From the phone came the blare of a car horn, the exertion of Lily's flight as she powered up the hill to the station.

He'd been scared was the reason. He'd clung to her because he was terrified. Not of Quentin or the cameras, but of the chaos in his head. So tell her that truthfully. But he couldn't focus on speaking because, even now, something was compelling him to duck into this side street, head for the sea.

'The thing is, Lily—'

But the phone was dead. She'd killed the call, and when he rang back he was put through to voicemail, and still he had nothing coherent to say.

Harry

Oh, relief and jubilation! Across the road, my son Richard is stumbling, with Scotty riding him piggyback. Two heads close together, blond and brown curls intermingled.

I fling myself joyously about. 'Scotty, oh Scotty, thank you!'

Richard reaches the pavement and stops dead, staring at Henry V. His hands go to his head as Scotty dismounts.

'This is just awful,' says Scotty. 'I can't bear it. I should never have meddled.'

'Yes, you should. Yes, you should. What's he doing? Has he recognised Henry?'

'More than recognised him. The poor soul's in shock at the sight of him, doesn't know which way is up. He's a nice boy.' Scotty peers into Richard's eyes. 'What a horrible abuse of my power.'

'Look, tell me later,' I say.

'I may have ruined his chances with the woman he loves.'

'Blue eyes. Blonde hair?' I remember her stepping in front of the bicycle.

'No, brown. Lovely woman, long brown hair and a birthmark. I've put her right off him. Betrayed my vocation.'

Richard sways on the pavement, hands clamped to his skull, moaning softly and staring out to sea.

'I'd love to hear later, Scotty,' I say. 'Really I would, but first, please – you have to finish the job.'

He looks at me, blinking. 'I've brought him here, haven't I?'

'Yes,' I agree, leaping up and down above Henry V. 'Here, the wrong side of the road. You still have to get us across.'

'No.' Scotty sinks to his knees, covering his ears.

'But please, don't you see? What you've done already, it's a complete waste if he doesn't carry me home.'

Scotty lifts his eyes to me in a look of great torment. Then he slowly gets up, puts his arms tenderly around Richard's shoulders and touches foreheads with him.

Richard's eyes focus. He looks down at the cat. Then he

steps forward, squats on the pavement beside me, and reaches to touch Henry's ear. 'Is he still alive?' Scotty asks.

'I think so. I hope so,' I say.

'Be quiet. I'm not talking to you. I'm putting thoughts in his head.'

Richard's hand moves to Henry's ribcage and rests there.

'Yes, yes, still alive,' Scotty says. 'Okay, let's get him home.'

Richard totters to his feet and looks at the traffic. Then he pulls out his phone.

'No,' Scotty yells in his ear. 'Home, I said, home. Not a cab. Not a vet.'

'Quite right,' I cry. 'The cat will die, I'll get stuck at the vet, and then—'

Scotty rounds on me. 'Shut up. Stop interrupting!'

At this, Richard lets out an enraged bellow. He sits down on the pavement and throws himself from side to side, moaning and smacking his head.

Scotty fusses around him. 'I'm so sorry. I was talking to Harry.'

He yelps and tugs at his hair.

'Have courage.' Scotty presses in, forehead to forehead. 'It makes no sense at all, I completely agree with you. Keep going just a few minutes. How I wish I weren't doing this to you, but you're going to pick this cat up and carry him over there to his home, and then, by all the powers that govern me, I promise I *will* let you go.'

Richard lumbers up, aiming useless swats at the air.

'Come on, lad,' I urge. 'Do as he tells you.'

He bends for the cat, easing his palms beneath the limp body and raising it high, like an offering to the gods. I rise along with it and hover about my son's head, wishing that I, too, could invade his thoughts to tell him how happy I am he exists, how I wish him nothing but well, how sorry I am for all the years I ignored him.

He steps to the kerb and waits while a couple of cars go by. There are tears in his eyes. 'What am I doing?' he wails.

Scotty is distraught. 'I've made such a pig's ear of this. I'd no idea how powerful I was. The poor, poor young man.'

I try to listen and care, but I'm far too excited, for at last the way clears and Richard is carrying me home. I fly ahead of him, like a kite in a strong wind, tugging him forward, Scotty trailing behind. My house was never more beautiful. Heightened, super-real, the three white-stuccoed storeys outshine the light of the streetlamps. The elegant pillared porch calls to me, but a stronger pull comes from above. Black against the stars is the line of chimneys where, in a first act of exultant homecoming, I shall dance again, now, now, now.

I strain on my leash as Richard crosses the parking bay and, yes, oh glory and gratitude, here I go, sailing across to a pillar. It's a mere hop, skip and jump past the porch to the house wall, up which I shoot, yelling, 'Scotty, darling, you're an absolute angel.'

A triumphant caper along the chimneys, a dive into the gulls' nest, sending them into squawks and flaps of alarm, then, quick, down the back for a lightning tour of the garden, before squeezing in through the cracks around the cat flap.

I am home. I am *home*. Jumping in delight at the Hockney, hurtling up the stairs, chasing my tail in the living room, out and up to the bedrooms, dashing from one to another, spinning and bouncing with joy. The relief! Was I ever so happy? I plummet down the stairwell, and hurrah, out through the keyhole, where—

Calm down. Calm down. I must put a lid on myself.

Scotty's eyes are so troubled, and Richard bends in a miserable daze above the bedraggled scrap of cat he has laid on the step. These poor, dear people are suffering for my sake. The cat is dying for my sake.

'Scotty, forgive me,' I plead. 'I'm so selfish, I know, but you wouldn't believe how much it means to me to be here. Thank you so much, my dear friend, my dear Mr Pickles 64123.'

He doesn't bother to answer. He barely glances at me. He has let go of Richard, but Richard is his only concern. A picture of stricken conscience, Scotty sits on the porch wall, hugging his pinstriped knees to that same T-shirt slogan – *To understand everything is to forgive everything* – his bare toes curling and uncurling, watching over my son as I should be doing.

Come on, I scold myself. Here's a chance to do my fatherly job. Defer celebration. Give my son's mental health my attention – and Henry V, my poor, sweet cat. It was my panic in your whiskers that distracted you from out-serenading the fox. I'm so sorry, forgive me, keep breathing, I beg of you. You have to survive and be well.

I hover above each in turn – Scotty, Richard and Henry – churning with remorse and goodwill. I pray to all the powers of the universe: all must be well now, all must be well.

'Oh no. My little friend. Is he dead? Did you run him over?'

The voice comes from behind us. I spin round, and here is Henry V's devotee from the side street, the buxom matron with the dimpled, round cheeks. She sees only Richard, who says, 'Not me. I just found him like this.'

'Ah poor puss, poor, poor pussums.' She's on her knees beside the little heap, stroking the bloodied fur. 'Hang on, though, he's warm. He's still breathing.'

'Yes,' Richard says dully.

She stands and peers into my son's eyes. 'Are you all right? Do you feel faint?'

'I don't know.'

She takes his arm. 'Sit yourself down. Here on the step. Head between knees. Breathe deeply and slowly.'

Scotty is off the porch wall, fluttering anxiously with me around the pair of them.

'Feeling any better?' the woman asks Richard.

'The cat needs a vet,' he whispers.

'And his owner.' The woman lifts her head, scanning the few lights still on in the terrace.

'He lives here, in this house,' Richard says, 'but it's empty. The owner died a few weeks ago.'

'Harold Whittaker's house?' she says. 'Harold Whittaker's cat?'

'Yes.'

'Problem solved,' she says. 'I'll go and fetch Simon.'

But Scotty throws his hands to the sky and implores, 'No, please don't do this.'

'What's the matter?' I ask him. 'Is Henry dying?'

'Not Henry. Me.'

Scotty's fading, but not in the usual way. There's no golden tinge in the air. Instead colour drains from him until he's a husk. His face, full of anguish, turns deathly white, then transparent, and then he is gone.

'Scotty,' I cry. 'Scotty, where are you? What's happened? Come back.'

Friday

Richard

'You're very kind, but no thank you.'

Simon was offering brandy, but Richard's more desperate need was to be on his own. The terrifying voice in his head had fallen silent, but it could be back any moment. He focused on being sober and rational, gathering himself to resist.

Simon was in plain need of brandy. He'd arrived wearing a silk dressing gown over pyjamas, almost in tears. 'Dear heaven, poor Henry. How did it happen? Did some speeding bastard just hit him and leave him?'

He'd been no more use than Richard himself. It was Maisie, the neighbour, who'd fetched Simon, found him to be useless, finally spoken to a twenty-four-hour vet and summoned a minicab. It was Maisie who'd nipped home for a fleece to wrap the poor animal in, and she who'd gone alone with the cat in the cab, leaving Richard and Simon staring after her from Harry's porch. She had waved aside Simon's protests with, 'Not at all. It's no trouble. He's the best cat in Brighton.'

To Richard's immense relief, he hadn't felt compelled to

go too, but who knew what mad impulse would hijack him next? No brandy, no more waiting on others: he was determined to assert his autonomy. Backing away, forcing a smile, 'I'll walk along the front to my mother's,' he told Simon. 'It'll clear my head. I'll be fine.' He willed this to be so. 'Let me know how he gets on.'

Clear of Simon, he concentrated on putting one foot in front of the other, testing his will and muscles for resistance, braced to fight any contrary pull. He re-crossed the road to the sea-rail and set off warily towards the pier. So far, so good.

'The young man's in shock,' Maisie had told Simon. Shock at what, though? It didn't make sense. And Lily, oh Lily. His heart buckled at the thought of what he'd done to her for no reason he could explain. Would she ever forgive him?

The muggy warmth of evening had given way to the cool of the small hours. A few dying fires glowed among the pebbles, and far off in the Channel a ship's light came and went. Richard paused to watch it and to listen to the soothing, slow rhythm of the waves. I've had some kind of seizure, he told himself. Somebody spiked my drink in the pub, or maybe I have a brain tumour. Frightening possibilities crowded into his mind. 'Act fast,' said those adverts about strokes. He should get himself checked out, but what would he say to a doctor? I did things I didn't want to do as if someone were making me. I found an injured cat, a cat that belonged to my dead father. It was as if I'd been led to it. And then I didn't help. I should have called a cab or a vet, but instead I carried it home to an empty house.

What would a doctor make of this? It sounded like nonsense. He would have to mention the voice he'd heard bellowing orders, pleading and offering apologies. Which would make him psychotic, wouldn't it? Richard drew in a breath and held it, blinked back at the fragile navigation light and tightened his grip on the sea-rail, daring his mind to mutiny again.

He remained a long time, staring out into the darkness, searching himself for anything worse than tiredness and hangover and shame and distress. Minute by minute these feelings loosened their grip and his trust in himself strengthened. His bike was miles away in Worthing and the trains had stopped running. He turned towards the pier and made his feet move again. He would do as he'd told Simon he would. He began to walk slowly west to his mother's.

In Hove, before turning inland, he paused to watch the dawn break. In a long moment of stillness, sea and sky emerged from the mist, shimmering silver-grey, east to west, above and below, as though he stood on the edge of a void. Walking to the sound of the sea had calmed him completely. The brainstorm had the quality now of a dream, and, apart from sleep deprivation, he felt like himself, as sure as he could be that he was neither ill nor mad. The new day was giving him certainty and purpose. The world continued to turn; the sun continued to rise.

He must put things right with Lily: that was the main thing. It was too early to call her – he'd kill time at his mother's, with luck manage to sleep a little – but at the first half-civilised hour he would ring and apologise, explain exactly what had happened, however odd it might sound. If Lily forgave him, then anything was possible and all might be well. If not, he'd be on the next train to London. He had to make things okay with her.

As he eased open the door and crept into his mother's house, he had a sense that something was different. The stale, dusty smells of his childhood were absent; instead there was the smell of clean washing. In the darkness, the hall seemed weirdly empty, and when he reached out, his fingers met no obstacles, instead found walls that for years had been lost behind towers of boxes and carrier bags. Here was a light switch. He tested it cautiously, afraid of blowing a fuse, but the ceiling bulb sprang into life, and he froze. What on earth? Was he in the wrong house?

Someone was watching. He turned sharply to meet eyes and a smile, but it was only Sid the Buddha, beaming welcome from the front room. The wooden statue took pride of place on an otherwise empty sideboard and wore on its bald head the barrister's wig last seen in a heap of miscellaneous junk in the hall.

Above the sideboard was another light switch. Turning it on, taking a step into the room, his jaw dropped. Empty space met his eyes, broad, high and wide, the few furnishings verging on Spartan. A sofa that he vaguely remembered from childhood had materialised from the chaos, and the chaos was nowhere to be seen. A yellow rug lay over the threadbare carpet, and a vase of sunflowers stood in the window. Most remarkable of all, on a small bookcase was a shiny flat-screen TV.

Richard closed and opened his eyes, but the vision remained solid and real. He backed from the room, intending to take a look in the kitchen, but some memory nagged him. That rug, that yellow rug was familiar. It was—

'Hello, Richard.'

He jumped half out of his skin. There on the stairs, in a long, white nightgown, was Claire. Was he hallucinating, losing his mind after all?

'You gave me a fright,' she whispered. 'I thought you were a burglar.'

She was real, but he was too shocked to make any sense of her.

'We wondered when you'd put in an appearance, but what time do you call this?'

She was teasing. She was happy. She looked like someone who'd won the lottery and was bursting to tell.

'What on earth are you doing here,' he managed to say, 'and what have you done with my mother?'

'Shhh.' She drew him back into the front room, closed the door and leaned against it. Glancing at the ceiling, she began to speak fast and quietly. 'The idea just came to me. I had to move with my lease running out, and I could see your mum needed TLC. She was going to slam the door in my face, but you wouldn't believe how that changed when I said I was having her grandchild and you didn't want to know.'

'Hang on. That's not fair. I've said I'll—'

'I know you have and you will, and she knows it too. She's on cloud nine that you're not going to Wales or wherever it was – she's been thanking me nonstop for that. It was the first thing I told her, and she was so grateful, clutching my hands, pulling me into the house, real tears, the whole lot.'

Richard was speechless. A new horror took shape in his mind. An unholy alliance of his mother and Claire? Too shattered to think straight, he sank down on the sofa.

'Look, don't worry,' she said, sitting beside him, taking his hand. 'The more I think about it, the more I agree with you. It's never nice being dumped, and I was scared about the baby at first, but being honest with myself, I can see that you're right.'

'You can?'

'Of course. I wasn't all that into you either. We're not really suited. The only, only thing, I promise you, that this is about, is I had to find somewhere to live. And where better, eh? I'll be needing a childminder, your mum's up for it, and my parents are no use in Norfolk.'

He stared, bewildered. 'A childminder? Mum? But she's batty – you said so yourself.'

'I was joking. Exaggerating. I hadn't met her, remember. She's fine, and she'll be fine with the baby, don't worry. I told you I was good with old people.'

'She's not old,' Richard said automatically, but he was beginning to smile.

'Too right. She can be good fun, your mum, when she's happy, so watch what you say from now on.'

'But the house?' He gestured amazement at the TV and the sunflowers. 'How on earth have you done this?'

'It's good, isn't it? Do you like it? I took one look around, and I offered her a deal. I'll live here, I said, have the baby here, and she could share in all that. You should have seen how excited she got. I'll be moving on somewhere eventually, I told her, but she would still be the grandma. The price, non-negotiable, was that she had to get shot of her bonkers museum, no half measures, once and for all.'

His fears were dropping away. This was nothing but good news. 'You're a genius!' he said. Suddenly anything seemed possible, except, 'Are you sure this isn't one of her acts?'

Claire grinned at him, lowering her voice to a whisper. 'Of course it's an act. She's a bloody actress. It's the I'm-going-to-be-a-proud-granny act. It's a great performance, maybe her greatest – don't knock it. And look – the stuff's gone – she can't magic it back again. She made a hell of a fuss at first, but I just said, 'Fine, I'm out of here,' and she soon changed her tune, and now she's started she's going to be okay. Seriously, I promise I'm not the disease, I'm the cure.'

She jumped up from the sofa, flinging her arms out and doing a twirl on her yellow rug.

The stuff was gone, gone for good. 'You've done it so fast.' Richard stood and moved through the room, touching the walls, marvelling at the space. 'I was here, what, only a week ago?'

'It's been wild,' Claire said. 'You wouldn't believe the week we've had, but I was afraid she'd wriggle out of the deal if I didn't get it done. I took time off work, filled a charity van – the skip's still outside, did you see it? I'm hoping they'll come for it before she starts fishing things out, but she hasn't shown any signs.'

'It's astonishing.'

'Yes, and a woman from the auction rooms came and cherry-picked too. Reckoned what she took might make a fair bit for us. There was a little bowl she got ever so excited about. A Chinese antique or something. Debs had a fit of laughing when she said it was valuable.' Claire was laughing herself. 'She's let it all go, hardly made a fuss about anything in the end. I agreed she could keep Sid of course, all the really personal stuff. Wow, her dressing-up clothes! We've found some lovely things in amongst all the tat. She's all right, your mum – she doesn't mind sharing.' Claire spun round again. 'Do you like this Victorian nightie?'

'It's beautiful.'

'The kitchen needs a complete makeover, but I've started on the bathroom.'

'Hang on, are you okay? Shouldn't you be taking it easy?'

'I'm fine, full of energy. No morning sickness, not once.'

'You must let me help, though.'

'That would be great, but there's one other thing I must tell you. I'm not sure how you'll feel about this, but, well, I needed a bedroom, babes, so I broke into yours upstairs, and I've kind of taken it over.'

'You're welcome. That's fine. I can't thank you enough.'

Euphoria swept through him. Lily's face sprang in his mind. He was dog-tired, but he couldn't rest until he'd spoken to her. There was no bed to crash in here anyway, so he'd go back to Worthing. He'd ring Lily from Worthing.

'Small steps,' Claire was saying, 'I'm trying to broaden her interests. We've been to the cinema, and she adores my telly. She's got hooked on cookery shows: we ate pan-fried duck breast last night. We've watched almost no Harry at all – she's fallen in love with Tom Hanks.' Good news kept tumbling out of her. 'And I found an address book – people she was at school with and so on. We might throw a party or go on a day-trip to see one of them.'

'I should have let you loose on her months ago.'

'Rubbish, it's the baby that's done it – she's counting the days to my first scan – plus huge relief you're not going away.' The floorboards creaked overhead. 'Thar she blows.'

He was eager to see the change for himself. He opened the door to the hall and called, 'Are you up, Mum?'

'Richard, *darling*,' she said. She was looking down from the top of the stairs, clear-eyed and alert despite her unmade-up face. 'It's so early. How *lovely* to see you. We're having a *baby*. Isn't that wonderful? How silly of you to run away from a baby. *Just* like your father.'

'Mum, you look great.' He opened his arms. 'You've worked miracles,' he murmured to Claire.

His mother's mules slapped on the wide, empty steps as she came down and accepted his hug. She had on a red silk kimono patterned with fire-breathing dragons. 'Now listen,' she said, 'can I make you some breakfast? Do you like blueberries? I've only just discovered them. Why did you never *tell* me about them, Richard? I've been wondering if they might go with porridge.'

'Sounds delicious,' said Claire. 'I'll give you a hand, Debs. No, you stay here, Richard. We'll bring it through. You look bushed, if you don't mind my saying. Put your feet up in the front room.'

He did as he was told, but only because that was exactly what he wanted to do. If last night's weird brain-event showed him anything, it was that from now on he must be in charge of himself. The trains would be running soon from Hove station. He would eat porridge and blueberries cooked by his mother – how novel was that? – then go back to Worthing.

He pulled out his mobile. His fingers itched to ring Lily, but it was still far too early. He couldn't wait to explain himself, to tell her how sorry he was. Lily was an open-hearted person. She would listen to him and believe him. She'd be glad about Claire and his mum. She'd be wary – anyone would be in her place – but lovely Lily would surely give him a chance.

Okay, that was the plan. First throw himself on Lily's mercy, then ring Simon to ask after the cat, and next, no more excuses, he must go straight to the café – what day was it? Friday? – and put things straight with Tiffany. She could have a half-share in the business or a proper wage, her choice. 'No rush, no pressure,' he'd tell her. 'Take your time to decide.'

He'd been missing the café, he realised. It was his business, his living, but also it had once been his dream. Perhaps it could be again. It was time to re-involve himself, contribute to Tiffany's plans, share her decisions. Time to serve some coffee, chat to some customers, see if Maurice had finished *War and Peace*.

Also, starting tonight, no more procrastination, no more alphabet-Google-soup, he would plan some actual travel before the baby was born. India. The decision arrived, firmly made, in his mind. This winter he was going to see India.

His mother put her head round the door. 'Tea or coffee?' she said. 'We've got real beans and one of those Italian machines. Claire's checked online, and she's allowed one cup a day.'

Lily

Somewhere in London, a charming, affable, well-educated, well-travelled, articulate, outgoing, talented, independent, attentive and hung-over man opened his eyes on the new day and gingerly turned his throbbing head to look at yesterday's blind date sleeping beside him. What a bore she had turned out to be. In five minutes, he'd be well-dressed and out of here.

Every date had gone bad lately. That disfigured witch who'd tricked him into buying her champagne must have put a hex on him or something.

Mrs Jones let the dog off the lead on the Common and sent a chewed tennis ball scudding across the litter left by yesterday's picnickers. Back in her kitchen, the family were grunting their way through bowls of cornflakes, their eyes glued to their smartphones, but she preferred to be out in the world.

The dog dropped the ball at her feet and she threw it again, shading her eyes against the morning sun. He lolloped off but got distracted by a boxer pup and a chihuahua who were disputing a stick, their owners yelling at them to desist.

By the time she'd fetched the ball herself and had a chat with the puppy's owner about the silliness of dogs, it was nearly eight o'clock, her small slice of freedom all too soon gone.

She re-attached the lead – 'Playtime over. No peace for the wicked' – and set course for home, catching her breath, because here came the woman with the birthmark, striding across the grass towards her, pulling not a dog but a suitcase.

It was only last night she had seen her on YouTube. 'Wow, Mum, come and look at this,' her daughter had yelled. 'It's Raspberry-face from over the back fence.'

She'd insisted her daughter explain what she meant by 'Raspberry-face', delivered her a lecture about respect for people with differences, and told her off for spying from her bedroom. But she'd watched the clip herself too, several times. It showed, not only her neighbour, but also dishy Quentin from *Tomorrow's Tycoon* hugging a young man, and Mariella whispering that this was Quentin's camera-shy brother. It was the fellow she'd seen here last Saturday, laughing and clinking glasses with her neighbour. He had her by the wrist in the internet clip, she looked more and more cross, and finally she broke free and ran off.

The dog halted, sniffing a cola can. The woman with the birthmark was approaching and passing, offering a radiant smile. 'Lovely morning,' said Mrs Jones to cover her stare.

'Yes, isn't it,' Lily replied.

At Clapham Junction, Lily chose a seat in the near empty carriage and smiled through the window at the commuters crammed on the opposite platform.

She'd slept badly and woken early, unsettled and cross with herself. She had misunderstood Richard, misjudged him, been completely wrong to get angry. Why be unnerved by a few cameras – what harm could they do her? He'd been brave to stop running, to turn and face what he feared, to try to make her face it too.

Giving up on sleep, she'd got up and gone to the laptop, daring to look on YouTube for *Tomorrow's Tycoon*. And yes, as she'd feared, there she was, struggling to free herself, running away, and it was she who had looked like an idiot, not Richard, standing there courageously silent.

Like an idiot yes, but not too bad otherwise, even full screen. 'What a beautiful woman,' Quentin said. She'd listened a dozen times to him saying it, and he wasn't being snide – he meant it. She looked fine in the blaze of TV light. More than fine. She'd never seen that before, never discounted the splodge on her cheek.

Richard discounted it – she'd noticed that from the start. She couldn't remember feeling so unselfconscious with anyone except her grandparents. She really liked that, and lots more, about Richard. More than liked, although – slow down – she mustn't be impetuous. Was she still suffering from post-Martin stress disorder? Karen from Martin's work was emailing all the gossip to her. He'd quit some hell-hole of a bedsit to shack up with Tamara. They'd given up pretending to arrive at work separately and started walking in together, Tamara simpering and smirking, Martin scowling and growling, daring anyone to snigger. *Not a happy bunny*, wrote Karen. *An idiot to leave YOU.* Which warmed Lily, and amused her, and had her telling herself she had no wish whatsoever to see Martin again. Whereas Richard...

'I love you,' he'd said as he'd caught up with her from the pub. A reckless, mad thing to say, but it had felt right at the time, more than right, wonderful. That was what she remembered this morning, not why she'd been angry. Then his text had pinged into her phone. *Are you ok? I couldn't be sorrier. Hope we can talk. Want to explain.* She had rung him straight back, cut short all explanation, said she understood everything, asked what was he doing today?

'Café. Then planning a trip to India. A real one, I promise.'

Just hearing his voice gave her goose bumps. He sounded so much like his father, she realised. 'I was a cow and a coward to run,' she'd said. 'Shall we start over? Shall I come back again?'

His delight swept her worries away. 'I can take today off, and stay the weekend,' she'd told him. 'May I help in the café?'

It was stupid and premature to talk of love, she warned herself now as the train began to move. She really must not, nor must Richard. They'd known each other only a week, and half of that time they'd been brother and sister. But she liked him. His lovely voice, his warmth, his sense of humour, his independent spirit, his take on the world, and yes – admit it – his arms around her, the welcoming smell of him.

He was attractive and sexy.

She was looking forward to seeing him.

She was going to give it a chance.

The train gathered speed, through suburban stations, past back gardens, shops, office blocks, cemeteries and small stretches of woodland and grass, burrowing through shopping centres and gliding over viaducts. Beneath a brick arch, as it whipped past overhead, the man with a van drove towards his next assignment without a thought in his head of Lily Caruthers.

Harry

'His punishment is neither your fault nor your concern. We expect our operatives to come under pressure from spirits. It is what they are trained to encounter. It was Pickles 64123's clear duty to resist you. He has shown himself unsuitable for this level of responsibility. I am here to inform you that you will be assigned a new mentor when your case comes up for review in eleven-point-five months' time.'

Barely looking at me, the woman speaks as though stringing together pre-programmed sentences. She gives off the same golden glow as my little curly-haired saviour and looks barely out of her teens. She has on silver sandals, and her slim, pert-breasted figure is draped in a banally angelic white-toga affair. She stands in my hall, her eyes vacant, her pretty arms motionless at her sides, while behind her the stairway sweeps up to the first floor like an invitation to heaven. I ought to fancy her, but I don't. Scotty's supervisor is exactly as he described her: a jobsworth with an eye on advancement, parroting unexamined nonsense.

'But where's the heart in all that?' I say.

Briefly her smooth forehead puckers. I'm not sure if she disapproves or is merely trying to access the correct response from the manual. 'A spirit's fate depends on the heart that he or she had in life,' she says finally.

I had feared, as she began listing Scotty's misdemeanours, that she'd come to throw me back into hell, but it seems I'm to be allowed to continue as I am. My son Richard found the cat and carried him and me home. Perhaps the universe cannot undo itself.

I was here in the hall when she materialised because I've been contemplating the Hockney. Not for its ever-pleasurable and reassuring image of myself, soon to be lost to me, but for its portrayal of my darling Henry V, who once sat so plumply and proudly alive at my feet. His painted green eyes gleam at me still. How I love him. Please Henry, be well.

'I've grown a heart in the afterlife,' I tell Scotty's supervisor. 'My cat, my son, my neighbour, my guardian angel. I care about all of them now. Doesn't that count just a little?'

I may as well put my case to a robot. Again there's a short pause before she responds. 'I trust,' she says, 'that Pickles 64123 explained during his introductory interview with you that the first level of attainment is emotional investment, the second is letting go.'

What can she mean? Dimly I remember some such words from Scotty on that terrifying journey in a van full of corpses. From his mouth they sounded softer, more poignant and profound, less of a non sequitur.

'Did he make sure that you understood that?'

'Yes, yes, he did, very clearly.' I mustn't land him in worse trouble, although I understand nothing. But then, maybe I do understand? I'm suddenly excited. 'Have I done it then – achieved the first level of attainment?'

She looks at me pityingly. 'Your *life* was your chance to do that,' she says. 'It's time now to accept and let go.'

She has me feeling spiteful. 'Did you come up the same way as Scotty?' I ask.

She looks blank.

'The same way as Pickles, I mean. Alive, then a spirit?'

'I don't see what relevance this has to your case, but yes of course, we all did.'

'So you must have had a heart once? Such a pity you lost the use of it.'

Her face twitches in a brief frown. She regards me for a

moment before her gaze loses focus. 'Today's interview is terminated,' she says, and she begins to fade out, leaving me none the wiser about poor Scotty's fate.

Next to arrive is Mrs Butley, who steps over the threshold billowing smoke from her nostrils and dropping keys and cigarettes into her bag. 'Tommy,' she calls as she wheezes up the stairs. I follow her up and then down again, cheered by her disgruntlement. 'Where the hell's the damn cat when he's needed?'

In the garden room she finds the cat carrier and props open its lid. Then she unlocks the French windows and steps outside, banging a spoon on a tin and calling, 'Tom, Tom, Tommy.'

Behind me another key turns in the lock, and I'm flinging myself at Simon, relieved to see him, anxious for news.

'Would you credit it?' says Mrs Butley, dropping ash as she emerges from the garden room. 'Just when Cat Rescue are coming, the pesky animal has to go walkabout.'

Simon closes the front door. 'That's why I'm here,' he says. 'I knew you'd be worried. The poor creature was run over last night. He's at the vet, in a very bad way. They don't hold out much hope.'

His eyes glisten with emotion – he always had a soft spot for my Henry – but Mrs Butley is not to be moved. 'Typical,' she says. 'All my trouble finding someone to take him, and I shall have to stand them down now.' She's grumbling her way up to the living room, where the landline phone is.

Simon stays in the hall, where he and I gaze sorrowfully together at Henry by Hockney. He blows his nose when he hears Mrs Butley returning. 'I do have one piece of good news,' he says mournfully.

'Oh yes?'

'This painting doesn't have to be sold, after all. I emailed a photograph to the Royal Shakespeare Company, with dimensions and so on, and they rang back at once to put a halt on the sale. Harry left plenty enough for his new Dorchester theatre, it turns out, and they think the portrait will look nice in the foyer.'

I can't believe what I'm hearing! Why did I not think of it myself while I lived? I should have earmarked the Hockney for exactly this purpose. Rather than haunt this empty shell of a house, I can follow *Harry and Henry V* to Dorchester and spend eternity in my very own most wonderful and glorious Whittaker Theatre!

'Nice for some,' snorts Mrs Butley.

'"Rather splendid" was their actual phrase,' Simon says.

'An effing disgrace is what it is,' she comes back at him. 'The conceited old bugger. A fortune to throw about, and what does he do with it? A sodding great memorial to himself, and not a penny for the likes of you and me.'

The ungrateful hag. She's had a thousand pounds and several bucket-bagloads of small lootables.

Simon sighs. 'Actually,' he says, 'I'm coming round to the idea of the theatre. I agree his motives were grossly egotistical, but so many people are going to enjoy it, Mrs B, and it will give work to actors and so on. Acting was Harry's life, after all.'

There's no persuading her. 'Charity begins at home,' she says with the air of someone inventing the idiom. She's as grossly egotistical as I am, which thought carries with it the pleasing corollary that her experience of the afterlife may be not unlike my own.

My dear, forgiving, loving and understanding friend Simon

spreads his arms, smiling. 'They're thinking of copying this hall and staircase for the foyer design,' he says, 'to give the portrait the right setting.'

Genius! I take a spin round the hall, looping the loop twice past the brilliant Hockney. My dear Royal Shakespeare Company, a million thanks. I was never more inspired than to leave my money and the guardianship of my memory to you.

Three years later

'In other news, the immortal actor Harry Whittaker will be remembered tonight when the new theatre he bequeathed to the nation opens in Dorchester. Over now to our arts correspondent, Gerry Matterson.'

'Thank you, Angela. I'm in Dorchester, gazing up at the splendid new Whittaker Theatre. As you can probably hear, there's a real buzz outside. So many celebrities arriving, there should be a red carpet...'

Richard

'I've been telling them they ought to rename the café "Breakfast@Tiffany's",' the soup woman was saying to Simon. 'Don't you agree? Like the film, but with the twirly "at" sign.'

Simon glanced over his shoulder and met Richard's eyes. 'Ingenious,' he said.

'They won't *listen* to me, though,' she persisted, 'so tell me honestly, what do you think, Mr Foyle?'

'Please, you must call me Simon.'

Simon, heroically burdened with Richard's mother on one arm and the soup woman on the other, led the way up Dorchester High Street. Richard intervened, smiling firmly.

'You have great ideas – keep them coming, Veronica. It's a wonderful name, but the trouble is, it doesn't fit with the food we do.'

'It's up to you,' he'd murmured to Tiffany yesterday when Veronica's back was turned. 'You're the best judge of what name will bring customers in.'

She had shaken her head. 'It's a rubbish suggestion – we're not a greasy spoon, and if I've not heard of some old movie, who else will have done?'

'It's an awesome idea,' she chipped in now, from behind Richard, 'but we're mainly coffee and cakes, that's the problem.'

'And soup,' Richard added. 'That was such a winning idea of yours. We haven't looked back since the day we put soup on the menu.'

They were making slow progress up the high street. Little Harry had so far insisted on toddling all the way from the car park, refusing to be carried or pushed in his buggy, and every now and then the party had to halt to let Claire catch up.

Richard squeezed Lily's hand. The pace suited her, heavily and radiantly pregnant beside him. There was no hurry and nothing to worry about. The invitations said arrive any time between five and six. He turned to review the rest of the procession. Tiffany just behind in her rainbow-coloured minidress and yellow Doc Martens, her hair pink as ever. Her new boyfriend, Zed, had dyed his for the occasion, electric green with blue highlights that dazzled Richard's eyes in the afternoon sun. Beyond them Veronica's husband and daughter with Quentin. Lastly, way down the hill, straggling in the rear, Claire and little Harry.

Spring flowers bloomed in the window boxes of the pub they were passing, where the locals spilled onto the pavement, pints in hand. The drinkers' eyes followed them. They were gawping at Lily as ever, at Tiffany's clothes and Zed's hair. No one spared Quentin a glance, Richard noticed. His brother rarely got recognised these days. His hairline was receding and he'd grown a beard to make up for it. He wasn't too bad a chap, for all his superficial charm and megabucks. They sometimes sank a brotherly pint together in The Hand in Hand, and no one took any notice.

Veronica, with her nose into everything, had brazenly insisted on coming with them today, so Richard, rather mischievously, had invited Maurice along too, offering to kit him out for the occasion and give him a bath. But Maurice had declined with disdain. He had no use for new clothes or inane chatter with luvvies when he had *Moby Dick* to get on with. He'd spent much of yesterday objecting to the one-day closure and threatening to take his custom elsewhere. When asked for his opinion on 'Breakfast@Tiffany's', he'd growled threateningly that 'The Eclectic Café' was a fucking pretentious name, but at least it didn't make him want to heave.

Veronica wasn't about to give up. 'But it would be so brilliantly apt,' she said, 'now that Tiffany's in charge at last. Don't you think, Simon?'

The café partners had recently become three. Simon, their new backer, was about to open a second Eclectic Café in Brighton in what used to be his antiques shop, and Richard was spending most of his time helping to fit it out and get it off the ground. His South Downs cycle-tour business was taking another great chunk of his time, so Tiffany was running the Worthing café pretty much single-handed again.

'Nonsense,' chipped in Richard's mother. 'No breakfast. No diamonds. No Holly Golightly.'

'I'm afraid you're outvoted, dear lady,' said Simon.

'Of course we do breakfasts,' Veronica said, but she was waving a hand, palm out in front of her face, in defeat.

'Little Harry looks tired,' said Lily. 'How about a piggy-back ride from his daddy.'

'Good thinking,' said Richard and set off down the hill.

The child sat on the pavement, shaking his head violently at Claire. Richard quickened his step. He'd done his best to veto the name Harry but had been outvoted by Claire and his mother. He shouldn't have worried. It was weird how the name meant, now, not his father but this delightful little boy, who flung up his arms. 'Daddy, daddy. Piggy-backy.'

He swept him up to his shoulders, and they made better progress. He kissed each of the fat little arms wrapped around his head. What would old Harry have made of this family party, he wondered.

His mind had been half on his father all day. On the drive down, hearing his mother in the passenger seat sing happily along to Classic FM, shooting smiles over his shoulder at Simon and Lily in the back, he'd been marvelling at all the changes since Harry had died. Everything was good in his life now. His dismal Worthing flat was a thing of the past. Instead he was with Lily in Brighton in the nice little house they'd chosen together, from where she commuted to her statistics in London. His debts were paid off, and the café and the bike-tour business were blossoming. India had been fabulous, and the two Eclectic Cafés had several carved elephants to complement Simon's unsaleable antiques. Richard still sometimes googled elsewhere, but his wanderlust for the moment was sated.

He squeezed Harry's legs tight against his ears in a fit of euphoria. Because yes, at last he was who he wanted to be, doing what he wanted to do, free to go where he wanted to go, always glad to come home.

He wasn't the only one. Everybody was having better luck and more happiness than three years ago. Who would have guessed that Claire would strike up that unlikely friendship with his mother and turn her around? That Quentin would put his winnings towards buying and converting the Marine Parade house as part of his growing property empire? That his mum, investing his grandparents' money sensibly at last, would be cosy in the ground-floor flat there, contentedly tending old Harry's garden, sallying forth to her cookery evening classes and holding dinner parties for her book group? That Henry V would have survived despite losing a leg and be spending his evenings purring on Maisie's lap just round the corner? That Simon would be rescued from bankruptcy by a couple of rare maps he'd spotted in a car boot sale? It was as if Harry left a blessing on everyone.

'I can't wait to see all the famous actors,' said Claire, smiling up at him. 'Do you think there'll be TV cameras too?'

'Bound to be,' Richard said.

The ground was levelling out. The others had reached the top of the hill and disappeared past the corner, and soon they were turning the corner too, showing their invitations at the security barrier. Beyond the barrier, in a small grove of pink cherry-blossom, stood the new theatre, as elegantly striking as the plans and photographs promised: three gleaming white storeys in Regency style, with the theatre name picked out in black along the lintel of the colonnade and a display of gold-and-pink posters for the all-star inaugural production of A Midsummer Night's Dream.

Champagne flutes in hand, a crowd of the great and the good had spilled out through the doors to chatter among the cherry trees in the evening sun. Everywhere Richard looked he saw faces from stage, screen and television. Little yelps of joy escaped Claire: 'Oh... oh... *oh!*'

Against this illustrious backdrop, a well-known arts presenter with her accompanying cameraman was interviewing an old guy in a toupée and a plum-coloured jacket. Richard smiled as he passed them, remembering the awfulness of Harry's funeral and counting his blessings again.

Harry

This is sensational! I shall run out of superlatives. Tearing up and down between the circle bar and the foyer, hitching rides on the waiters' trays of champagne and canapés, hopping between the sparkling earrings that adorn many a pretty lobe, I'm bellowing jubilantly, for no one to hear, lines from this daft, deft, jolly play that carries me back to my days fresh out of RADA on the repertory circuit. I have watched in rehearsal until I know every line once again inside out.

> *Hippolyta, I woo'd thee with my sword,*
> *And won thy love doing thee injuries;*
> *But I will wed thee in another key,*
> *With pomp, with triumph, and with revelling.*

The production is ludicrous, the director more concerned with innovation than authenticity, and the drinking abilities of my frazzled ex-wife Miriam, who is playing Titania, are surpassed only by her talent for missing cues, forgetting her lines and viciously badmouthing me to other members of the cast. But nothing can tarnish my delight in this felicitous day. My beautiful theatre is open, and everyone, but everyone is here: my thespian rivals, all of whom I outshone, and a whole marvellous throng of deliciously unfrazzled, good-natured women whose hands I have kissed and whose beds I have shared.

Julian, my agent, has come of course – he's somewhere outside in the crowd. Right here by the stairs, all the way from la-la land, is the jumped-up little director who stopped my heart with his impudent advice on my Lear. And ingratiating himself with the director, who's this? None other than the slick, arrogant hospital consultant who gave up on the job of starting my heart again, patted his hair in a mirror and swaggered off to tell the world's media I was gone.

Ha, the lot of you! I am *not* gone, not at all. Nor am I shut in an urn, or stuck in a filing cabinet, or tossed on a rubbish heap, or adrift in the world's oceans. No, here I am, in my very own Whittaker Theatre, gliding among the guests, caressing the women's décolletage, only wishing I could smell their perfume and finger the silk of their dresses.

Alongside the staircase, there it is, the object that delivered me to this haven – Hockney's portrait of my glorious maturity. It dominates the foyer and draws tender glances and murmurs of approval. White-haired but imposing in green, tailored trousers and sapphire-blue shirt, I challenge the viewer, and the gleaming green eyes of Henry V shine out too, the image to the life of the best cat I have known. The years have flown by since I saw his little body driven off in the arms of that rosy-cheeked neighbour. What a relief it was, before I bade farewell to Marine Parade, to hear that he was out of danger. I hope he lives still.

A ripple of nostalgia has me floating upwards, away from the staircase and the chattering crowd to the splendid chandelier above the whole gathering. There are days when its glitter is a poor substitute for the white horses on Brighton's turquoise sea. When the time came to leave my beloved home, it took all my strength to go with the Hockney into polystyrene-wrapped darkness in the back of a van, expecting to be shut away from the light for years while this theatre was built, grimly bracing myself for the silence and sensory deprivation. Instead, imagine my joy when the portrait was swiftly unpacked to hang in pride of place at a grand memorial service in Westminster Abbey, solemnly looked on by royalty, heads of state and the living stars of the theatrical and Hollywood firmaments, many with tears in their eyes. From where, even better, we were off to the National Portrait Gallery, to be central attraction among many likenesses of me in an exhibition opened by Hockney himself. For three months, the world and his wife stood in wonder before me and spoke with reverence of my towering genius.

My good luck never-ending, there was still more delight on its way. Off next went the painting on loan to the Garrick Club, where I had the immense pleasure of seeing actors gather, of hearing them backbite and gossip and gripe, and better even than that, of sharing their excitement at the progress of this wonderful theatre. Because yes, all the while, up ahead, the prospect of finding a new home here glowed ever more brightly. Blissful as I was, eavesdropping at the Garrick, I was impatient to inhabit this monument to my grace as an actor, to all the moments of epiphany I brought forth on the boards and the screen. To witness the portrait hung at last in this foyer, where the first-night audience gathers now on a chequerboard of black and white floor-tiles and drifts up the curved Regency staircase towards the bar and the circle. To be free to unhitch myself from the portrait at last and explore the building that embodies my life's most profound emotional investment, free to roam its stage and rehearsal rooms, its boxes and balconies, its delightful exterior, its grove of now-blossoming cherry trees, its views over the rolling green hills, its roof beneath the Dorsetshire stars.

All my adventures for this! Yes, I'll settle for this. In so many ways I couldn't be happier. When, rarely, I begin to be bored, or to hanker a little for Brighton or some other place in the wider world I have known, meditation has calmed me. I am safe here, where there is so much to console and to interest me. I have infinitely more than the universe in its blind wisdom thinks I deserve. I've been sending thanks, not complaints, up the line.

There is my one real sorrow, however. I miss Scotty so much and worry what has become of him. I descend from the chandelier and weave my way again through the crowd, trying to shake off the remorse that grips me whenever I think of him. Twice now, on the anniversary of my death, a rather nervous substitute has shimmered into being beside me. I forget his name, let's call him Smith, followed by a number as long as your arm. The little chap has the potential to be quite engaging, I think, but he's too fearful of blotting his copybook to let his guard down. I answer him, with no irony, that I'm fine and contented and grateful. I ask him questions about his own situation that have him blushing and changing the subject. I wish him good luck with making sense of it all. I ask after Scotty.

I worry very much about Scotty. 'Please find him,' I've begged Smithy both times that I've seen him. 'Please give him my love. Let me know he's all right.' But the lad says it isn't his business. 'More than your job's worth?' I came back at him last time, neither expecting nor getting an answer. 'Live dangerously,' I added as he faded into thin air.

'Hello, Pickles 64123. Are you receiving me?' Now and then I have beamed this into the ether, but only silence comes back. My dear little friend paid some awful price for my redemption. I hope his punishment was not too dreadful or prolonged, that he is done with it now and back where he's needed, bestowing his insouciant charm on some other suffering spirit.

Today though, I refuse to be melancholy, and here, on cue to distract me, is another face I've been hoping to see. In through the door comes my excellent friend Simon Foyle, relaxed and smiling, unscarred by the wrongs I once dealt him. I swoop forward to greet him, and, good heavens, can this be Deborah Lawton beside him? No longer the faded ragdoll I saw drowning in junk mail, squabbling over bin bags and stealing my china. Something or someone has stripped the years off her. Her eyes are brightly intelligent, her evening dress understated and chic. At last there's an echo of the sweet lass I seduced long ago. *Now, my Titania; wake you, my sweet queen?*

'Just *look* at the picture, Simon,' she says. 'Doesn't it look *wonderful* here? I'd forgotten what a lovely picture it is of *darling* Henry V. And to think – those black and white tiles are now *mine*.'

More new arrivals flood in, smiling up at the portrait and around at the crowd, accepting champagne from the waiters. Among them is the woman with the strawberry birthmark, whom I remember seeing in my solicitor's office and again at my house. I paid no mind to her then – I was far too preoccupied – but now I'm wondering, who can she be? A child of mine, possibly; there were three after all.

Not least, Richard. I dance to the door again, high on anticipation. For if Deborah is here, surely Richard must be.

Could this be him now, with a beard? I zoom in for a close-up, but still I'm unsure. He's disconcertingly not as I remember him. The woman hurrying to catch him up – I know her – yes, indeed! – it's the pretty girl who stepped into the path of my son's bicycle. She stares at the faces around her and says, 'Omigod, wow. Quentin, look, it's James *Bond!*'

Quentin? I dither, straining to decide if this is Richard or not.

Then I see him! The son I remember so clearly is coming in through the door. I have pictured him often, remonstrating with his mother, angrily cursing me, pedalling like fury, bellowing at Pearl Allen that I should have taken him to McDonald's, standing guiltily in my hallway, and then, distressed and half-crazy, stumbling across Marine Parade with Henry V in his arms. Richard, my dear son, hello.

On his shoulder rides a small, grinning boy, and at his side someone else is grinning, straight at me, for all the world as if he can see me. For a moment I am not ready to believe I am seen, then recognition floods through me.

'*Scotty!*' I shout. 'Oh, Scotty, Scotty! Would that I had eyes to weep with, arms to enfold you.'

He steps forward, punching the air. 'I hoped you would be here! I'm so happy to see you.'

He dances around me, and I in sheer delight around him, drinking in his sweet face, his bare feet, crumpled pinstripes and inevitable T-shirt, whose slogan is: *With our thoughts we make the world.*

'Nowhere near as glad as I am,' I say. 'Where have you been?'

'With your son.' He pats Richard's cheeks. 'Attached to him as firmly as you are to this theatre. They hauled me back that night and gave me a massive dressing-down for abusing my powers. I had meddled with fate and caused Richard distress – the poor lad thought he was losing his wits or mortally ill – so to make amends they sent me straight back to him, and I can't leave his side.'

'His guardian angel?'

'In a manner of speaking, though I've no power or influence. I'm just an observer, like you.'

'Oh dear. I'm so sorry.'

'Not at all. You were making such excellent progress. I'm really glad that I helped you.'

'You saved me from disaster – thank you, thank you – but you've lost your freedom.'

'Please, think nothing of it. I wasn't enjoying myself, as you know. They don't bother to ask – they assume I feel disgraced – and of course I am very sad that I can't visit my wife, but between you and me, I'm otherwise more than happy. Your son and his friends are such lovely people – I hope my presence puts a shine on their lives. I dare say I'll be pardoned eventually, confined to some backroom job until they're satisfied they can trust me out on my own again. I'll make sure to drop in on you then. No more special favours though, mind.'

'Absolutely, and why would I need one? Here I am in my very own theatre. And you knew it? You knew I'd be here tonight?'

'I hoped that you would. You weren't there the next time Richard went to the house, so I guessed you'd gone with the picture.'

'But you, Scotty? Are you really happy with him?'

'Your son is a fine young man.'

'And who's this on his shoulders?'

'Your grandson.'

'My grandson? Of course.'

'They call him little Harry.'

I'm speechless. Astonished. Delighted.

Scotty is starting to explain the relationships here, and the living arrangements, and how Henry V is alive, but I can't take my eyes off this self-assured child with his flashing eyes and bright curls. My grandson, and they've called him Harry.

The play is over, and the audience are surging through the foyer and away through the doors, swallowed up one by one into the darkness. Scotty and I have talked incessantly throughout the performance, sitting one on each of Richard's shoulders, telling each other our stories since last we met. Now Richard and his companions must leave, Scotty with them, and who knows when I shall see any of them again.

I am Lear, who has given his kingdom away, or Bottom, in a dream I shall never awake from, wearing the head of an ass I shall never throw off. The cast, high on their curtain calls, will be popping corks in their dressing rooms, but the party holds little interest for me any more. I am following Scotty, and Richard, and Quentin, and Simon, and Deborah, and Richard's lovely girl, her face splashed with port wine, and blonde Claire, and Harry, my grandson, as they drift out over the threshold into the night. I am at their side, flying around their heads, straining to understand all their conversations at once, until, 'No, Scotty, please don't let this happen.'

But he's backing away from me, following Richard. Waving farewell.

I am straining on my leash from the last cherry tree as, one by one, they turn the corner and vanish, deaf to my cries. I have barely begun to learn how to love them, and I am not ready to let them go.

www.sandstonepress.com

f facebook.com/SandstonePress/

🐦 @SandstonePress